Divided Treasure

Finding two bodies in a sweet factory dramatically alters the purpose of merchant banker Mark Treasure's visit to the North Welsh seaside town of Llanegwen. He has gone there – not entirely as a volunteer – to champion the cause of the workers whose pension fund is threatened through a takeover of their company. He stays to play a crucial part in unravelling the cause of the deaths, to expose an earlier murder, and to prevent yet another.

An engaging, red-headed chemist and a siren blonde widow are intimately caught up in the case, as is a superannuated curate, the stage-struck Gwyneth (one of the assault victims whose fates have a direct bearing on the outcome), plus a bevy of other well-drawn Welsh locals who add credibility to tale and setting.

Here is yet another of David Williams's intricately plotted whodunnits, lightly told but with an informed business background – this time about skulduggery in the pension business.

Treasure addicts will know that when the banker last went sleuthing in the author's native Wales the result, *Murder for Treasure*, was short-listed for the Gold Dagger Award, and of which the *Daily Telegraph* review concluded 'Mr Williams continues to astonish with his command, subtlety and assured comic invention.' With *Divided Treasure* he has set the scene to do that again.

David Williams
DIVIDED TREASURE

David Williams 1987

MACMILLAN
LONDON

First published in 1987 by
MACMILLAN LONDON LIMITED
4 Little Essex Street London WC2R 3LF
and Basingstoke

Associated companies in Auckland, Delhi, Dublin, Gabor-
one, Hamburg, Harare, Hong Kong, Johannesburg, Kuala
Lumpur, Lagos, Manzini, Melbourne, Mexico City, Nairobi,
New York, Singapore and Tokyo

British Library Cataloguing in Publication Data

Williams, David, *1926-*
    Divided treasure.
    I. Title
    823'.914 [F]   PR6073.142583

    ISBN 0–333–45223–2

Typeset in Times by Bookworm Typesetting Ltd, Manchester

Printed and bound in the UK by Anchor Brendon Ltd, Essex.

This one for
Patrick and Shirley Cosgrave

1

'I said no, Owen,' Gwyneth Davies protested, pulling her lips away from his. She grabbed Owen Watkins's groping hand before it could explore any deeper under her skirt. Then she directed the hand back to the unbuttoned front of her cardigan. She had nothing on underneath the cardigan, which should have been enough, all said and done. Elsewhere she had limits.

'Hard to get tonight then, Gwyneth?' he said, after the next kiss had run its passionate course.

'No different from any other night,' she answered, which wasn't strictly true. Even so, she was a virgin and intended remaining that way for the foreseeable future. 'And it's no use getting worked up standing in here, is it? Anyway, it's time I went home. Mam'll be worried.'

'Not much to be worried about, if you ask me.'

'Isn't there, then?' She smiled, opened her mouth to be kissed again, and began making enthusiastic noises about what he was doing to one of her nipples.

Gwyneth was a practical girl – just sixteen, still at school, fond of boys, and indulgent with them up to a point. She was pert with a small frame, neat little figure, short dark hair and big, eager blue eyes. She was doing well at school, notably in commercial subjects, but her sights were set on a stage career. She was thinking of changing her name to improve her prospects. She was thinking about it now as it happened. Being touched up in a bus shelter, on the windy sea-front at Llanegwen, on a Friday night in early April didn't exactly crease you mentally – and no offence to Owen.

'D'you like Gwendolene?' she asked a little later, absently rebuttoning the cardigan.

'Don't know her, do I?' he replied, trying to undo it again.

'Don't be daft. I mean the name Gwendolene. I might change to that.'

'It's all right. Bit English.' That response was almost mandatory in North Wales whether or not you were Welsh Nationalist. It showed the right attitude about the ruling establishment in London. 'You don't want to go on the beach, then?' There was no harm in his asking – but not much hope in it either. Gwyneth had decided against the beach the moment they had got off the bus back from Pentre Beach – that was the bigger town, next to Llanegwen. 'Wind's dropped a bit,' he added hopefully.

'Go on, it's blowing a gale. And I said, it's time. After eleven. I told Mam I'd be home straight from the pictures.' She pushed him away from her, zipped up her anorak, then, taking his hand again, pulled him towards the deserted road. Their bus was the last to take the loop road up to the narrow Llanegwen promenade at this time of year. There wouldn't be any other late traffic up here – and not much down in the town either.

Owen glanced back at the straggle of single-storey buildings dotted along the bleak and otherwise uninhabited shoreline behind the banked shingle – the café, the beach shop, the small amusement arcade, and beyond those the wooden-sided sailing club. There was no sign of life or light in any of them. It was the sailing club he was interested in.

A year older than Gwyneth, he was a fair, lanky youth with long, straight hair, a wide, thin-lipped mouth, and very little chin. He looked half-starved, which he wasn't – just naturally thin. The perpetual innocent smile, combined with the hint of brave endurance in the eyes, engendered the impression that he was both deserving and hard done by.

Mothers – with the exception of his own – felt sorry for Owen Watkins, and protective towards him. Their daughters weren't always so malleable in their own way. Gwyneth's mother, the divorced Mrs Blodwyn Davies, liked Owen a lot. It was through

8

her he got the odd jobs at the sweet factory where she worked. It was why he hadn't grumbled about getting Gwyneth home. He valued her mother's good opinion.

Owen had left school before Christmas and hadn't found a regular job so far. Everyone knew work was hard to come by – especially if you didn't want to be a trainee waiter in one of the hotels in Pentre Beach or Llandudno. Dead-end stuff that was, whatever they told you at the youth employment place. He was down for a proper catering management course at one of the polytechnics. That had a bit more promise to it. But it wouldn't be till the autumn. Meantime he was coping on the dole – and taking what opportunity offered. Except it was no use looking for opportunities in Llanegwen. You had to set them up.

'Come on then, let's run for it,' cried Gwyneth.

Hand in hand they raced up onto the flat steel bridge opposite and across it into Sea Road. This would take them to the town centre, passing the church at the end. There the road joined the High Street that ran parallel to the promenade, but half a mile inland.

There were no houses on the seaward side of the bridge – the centre one of three road bridges recently extended to span the new expressway as well as the old railway. For generations the railway had separated the town from its foreshore. Now the modern road bypassed Llanegwen in a similar way. The expressway was considered a blessing by most of the town's ten thousand inhabitants. It took all the through coastal traffic between Chester in the east and the island of Anglesey in the west – all the cars that used to clog the narrow High Street, particularly in the holiday season.

Some shopkeepers complained that the road also took all the passing trade, but you can't have everything.

Beyond the bridge, the couple passed a succession of neat if almost indistinguishable streets of modern bungalows that spread out on both sides, on gently rising ground. There was no illumination in the buildings here either – as if the wind blew all the house lights out before eleven o'clock.

Llanegwen is in the centre of the North Wales coastline. Two

9

centuries ago it had been a genteel watering place. Later it had scorned developing as a modern holiday resort, in contrast to its jumped-up, brasher neighbours. Once there had been some light industry, but even the slaughter house had closed now. It was rumoured the sweet factory was about to do the same. But it was still an attractive, healthy place for respectable people of modest means – even though most of them were elderly and retired, or else about to be both.

'Like the grave, this town,' said Gwyneth as, breathless, they reached the High Street. They stopped at the corner, out of the wind, in the doorway of an estate agents'. 'G'night, then.' She kissed him on the lips, but not so that it would start anything.

'Sure you don't want me to take you right home?'

'Positive. See you.' Really she was tired of him for now. She darted across the empty road.

They often parted here if it was too late for him to be asked in to her place. She lived in Sheep Street, two hundred yards to the right, behind the shops. There was another bungalow development covering the hillside beyond that, but the houses in Sheep Street were older. Owen's home was some way in the other direction and below the High Street. She waved from the far pavement. He waved back.

Gwyneth was deep in thought as she turned into Garth Lane. It was a short cut – narrow, running between two shops, then the high garden walls and the backs of houses in the next road, her road. She was as close as that when it happened. There was no light in the lane.

The man had been standing well back in a gateway in the wall. She'd passed him without seeing. His icy left hand came from behind. It clamped tight over her mouth and nose. He kept it there while he pushed her hard against the wall, forcing her to the ground while she was still off balance. He finished straddled on top of her. It all happened in seconds.

A wool Balaclava covered his head and face. Through the slits, mad eyes bored into hers, close up to hers. His breath came in short, straining grunts like a ravenous animal. He brought the carpet knife up in his free hand so she could see it. She strained back as he wiped the cold blade slowly down her cheek. She stopped struggling, not knowing if he had already cut her.

'Make a sound, you get cut. Understand?' His voice was forced – a breathy hiss.

She blinked obedience, not daring to move, choking back sobs, dreading what was coming, but trying to prepare for it.

Slowly he took his hand from her mouth. She didn't scream, but began: 'Please don't – Huh!' She stopped, stretching her neck taut as she felt the blade flatten against her throat.

The dead weight of his body on hers increased as he slowly transferred the knife to his left hand. He made the switch close to her face.

He ran his other hand down her body, unzipping the coat, pulling open the cardigan, pawing at her breasts. The grunts of his breathing got longer and louder.

Despite her horror, now the first shock was over the fear no longer paralysed her. She was making herself take stock: she'd been taught to do that.

The cold air increased the sense of her nakedness – her vulnerability – as he pulled her skirt above her waist, tore at the top of her tights, dragging them down, the panties with them. She swallowed to control the nausea when his fingers reached the soft, bare skin at the top of her legs. Now he was doing something to himself. The weight of his middle lifted from hers.

Suddenly a light came on behind them, taking the man completely unawares. It was in a curtained, upper-storey bathroom, making him look over his shoulder sharply. It only lit a small section of the lane but it was enough to distract. As he turned his head, his left hand moved well away from the girl's neck.

It was a chance, and she took it.

She hit hard outwards at his left wrist, jabbing two fingers of her other hand at his eyes. In the same instant she jacked a knee up into his crutch. It was what Miss Hughes, the games mistress, had taught them to do – with demonstrations. The girls said Miss Hughes was lesbian: Gwyneth was beginning to understand why.

'Rape! Help! Rape!' she screamed.

As her assailant's head went back to protect his eyes, she punched the heel of her hand into the lower part of his face. He recoiled further with a groan: more marks for Miss Hughes.

The knife had dropped with a clatter. Reaching, then searching for it put him more off balance and away from her. Grasping at the wall, she began pulling herself from him, trying to scramble to her feet. She heard a window go up; another light came on.

For a brief moment she was free, blindly staggering away from him. Then she tripped over her tights, falling on her face, crying in despair. Frantically she tried to haul herself up again, but he was already on her back. Why didn't someone help her?

'Help! Help me! Rape!'

'Please?' Incredibly, the word he breathed from behind her ear was a sobbed entreaty – except his ravening hand had again found the centre of his lust.

Heedlessly, she threw herself to one side, and with all her strength jabbed one elbow hard where she hoped his mouth would be. There was sharp impact, and a gasp of pain. His hold dropped away.

Struggling desperately to get to her knees, she thrust herself forward, but her legs were still under his.

Now with every new touch of cold stone on her bare flesh she imagined his knife was plunging into her.

Then suddenly her legs came free. She was crawling on all fours – dragging the tights from around her knees.

At once she was up. There was blood on her hands, a searing pain in her leg. She dared not look back while she could still hear his panting close behind her. And still no one had come to help.

If only she could make it to the High Street now. She ran, sobbing, screaming towards the light.

12

Owen Watkins had not intended going home. He was already halfway back to the beach when the assault on Gwyneth Davies took place. He was well out of earshot of her screams. On a still night it might have been different, but the wind was off the sea and carried all noise inland – like the scurrying clouds that made the moonlight fitful.

He was wearing sneakers, and jogged along silently. When he got to the bridge he sprinted across, head down, and stopped at the far end, crouched like a commando. There was no one in sight in either direction along the promenade.

Later he checked the scene again from the bus shelter, pretending he was reading the timetable. Then, satisfied the whole area was still deserted, he moved swiftly across the pavement, over the banked shingle, and down onto the stretch of smaller pebbles and the wet sand strip below. The tide was on its way out. It had turned an hour before.

His goal was the sailing club – the fifty-foot-long, oblong hut set in a fenced enclosure. Painted white, it had shuttered windows and a green composite roof. Its shorter ends faced inland and towards the sea.

On the promenade side was a small private carpark. There was a rockery too with a flagpole in the middle, adding a bit of credibility, though it was years since the club had owned a flag of any kind – or since the pole had carried a halyard to fly one by.

At the sea end, the last third of the building was free-standing on pillars. It jutted out over the sloping shingle and finished in a substantial, balustraded balcony, wider than the gable end itself. There were steps in the middle. The underpart of the balcony was used as an open, winter-storage space. It was racked for dinghies.

In front of the club-house was a flat concrete hard for boats, and, beyond that, a narrow slipway down to the sand, running under the padlocked gateway of the surrounding enclosure. The front part of the enclosure theoretically constituted a trespass on foreshore – common land in Britain – but it had been doing so for years, and no one had objected, not least because the fence looked easy to scale.

There were only two dinghies secured on the hard, masts stepped, booms secured and halyards flapping in the wind. It was early in the season yet. Most of the boats hadn't been taken from winter storage – either from under the club-house or from inside the building, half of which was also used for laying up craft and tackle in the off season. Only three or four of the dozen boat-owning members were keen or proficient enough to go out before April – and so far the weather had been too poor even for them.

It was a very small club, hardly meriting the title, being little more than a convenient boat store with a small bar. It wouldn't have existed at all except it was company subsidised – by G. L. Evan Ltd, the Llanegwen confectionery manufacturers. Years before the then chairman – a keen sailor – had leased the land from the local council, put up the building and provided some club dinghies, all available at a nominal membership subscription. It had been an exercise in community relations, except too few members of the community had related to it. Nowadays it survived partly because the subscriptions had been increased, but also because the less affluent company still underwrote annual losses.

It was the bar cupboard that interested Owen. On the previous Saturday morning he'd been casually employed on the weekly delivery round for a local cut-price liquor store. The sailing-club order had been a mixed dozen bottles of spirits – whisky, gin and vodka. On arrival he'd been told to take it in and stow it at the bottom of the cupboard behind the bar counter, on the right of the door from the balcony. Several members had been about, but busy outside getting boats ready for the season. He had noted that the cupboard lock was defective – also the latch of the casement window beside it. Only the window shutter made everything look secure, but that was removable from the outside.

Owen didn't thieve persistently, but it happened he had a ready cash outlet for liquor at prices below even those levied by

14

his temporary employer, and no questions asked. The opportunity, in ideal conditions, to repossess some of those bottles
was too good to miss. He had only let it lie for nearly a week
because a lapse in time would help separate him from suspicion.

He quickly scaled the perimeter fence, then climbed the steps
onto the balcony. In seconds he had taken down the shutter,
opened the window and entered, pulling the window shut after
him. The lock on the cupboard was easily sprung.

The liquor was not in the box where he had left it, but
arranged on a shelf above. That was good: someone had
rechecked it, so the delivery boy couldn't possibly later be
blamed for discrepancies.

He stuffed six bottles inside his anorak – two whisky, two gin
and two vodka. Apart from being all he could conceal about his
person, by limiting his take to the back row of bottles there was
a chance it could be some time before anyone noticed the loss.

He had already closed the cupboard when he heard a
throbbing motor close by, then footfalls on the balcony steps.
He ducked down behind the bar, which was at right angles to
the door.

The footsteps were heavy enough to be those of a patrolling
policeman, but the scratching at the lock suggested a burglar.
Then he heard a key sink home and turn in the mortice. Next a
figure entered, snapped on a hand torch, and shuffled past the
bar counter.

Because the vertical wooden slats of the bar-front had
separated with age, Owen had a partial, moonlit view of what
was happening.

The figure was dressed in a yellow, hooded weather suit and
long rubber waders – all very wet. Because the hood was pulled up
over the head, the observer couldn't yet determine the sex of
the newcomer.

There was a partition wall, with a door in the centre, that
divided the seaward end of the building – the bar and locker
area – from the rear part. The door wasn't locked. The figure
thrust through it.

Owen decided against flight. The other person might

15

reappear immediately, but hadn't been alerted by the missing shutter, and hadn't turned on the ordinary lights. The last point at least suggested the visit might be as clandestine as Owen's, if not as unauthorised.

There were noises of something heavy being shifted in the rear section. Then the figure came out, arms around some rolled-up sails, a rudder and a tiller. The flashlight beam had been extinguished. There was some wrestling with the main door while the bundle was pushed through. Then the door was closed and locked. To Owen's relief, the person then noisily thumped down the steps. A minute later the boy cautiously opened the window wide enough for him to put his head out.

The visitor was busy on the concrete hard and facing away from the building. The sails and other gear had been stowed in the larger of the two wooden dinghies, which was now being manoeuvred onto and down the slipway, and through the now open gate to the enclosure. After repadlocking the gate, the figure disappeared from view, running the boat down to the water.

Owen slipped through the window, and, staying low, closed it, without replacing the shutter. He crept on all fours to the front of the balcony where he could see through the balustrading, confident he wouldn't be seen himself from this better vantage point.

There were two vessels in the water. The sailing boat had been secured to the side of a similar-sized, inflatable rubber dinghy, mastless and with an outboard motor upended over its stern. The yellow-clad visitor had guided the boats out of the shallows and was adeptly getting aboard the mastless one, near the stern. Swiftly the figure grasped a paddle and continued to propel the two vessels seawards against the wind. A few moments later, the outboard motor was lowered into the water and jerked into life.

Owen Watkins adjusted the bottles in his anorak and prepared to leave. He was puzzled by what he had just witnessed, especially by the apparent stealth involved.

He knew who owned the sailing dinghy, which prompted him to believe it wasn't exactly being stolen – at least not in the way the liquor was being stolen.

When the figure had turned to lower the outboard motor, the face had been fully exposed for the first time to the sharp-eyed watcher. Although it wasn't the face of the dinghy owner, it was a face both Owen and the owner knew well.

It was seven ten a.m. on Thursday, May 13th when Molly Forbes, celebrated actress-wife of Mark Treasure, the merchant banker, opened the bedroom curtains. She paused at the window, intrigued by what she saw in the street below – in the tree-lined Cheyne Walk, across from London's Chelsea Embankment.

'Darling, you're not expecting a party for breakfast?' she enquired.

'Certainly not. I'm looking for a pair of dark blue socks,' her husband answered with determined inconsequence from the adjoining dressing room. 'A matching pair,' he added darkly.

'Meaning you've found an odd pair. Try some black ones. Mrs Pink sometimes mixes up the colours.' Mrs Pink did the laundry. Molly was still staring intently through the window, the famous head balanced high on the delicate, slim neck. Absently she cupped the edge of the short brown hair, then more consciously adjusted the sweep of the ruffed neckline on the primrose negligee.

At thirty-nine, the vivacious actress was arguably more striking than beautiful – and maturely unconcerned that there could be anything ominous or even significant about her next birthday anniversary. 'I think Mrs Pink's going colour-blind,' she went on, then added on the scene below: 'How extraordinary.'

'No, it isn't,' Treasure rejoined, but still about Mrs Pink. 'Faculties are bound to dim with age. It'll come to all of us,' he offered, in the certainty that it wouldn't be coming to him for a long time yet. 'Ah!' he completed, indicating he had undone enough pairs of rolled-up socks to have found a match.

'Perhaps you should come and look at what's going on in the street,' said Molly slowly.

'What?'

'People getting ready for a demo, I think.'

'Uh-huh. In a moment.' He'd hardly begun dressing. He found demonstrations less than compulsive, and only hoped that this one wouldn't be holding up the traffic when he was ready to leave for the bank.

'I'll just go and put on the coffee. Back in a moment.' Molly took another quizzical look at the scene below.

It was several minutes before Treasure came out of the inside dressing room and, while in the process of knotting his tie, remembered to look out of the window. What he saw prompted him to go back for his distance spectacles – in the cause of total accuracy more than in acknowledgement of a waning faculty.

Immediately in front of the terraced Regency house was a small paved courtyard, ending in high iron railings with an ornamental gate in the centre. On the pavement, beyond, a group of people was now lined up facing the house. Its five members were not part of a marching column: they were fairly still, and holding up three strutted placards between them.

In hand-drawn black letters one of the outside placards read: GRENWOOD, PHIPPS STRIPS, while the one on the other side read: SHUN REGAL SUN.

The placard in the middle asserted: TREASURE TAKES TREASURE.

Since Mark Treasure was chief executive of Grenwood, Phipps, the merchant bankers, and non-executive Chairman of the Regal Sun Assurance Company, the first two messages were enough to establish that the demonstrators had chosen the right house. Further confirmation of this fact was unnecessary – and doubly so when it was indicated in a personally offensive and possibly actionable form.

'Ah, you've got your glasses on. What do the banners say? I

19

couldn't see them properly before,' said Molly, newly returned. 'With or without glasses they say nothing that makes any sense. And when I—'

'Ah, they've seen us. They're waving. That's an attractive girl in the front. She's coming in. Oh, they all are.'

'Damned nerve.'

'D'you suppose they're collecting for something? Looking for sponsors?' Molly offered lightly before she had deciphered the messages. 'No, I see,' she added when she had. She cleared her throat. 'Why don't you finish dressing while I deal with them, darling? Really they look harmless enough. It's probably a mistake. Or some kind of joke.' She had disappeared before he could comment on the unlikelihood of either postulation. It was then that the telephone rang in the bedroom.

The banker was engaged with the caller for the following ten minutes. It was the Emir of Abu B'yat ringing from his palace – at eleven twenty local time – and requiring Treasure's personal confirmation that his agents were right to be buying one of the larger hotels in London's Mayfair.

The inconvenience of an early-morning call was a small price to pay to keep the evident confidence of a Middle-Eastern ruler. Nor was the call entirely unexpected, so that Treasure was well briefed in the matter. The result – that the deal would go through – naturally accorded with Grenwood, Phipps's earlier advice to the Emir's agents. In time it was further to increase respect for the bank from one of its more valued not to say affluent clients. Most immediately, though, the exchange produced a cosy sense of satisfaction in the mind of the bank's chief executive, content as anyone might be who effectively arranges a multi-million-pound deal before breakfast.

Self-congratulation tending to be an excluding as well as a heady indulgence, the demonstrators had quite gone out of Treasure's mind. They were to return to it abruptly.

On sunny mornings in season, the Treasures took breakfast on the terrace overlooking the garden at the back of the house. Conditions were perfect for this today – and the location a good deal more practical than the breakfast area in the kitchen in

20

view of the numbers involved. For when Treasure appeared, he found his wife at the rectangular wrought-iron table dispensing orange juice and coffee while engaging in animated conversation with five seated strangers. The people were, of course, identifiable as a group, though, tactfully, there was now no sign of their banners.

When he came on the scene, nevertheless, the banker judged this invasion of his privacy to be pretty cavalier – not mitigated by the fact that his wife was evidently party to it.

'You don't say?' Molly was uttering incredulously to the older of the two females in the party who were seated on either side of her. Then she waved at her husband. 'Darling, I knew you'd want to ask these good people in. Just wait till you hear their story. Now, come and be introduced.'

The good people didn't appear nearly so convinced of Molly's sentiments as she did. The three men looked especially doubtful. They had come to their feet at Treasure's entrance. One was elderly, tall and lined, with well-brushed, thinning hair, a slim moustache and an upright bearing, despite his years. He had on a dark serge blazer, with a gold emblem on the pocket, and what looked like a regimental tie, fairly faded.

The second man, in a crumpled suit, was small, skinny and in early middle age. He was wearing his pomaded hair parted in the middle, steel-framed spectacles and a furtive expression. His gaze was downcast. He was holding a badly rolled umbrella in front of him with both hands, its point hovering uncertainly over his feet as though he were deciding which toe to stab.

The third male, in open-necked shirt and blue jeans, was in his late twenties. He was big, fresh-faced and muscular, with close-cropped blond hair. Treasure hoped the beads of sweat on the freckled forehead indicated a due sense of embarrassment. The young man ducked to one side to fetch an extra chair for the banker.

'How kind of you, Mr . . . Jones, Mr Brenig Jones,' said Molly, beaming at him. 'Now, Mark, everyone comes from G. L. Evan Limited in . . . er . . .'

'Llanegwen, North Wales,' prompted the older woman.

'Thank you. Where I'm certain we know someone,' Molly responded with a vague frown before continuing. 'This is Mrs Blodwyn Davies,' she declaimed, indicating the speaker, and savouring the consonants.

'Pleased to meet you, Mr Treasure, I'm sure,' began that same lady. 'What a lovely man,' she added towards Molly, with a candour that Treasure found more disarming than complimentary.

Mrs Davies, about Molly's age, owned an operatic gypsy voluptuousness, with flashing eyes, a cushioned cleavage, and a shock of raven hair, all orchestrated by jangling jewellery and a rich contralto voice.

'I'm in accounts,' she vouchsafed, as though the information would be valuable. The ample bosom tested the buttoned closure of the bright red blouse intended to confine it. She gestured with her right hand towards the auburn-haired young woman on Molly's other side: 'This is Miss Marian Roberts, chief chemist, university graduate, BSc and more.'

The accomplished and stunning Miss Roberts gave Treasure a fairly wintry smile, but didn't speak.

On an encouraging nod from Molly, Mrs Davies continued with the introductions. 'This is Mr Basso Morgan, DSM, late supervisor, confectionery blending, but now retired from the company, also from the Royal Welsh Fusiliers where he served with distinction in the war. He was a full sergeant.'

'How d'you do, sir. Very kind of your wife to invite us in like this,' rumbled Morgan, and showing what Treasure considered a well-overdue regard for the niceties.

'Then comes Albert Shotover, manager, despatch department. Mr Shotover's a widower.' During delivery of this gratuitous snippet on Shotover's marital status, the speaker was regarding her subject with especial tenderness. Unexpectedly, he responded with a nervous upward and downward movement of the shoulders so violent it threatened to send the umbrella point through his left toecap. 'Mr Shotover's not Welsh like the rest. From Manchester originally. But his heart's in the right place, isn't it, love?' Mrs Davies concluded.

Shotover made an agreeing noise before briefly looking up to tender: 'It's right nice of you to ask us in, Mr Treasure.'

Mrs Davies beamed again. 'And last but not least, as your wife said, this is Brenig Jones, staff mechanical engineer. Also highly qualified,' she announced, completing the cycle. 'Well, that's done. Now it's up to Marian. Miss Roberts is our chairperson, Mr Treasure. Elected by the whole staff. She has something to tell you – from all of us in Llanegwen,' she ended, like a message in a Christmas card.

'I see,' Treasure replied neutrally and without seeing at all. 'Please carry on, Miss Roberts.' He sat down, motioning the men to do the same, and accepting a cup of coffee from Molly. He gave a courteous smile to the red-head whose appearance at least he found diverting. She was quite tall – slim but not willowy – and he guessed her age at about twenty-six. She was definitely a beauty, with large almond eyes, and a delicately chiselled profile. She was dressed in a chunky, white, v-necked sweater and blue skirt, the sleeves of the sweater pushed up, accentuating the slender wrists and hands. 'I hope this won't take long,' the banker added. 'I'm afraid I'm late already. Perhaps we could begin with an explanation of the banners?'

The girl again proffered the cool smile. 'As you know, Mr Treasure, G. L. Evan Limited has been taken over.' She had ignored his request, but not pointedly. Her accent was cultured Welsh, the tone melodious.

'I didn't know. But never mind.' He noted the stir and head-nodding this comment produced from amongst the delegates.

'If you really didn't know, that explains a lot. We've tried every way to get in touch with you.' Miss Roberts pushed back her chair a little from the table, crossing the shapely legs.

'If I tell you I don't know something, you can rely on its being the truth,' Treasure replied easily and without rancour. He helped himself to toast. The athletic Brenig Jones promptly moved the butter dish over in front of him.

'I'm sorry. I didn't mean . . . We really have tried all ways to reach you,' said Miss Roberts.

'The mail or telephone might have been more convenient than picketing my home. For all of us.'

'We tried both and got the brush-off.'

'Coming here this morning was a last resort, Mr Treasure.' This was the elderly, blazered Basso Morgan. 'And it was a very quiet picket. You could say almost hush-hush.'

'We kept the signs covered till we got outside the house,' Brenig Jones put in rapidly and leaning forward in support. 'We all came in my Ford Transit, see? It's parked just round the corner. The men came all the way in it from Llanegwen last night. The ladies came separately. We collected them this morning from Mrs Davies's married daughter in Putney. We didn't march or anything with the banners. No one saw them. Not to speak of. They were just to catch your attention, like.'

'They did that all right, Mr Jones.'

'It was like Mr Morgan said. Our last resort. Bit embarrassing, but here we are.' The young man took a deep breath, looked a touch defiant, and sank back, wiping his glistening forehead.

'I'm afraid I hardly know your company, nowadays,' said Treasure. 'I remember it's in sugar confectionery, of course?' The coffee was doing wonders for his earlier ruffled disposition.

'That's right, Mr Treasure.' It was Miss Roberts who answered. 'Or rather it was. It was taken over by Segam Holdings four weeks ago. They mean to close it down. They haven't said so yet, but that's the truth. So we shall all be out of work.'

'I know Segam,' put in Treasure. 'Private company in property development, isn't it?'

The young woman nodded. 'They'll be claiming they bought G. L. Evan Limited for the land the factory's on, the break-up value of the machinery, and the tax losses. That's what they'll say eventually. That the business couldn't be saved. But they've paid nearly two and a half million pounds for it.'

Treasure looked up from his cup. 'How d'you know that? Development companies don't usually volunteer that kind of information.'

'It's true, Mr Treasure.'

24

'We know all right,' Mrs Blodwyn Davies from accounts added pointedly.

Treasure frowned. 'How much land?'

'Five acres of good building land for housing. It's at the back of the town,' answered Miss Roberts.

'With building permission?'

'No, but they'll get it. From the local council. The Evan family could have got it if they'd tried. They couldn't be bothered. The factory itself only occupies one acre. That'll be knocked down, we think. With building permission the land should fetch two hundred and fifty thousand pounds.'

'That's all? Is that why you're suggesting Segam paid too much for the whole show, Miss Roberts?'

'One of the reasons. Some of the machinery's old. Only good for scrap. The brand names are practically unknown outside North Wales, even though the products are excellent.'

'You mentioned tax losses?'

'Just under half a million pounds.'

'A useful asset to a company that can set them against profits.'

'We're advised the whole lot's worth about a million pounds, Mr Treasure. That's for everything. Segam have paid more than twice that. But we know what they're up to.'

'And you're here to tell me, Miss Roberts, though I still can't see why. Of course, I sympathise with your situation.' He bit into his toast.

'There's surplus money in the company's pension fund. We think more than three million pounds. Segam mean to wind up the fund, leaving enough money in it to pay only minimum pensions, and transfer what's left to the company. To steal it from the pensioners without anyone knowing.'

Treasure took a moment before replying. 'That's not as easy as you might think,' he said deliberately.

'But possible?'

'The money couldn't just be stolen. The pension fund must have trustees. Responsible, independent people appointed to protect the interests of present and future pensioners, the beneficiaries. Those trustees would have to know about any

25

. . . any attempt at irregular appropriation of monies. They'd stop anything illegal. That's their main function.'

'There are trustees all right, Mr Treasure. But they're not stopping anything. Quite the opposite.'

'I think that's the shocking part, Mark,' put in Molly. 'If there's extra money, shouldn't it be going to deserving pensioners?'

'In principle, yes. Have pensions been improved recently?'

'They've never been improved, Mr Treasure.' Basso Morgan put in quietly. 'I'm a pensioner.'

'I see. And is it generally known there's a substantial surplus in the fund? You say three million more than they need to meet the fund's present commitments. To pay the pensions.'

'They deny there's a surplus,' Marian Roberts replied with spirit.

'Who's they?'

'One of the trustees for a start. George Evan. He's chairman of G. L. Evan Limited. He's still chairman, even though the company's now owned by Segam Holdings.'

'So who's right about the surplus? You or Mr Evan?'

'There's proof we're right, but it's being suppressed.'

'And we feel that's the beginning of the end.' This was Basso Morgan again. 'Once the money's transferred to the company that's the last the pensioners will see of it. Understand, we're little people, Mr Treasure. We can't afford to hire lawyers to fight for us.'

'Hear, hear,' Albert Shotover put in loudly and unexpectedly, fingering his toothbrush moustache.

'And you have proof there was a recent expert valuation of the fund? By an actuary?'

'That's exactly what was asked for,' said Miss Roberts. 'And it was reported on verbally, then cancelled. Those responsible for the cancelling are the ones who intend to strip out the surplus money.'

The banker pushed his cup away. 'Or take the treasure, as you put it so succinctly on your banner.' He smiled before

26

continuing. 'I assume that Regal Sun Assurance manages the pension fund for the company?'

'That's right.'

'And since I'm chairman, you figured the insurance company and I were responsible for what you allege is happening? I understand your feelings.' He paused. 'I can find out if a valuation was ordered, and if it was, what happened to it. Do you know who asked for it in the first place?'

The others looked to Marian Roberts who answered: 'One of the trustees. Joshua Evan, a director of the company. Nephew of George Evan, the chairman.'

'Was it Joshua Evan who got the verbal report?'

'Yes. But it was his uncle who cancelled the written one. Joshua wouldn't have done that.'

'So why has he allowed it to happen?'

She swallowed. 'He's dead. Drowned in a sailing accident. At the beginning of April. A tragedy in more ways than one. Joshua would never have deprived pensioners of their rights. He wouldn't have allowed the Segam takeover to go through either. And he controlled enough shares to stop it. That's if you include the ones held in the pension fund itself which he jointly controlled with the other trustees.'

Idly, Treasure noted that while Miss Roberts held everyone's gaze when she was speaking, she kept Brenig Jones's even when she was silent.

It was Jones who spoke next.

'Joshua Evan died on April the fourth. On the morning after Mrs Davies's daughter Gwyneth was nearly rape—'

'Was brutally attacked by a maniac in the street,' Blodwyn Davies interrupted loudly. 'And Mr Treasure doesn't want to know about that, thank you, Brenig. The point is, Joshua Evan told Marian how he knew there was extra money in the fund. And that was long before he died. But there's nothing in writing.'

'And his uncle was a co-trustee?' This was Treasure.

'Not at the time. He became a replacement trustee. Instead

27

of Joshua,' said Miss Roberts. 'Nominated by the board of G. L. Evan after Joshua died.'

Treasure nodded. 'How many other trustees are there?'

'Two.'

'Have you approached them for information, Miss Roberts?'

'Yes. They just fob us off, saying pensioners will be told everything in due course.'

'When it'll probably be too late,' Mrs Davies added. She turned towards Molly. 'We think they're just in league with the chairman and Mr Ranker. He's the managing director. Mr Ranker's only been with the company a year. He had shares, as well.'

'Are the other trustees also directors of G. L. Evan?'

'No. They're outside professional advisers to the company,' answered Miss Roberts. 'They're—'

'Good,' Treasure interrupted. The other trustees were probably the company lawyer and its accountant. He'd find out shortly. Meanwhile he saw no purpose in prolonging this discussion with a well-meaning, conceivably half-informed and evidently biased group – and certainly not without getting more information on those they were possibly libelling. 'Look, you've made your point in coming,' he went on. 'I'll do what I promised. I'll see you get all the information that can properly be released to you, and quickly.'

'Which means?' This was Marian Roberts sounding doubtful.

'It means no one's going to take money out of your pension fund without authority. Meantime I'd be glad if you'd stop maligning me and Regal Sun Assurance on banners or in any other way. Incidentally, knocking Grenwood, Phipps in that manner was pretty unfair. The bank has nothing to do with the matter.'

The others looked at Marian Roberts for a reply. 'That's not exactly true, Mr Treasure,' she said. 'The bank is one of the other two trustees. We thought you'd know that.'

'More coffee, anyone?' asked Molly brightly, breaking the awkward silence.

3

'So how the devil did the bank come to be a trustee for the G. L. Evan pension fund in the first place?' demanded Treasure. He was behind the desk in his office on the third floor of the Grenwood, Phipps building in Old Broad Street, in the City of London – the area known colloquially as the Square Mile.

Stanley Wigid, seated on the other side of the desk, gave a nervous cough. He was seldom summoned to see directors of the bank – and to his way of thinking, seldom was quite often enough.

'The appointment goes back some time, sir,' he uttered. 'I took it on when Smithers retired. That was eight years ago.'

Every company pension fund has trustees, appointed independently to protect the financial benefits due to existing and future pensioners. Sometimes a trustee can be a corporate body – such as a firm of accountants or lawyers, or, as in this case, a bank. Even so, it is still common, and sometimes required, for the firm to nominate a person in its employ to be the named trustee.

The ageing Stanley Wigid had long since settled into his time-serving role as the odd-job executive of the bank's trustee department. His work was usually conscientious but went largely unnoticed, which was precisely how he liked it to be. His consuming interests were in the growing of roses in his garden in Tunbridge Wells, and the performance of the Kent County Cricket Club. He was entirely without ambition, and in consequence made no enemies amongst upwardly mobile colleagues.

When someone in the department was required for a role

devoid of prestige or benefit for the holder, and not much for the bank either, it was Stanley Wigid who usually got the job.

'We first became connected with G. L. Evan Limited when we were still expecting to handle their flotation, Mr Treasure,' he added as an afterthought.

'They were going to be a public company at one time?'

'Oh, yes. That was nearly thirty years ago. But two sets of bad annual results nipped that in the bud.' Wigid was given to horticultural and sporting metaphor, as well as natural obsequiousness. 'G. L. Evan has stayed a private company. A pension scheme had been arranged in advance of the flotation plan.'

'To be managed by us?'

'That's right. Except when the company didn't go public we took the view the scheme would be too small for the bank to handle.'

'Which it must have been in the first place, but we didn't say so because of the other business?'

Wigid nodded. 'The pension scheme was bedded out with the Regal Sun Assurance. Into their managed fund. A long time before you began your innings as chairman there, Mr Treasure.' He finished with that half-patronising smile which is part of the unchallenged prerogative of the elderly underling.

Most medium-sized British companies appoint insurance companies to handle their pension funds. Usually a company's regular pension contributions will then be added to a 'managed fund' of investments set up by the chosen insurance company to service any number of its clients. Such a fund thus becomes a pool of money made up from the pension premiums of many companies, and 'managed' in the interests of all of them. Each company gets the share of the fund that equals its contributions, while they all get the benefit of a large-scale investment operation.

Treasure frowned. 'But why were we still invited to act as a corporate trustee?'

'I believe we offered. I think to keep a live connection going. It's been our only one with the company ever since. There's

30

never been any more talk of a public flotation.' Wigid paused. 'Of course, G. L. Evan was taken over recently. By Segam Holdings.'

'So I now understand,' Treasure responded stiffly, but without elaborating.

'The bank wasn't involved, sir. Not so far as I know.'

'Not directly, no. I gather there are two other pension trustees besides you?'

'One is Mr Chard of Chard and Co, accountants in Pentre Beach. They're the company auditors. The third trustee has to be a G. L. Evan Limited director. It was Mr Joshua Evan until just before the takeover, but he died in an accident. He was quite young. Their chairman's taken his place.'

'How often do the trustees meet?'

Wigid swallowed. 'We've never actually met. Not physically. Matters are handled through correspondence. Or on the telephone. That's not uncommon, Mr Treasure, when the parties are some distance from each other. If the two er . . . local trustees had disagreed, I daresay—'

'You'd have gone up and had a meeting.' Treasure interrupted. 'I see. Did you hear of any disagreement before the takeover?'

'Oh, no. Nothing like that.'

'Who usually initiated improvements in pensioners' benefits? The trustees or the directors of the company?'

'The directors. It was they who'd have to provide the money for improvements, so naturally . . .'

'Not if there was a surplus. Spare money in the kitty. Surely in that case improvements could be funded without asking the company for extra money?'

'Ah, it depends what's meant by a surplus, Mr Treasure.'

'I should have thought the definition was fairly obvious. If a pension fund has more money than it needs to meet its obligations, it's got a surplus. Or am I oversimplifying?'

'No. You're quite right, of course. It's just that . . .' Wigid paused, more uncomfortable than confused. 'Quite right,' he repeated lamely.

31

'In fact, have there been any recent improvements in benefits?'

The other looked surprised. 'Oh, yes. Oh, certainly. Just before I took over as a trustee. Widows' pensions were introduced. Also death-in-service benefits.'

'But the pensions themselves weren't improved?'

'Not exactly, no.'

'And that was over eight years ago?'

'They were substantial improvements, Mr Treasure.'

'But there haven't been any since? For instance, pensions have never been increased to match rises in the cost of living?'

'In some cases there's an obligation under the law now to do that—'

'Relating only to deferred pensions,' Treasure broke in briskly, because he didn't intend to be side-tracked. 'I meant for existing pensioners.'

'In times of excessive inflation, the trustees have discretion to increase pensions by up to five per cent.'

'But they've never used that discretion?'

'Oh, it's been considered several times. But each time it was thought prudent to delay any actual change. To avoid too heavy pruning of reserves. That was the view of the directors.'

'And the trustees always went along with it.' Treasure frowned. 'When was the fund last formally valued?'

'Ah, the Regal Sun is doing that now.'

'A valuation asked for because of the takeover?'

'Before that, Mr Treasure.'

'By whom?'

'By the trustees.' Then something in Treasure's eyes made him add, 'By Joshua Evan in the first place.'

'But it wasn't ready before he died?'

'I . . . I didn't hear it was. There were some queries. From the Regal Sun actuary doing the valuation. Technical queries. Nothing fundamental, but they held up the work. It'll be ready soon.'

'When was the last formal valuation?'

'Ah, that was three years ago.'

'Three? It's not done more often than that?'

'No. I think you'll find three years is quite usual. The last time the actuary reported, the assets were more than sufficient to cover all obligations. Nothing much has happened to alter things since.'

'More than sufficient meaning there was a surplus in the fund? How much?'

Wigid shuffled the papers he had brought with him. 'If I'm not mistaken it was estimated at a little over two million pounds. Yes, here are the figures. Total value of the fund four point eight million. Total obligations two point five million.' He glanced up and blinked before continuing: 'Leaving a . . . a theoretical surplus of two point three million pounds.'

'And what kind of average annual growth do you look for in the fund? Better than twenty per cent?'

'Somewhat less, sir. About fifteen per cent a year to be on the safe side. Of course, even that can't be guaranteed.'

'But fifteen per cent would mean your surplus had increased in the last three years to well over three million. A shade over three point five million, I'd guess.'

'I'm sure you'd be right, Mr Treasure. Mental arithmetic's not my strong point. But we'll see from the report. It's due any day.'

'Some of the G. L. Evan pensioners and employees think the main purpose of the Segam takeover was to strip out the pension-fund surplus.'

Wigid became visibly less tense. 'Segam would have a job on. The trustees are bound by the trust deed and the law. Before there could be any . . . any pruning of the fund, we'd see to it the bulk of that money is shared between the beneficiaries.'

'It's not pruning they have in mind, Wigid, it's rooting out,' Treasure corrected, using the other man's idiom. 'Anyway, I'm glad the pensioners can count on you. Miss Marian Roberts is their spokeswoman. She wrote me in despair four weeks ago apparently, saying she'd already failed to get a response from you and the other trustees. I was away at the time. Miss Gaunt, my secretary, referred the matter to you. You took the letter

33

and promised to deal with it. Have you? Miss Gaunt forgot to ask you.'

'Oh, that's well in hand, sir. You see the takeover altered things. I gathered from the tone of those letters this Miss Roberts must be a bit of an old battle-axe. Amateur lawyer, I should think. Had a nerve writing to you, I must say. That's why I decided to stone-wall—'

At that moment Miss Gaunt knocked and entered. 'Mr Hartley is on his way up, Mr Treasure. You did say as soon as he arrived,' she added, to justify the interruption.

Middle-aged, dependable Miss Gaunt was rarely reproved by her employer. But it had happened first thing this morning, over her failure to follow up on Wigid's action. Miss Gaunt was still suffering from remorse. It was unlike her to have slipped up on a point of standard practice, apart from missing a genuine *cri de coeur* when she read one – she blamed herself as much for that as for the other part. A devout and caring Christian, she felt she had failed not only her employer but also in charitableness to the deserving pensioners.

None of this prevented Miss Gaunt having an uncharitable thought about Stanley Wigid whose reputation for thoroughness she had always considered overrated. It was his slackness that had caused the trouble today. She had barely acknowledged him when he had passed through her office earlier.

'Morning, Mr Chairman. Cheer up, Miss Gaunt. Let's have a smile then, Stanley. It's a grand day.' Peter Hartley, raffish, long-limbed and angular, brushed past Miss Gaunt spreading bonhomie in a warm Yorkshire accent. 'Trouble at mill, is there? Well, have no fear, Hartley will sort it out.'

Peter Hartley was a young high flyer who could risk styling himself a problem solver before he knew the question. He controlled Regal Sun's managed fund, and was responsible for the investment of multi-millions of pounds in pension premiums. His own success was awesome – and so was his salary.

'Thanks for coming over, Peter,' said Treasure. 'A phone call would have done.'

'Long walks are good for me.' The Regal Sun Assurance

34

headquarters was on Cornhill, two hundred yards away. Hartley collapsed into a chair like a puppet with only its head still under active control.

'G. L. Evan Limited mean anything to you, Peter?'

'Naturally, Chairman. They're revered participants in our managed fund. Stanley here's one of their trustees. That right?'

Wigid was nodding, but not glowing at the recognition.

'Obviously you know they've just been bought by Segam Holdings,' Hartley added.

'Possibly because Segam has an eye on the surplus in the pension fund,' said Treasure.

'Another pension predator? Is nothing sacred in this grasping world?' The lanky young man rearranged his limbs with one heave. He still resembled a crumpled puppet – but now collapsed in a different direction, arms hanging limply outside his chair.

'I was just about to ask how you come to hold G. L. Evan Limited shares in your fund?' Treasure responded.

'They weren't actually in the fund. We can only hold shares in public companies. Evan is a private company. We did hold some of their shares outside the fund though. Had to get special permission from the Inland Revenue to do it. They were held as an administrative convenience for the G. L. Evan trustees. That's Stanley and two cronies.'

'That's right,' Wigid put in lamely, wishing he'd thought to volunteer the same information earlier.

But it was still left to Hartley to enlarge. 'Happened some years ago,' he continued. 'An Evan family shareholder died somewhere abroad. Australia, I think. He held ten per cent of all the shares. He chose to bequeath them to the staff pension fund. Probably didn't care for his relatives, or perhaps Stanley knows a better reason.'

Wigid coughed. 'The will stated it was to establish a block of shares outside the control of the Evan family or the firms' directors. For tactical use by the pension trustees if . . . if occasion arose.'

Treasure frowned. 'Tactical use? In case of a takeover bid?'

35

'That would be one use, Mr Treasure,' Wigid conceded.

'The shares were sold four weeks ago to Segam, of course. At the direction of the pension trustees,' said Hartley.

'At your direction?' Treasure looked across at Wigid.

'I didn't oppose the sale.'

'And Segam's paid for the shares?'

'Yes, at twelve pounds a share. Sounds high, but then it's a private company. There had never been any cause for splitting. There were twenty thousand shares involved.'

'And the proceeds? The two hundred and forty thousand pounds?'

'Given to prudent Peter Hartley for investing in his managed fund,' Hartley chipped in with a grin.

'Further increasing the G. L. Evan surplus,' remarked Treasure. 'Interesting. Did either of you know that Joshua Evan was against the takeover? Before he died.'

'Is he dead?' This was Hartley, surprised.

'Afraid so. In an accident. I was told this morning that his own shares, and those of some remoter family members who supported him, plus that ten per cent, came to enough to stop the Segam deal going through. He had better than fifty-one per cent of the shareholding ready to vote against.'

'I didn't know that,' said Wigid weakly.

'Well, I knew he was originally cool about the deal,' said Hartley. 'Happens he rang me about it. When it first came up. Thought I'd mentioned it to you, Stanley. I'd never met him, but he rang me two or three times over the years. Only once about the takeover. Haven't spoken to him since. Not surprising if he's no longer with us. When the deal went through, I assumed he'd changed his mind. Didn't know he'd died.'

'Who actually authorised the sale of the Evan shares held by the pension fund?' asked Treasure.

'I think the transfer was signed by Michael Chard and you, Stanley, wasn't it?' Hartley answered, looking at Wigid, who nodded but without enthusiasm. 'Chard's now sole partner in the company accountants,' Hartley continued. 'We only need two trustees to sign formal documents. Otherwise I'd have known Joshua Evan wasn't around any more. Is there a new trustee yet?'

'Yes. George Evan, the chairman,' said Wigid. 'I agreed to the sale, Mr Treasure, because there was no purpose in not doing so. I'd have been outvoted by the other two. In any case, I still think we acted in the best interests of present and future pensioners. Segam want to put new life in the company. Get it back on its feet.'

'Why d'you say that?' This was Treasure.

'George Evan, the chairman, told me so. When he rang me about supporting the sale. Said that as trustees we should accept the Segam offer for the shares.'

'You have that in writing?'

'No, Mr Treasure. But he wouldn't have told me—'

'Some people who came to see me this morning take a different view,' Treasure broke in. He then went on briefly to describe the meeting. Wigid was shocked. Hartley was surprised and, in places, slightly amused. 'Miss Roberts and her colleagues believe Segam intend to liquidate the company as soon as they've stripped out the pension-fund surplus,' the banker concluded.

'Segam paid a high price for the company if they just mean to close it,' countered Wigid.

'But which they could afford to do if they get hold of that pension-fund surplus,' said Treasure. 'And it seems to me we may have aided and abetted them.'

'You don't think that's an overstatement, Chairman?' This was Hartley. Wigid had remained silent.

'It may be. Perhaps I don't have enough facts yet. But Miss Roberts seemed to know what she was talking about.'

'So we may have been guilty of deserting the pensioners and widows in our charge,' said Hartley.

Treasure glowered. 'It's a great mistake for financial institutions like ours to ignore the rights of little people. For our sake as well as theirs.'

'Unacceptable face of capitalism, Chairman?' smirked Hartley.

'Exactly. Before breakfast this morning I spent some time

37

sorting out a problem for one of the bank's larger private customers, someone who trusts us implicitly. I hope I gave him the right advice. Later I grudgingly gave half an ear to the problems of this group of people who are also customers of the bank, in the sense that we're one of their pension trustees. At the moment they don't trust us implicitly. Or even at all. I need to know why, because they've just as much right to rely on our judgement as the bigger fish.'

'I'm against sin too,' said Hartley with an irreverent chuckle. 'And in favour of motherhood. Not always any profit in either cause, I'm afraid.'

'But in this case potentially a very unsavoury press pending for Grenwood, Phipps and for Regal Sun. What if it later comes out we've let Segam get away with barefaced robbery? That's what many respectable actuaries call pension-fund stripping.'

'The trustees won't allow—' Wigid began.

'The trustees haven't opposed the sale of the company, haven't listened to the warnings of the employees, and at best will probably have to compromise over the carve-up of that surplus.' For the first time Treasure showed real irritation.

'I agree it seems bad in public-relations terms,' said Hartley leaning forward and for once looking serious. 'But is it a bit late to be playing the white knight?'

'I assume the sale can't be undone. Possibly Segam will end up with some of that surplus – but not before we've done our best to have the pensions improved. It may also be possible to do something about saving the company from closure. Nearly two hundred jobs are involved. Altogether I think Segam should know they're not getting a walk-over.'

'I could write them a letter straight away,' Wigid offered with an unconvincing show of aggression.

'I don't somehow think a letter's going to be noisy enough,' said Hartley quietly.

'But there may be plenty of noise from other quarters by the weekend,' said Treasure. 'On Saturday morning G. L. Evan employees are planning to hold a mass meeting. A protest meeting. They're inviting the press and television.'

38

'What sort of turn-out d'you think they'll get?'

'Difficult to say, Peter. Their member of parliament's promised to be there.'

'Would you like me to attend, sir?' asked Wigid.

'Very much so. But it won't be necessary.' Treasure paused. 'I've promised to be there myself.'

'Champion,' exclaimed Hartley.

Wigid's mouth opened but no sound emerged.

Treasure didn't trouble to explain that he'd made the promise on an impulse he now at least partly regretted. But since he had no plan to retreat, if he was going to set an example in responsibility he felt he might as well start getting his money's worth immediately.

4

'Mrs Treasure was great. Sort of gracious, I thought,' offered Brenig Jones from behind the wheel of his red Ford Transit van. He stole a glance at Marian Roberts in the regular passenger seat beside him, savouring her proximity. He normally used the vehicle as a mobile workshop: for the journey to London he had fitted two extra rows of bench seats.

It was late afternoon. The whole G. L. Evan delegation was returning to Llanegwen in the Transit. Young Gwyneth Davies was with them – collected from her married sister's house in Putney where she'd been staying, getting over what was usually called her nasty experience. She had been excused school for the first week of the summer term.

Gwyneth was sitting beside grandfatherly Basso Morgan on the first of the bench seats. Her mother was behind, where she'd been holding hands with Albert Shotover surreptitiously under a coat. Even so, everyone knew they were heading for marriage – or at least that Blodwyn Davies was.

'Think we can count on Mr Treasure coming up for the meeting?' Brenig went on.

'He has to come,' said Marian deliberately.

'You can bet on it,' called Mrs Davies, just as firmly, and patting her front with her free hand. 'Strong influence you were on him, Marian. He fell for you all right. You could see that.'

Brenig Jones scowled.

'Nonsense,' the young woman countered lightly. 'It wasn't a question of personalities. He'll check on what we've told him, find out we're right, then know he's got to support us. Do what he promised.'

'Good as having Joshua Evan back with us,' blurted Shotover. He followed with a defiant look, as though he had said something controversial.

'Not really. Not the same as that.' Basso had watched the reaction to the last comment in Marian's half-turned face. 'Bit late in the day too, that's the trouble.'

'The *Sunday Mirror* will come to the meeting all right,' said Mrs Davies. 'After they've developed the pin-up pictures they took of Marian.'

'They weren't like that? Not sexy? Were they?' This was Brenig Jones, affronted at the thought. There was laughter from the others, including young Gwyneth.

Jones minded their making fun of the way he felt about Marian, and the way he tried to protect her. He glanced at her again, dropping the gaze to linger on her legs. She was smiling too – laughing at him probably, which he reasoned wasn't fair at all. He gripped the steering wheel harder, and scowled at the unwinding M1 ahead. It wasn't right that she still didn't credit the depth of his devotion.

'You should have been there when they took the photos, Brenig,' Mrs Davies chided. 'The men were going crazy.'

When the others had been in the newspaper offices, Jones had been driving around outside in Holborn, looking for a parking place.

'So perhaps it's just as well you weren't there,' offered Marian. Chuckling, she put out a hand and lightly squeezed his bare forearm. As always, her touch sent an electric spasm through his whole body.

'Don't you believe them, Brenig,' put in Basso. 'Quite proper photos they were. Nicely posed, if you ask me. Naturally they made a fuss. Marian's a lovely girl. Good for the paper to have her picture gracing their pages on Sunday.' He rolled the 'r' in 'gracing', enhancing an already rich Welsh consonant. 'The reporter made plenty of notes, too.'

Shotover nodded earnestly. 'Grand stuff for the cause,' came out with nervous sharpness, like most of his utterances.

'They took photos of me as well, Brenig,' said Gwyneth, who

41

hadn't said much in the hour they'd been driving. 'Don't suppose they'll use them, but the photographer said I could have prints.'

'You were radiant, Gwyneth,' said Marian, turning around to smile at the girl. 'And much more photogenic than I am. The . . . the holiday's done you good, too.'

'You looked gorgeous, love,' said her mother, all indulgence. 'They might use your photo. The man said so. To add local colour. But fancy saying your name was Gwendolene!'

'It's my stage name, Mam, you know that.'

Basso Morgan gave a good-natured grunt. 'Better tell all your suitors then, Gwyneth. Don't want any mix-ups, do we? Does Owen Watkins know you've changed your name for instance?'

'He knows,' the girl answered quietly.

'Saw Owen yesterday morning,' said her mother. 'He was asking about you. When you'd be coming home. Nice boy.'

'Still feels right badly about what happened,' said Shotover. 'He knows he should have seen you home that night,' he went on, while feeling about under the seat.

'What you doing?' asked Mrs Davies quietly.

'Making sure my umbrella's still there.' His face was turning crimson it seemed from the effort.

'Well, it can't have gone far.' She shifted on the seat. 'It's natural Owen feels bad. But what's done can't be undone, can it?'

'Wish it could,' murmured her daughter.

'I saw Owen in the week,' Basso put in quickly, aware that they could have done without Shotover's earlier remarks. 'Well dressed, he was. I think he must have come into money.'

'Or got a proper job, perhaps.' This was Shotover again, now holding his umbrella with the point upwards.

'He's going to college in the autumn,' volunteered Mrs Davies, taking charge of the umbrella and once more adjusting the coat over their knees.

'Owen's lucky. I can't go to drama school for another year. Even if I get a place,' mourned Gwyneth.

'Want to get your proper schooling done first,' Basso put in sagely. 'Pass those exams.'

'Finish your shorthand,' her mother added.

'Shorthand!' echoed the girl contemptuously.

'Something to fall back on, love.'

'Well, it'll be grand having Mr Treasure. To do what Joshua Evan intended for us.' Shotover blinked between the phrases, and returning the discussion to the earlier subject.

'Mr Joshua could have stopped the sale. It's too late for that,' said Blodwyn Davies.

'That's right,' agreed Basso, again watching Marian Roberts.

'He could have. But would he have done if he'd lived?' This was Brenig Jones.

'He told you he was trying, didn't he, Marian?' insisted Mrs Davies, frowning, but only because she was searching for a soft centre in the blue carton of chocolates on her lap.

'He tried very hard.'

'So as to keep on the right side of everyone, probably,' Jones roughly countered the comment from Marian. 'He was weak. That was his trouble. Product of his class. And putty in his wife's hands. Everybody knew that.'

'She'd have been for the takeover, all right,' said Mrs Davies, unwrapping a coffee cream.

'I gathered he'd stopped being run by his wife,' said Basso carefully, wondering if Jones was showing ignorance or an astonishing lack of tact.

'Changed man over those last three months,' agreed Mrs Davies pointedly. Like Basso, she knew when Marian's influence had become uppermost with Joshua Evan. 'He'd started behaving like a manager. Pity they hadn't made him managing director.'

'Anyone'd be better than Paul Ranker,' said Jones. 'But Joshua had his chance for the job a year ago. And he blew it. He was family too. Big advantage.'

'George Evan wouldn't have him,' Marian pronounced stolidly, her gaze fixed on the road.

43

'You said Joshua was a good sailor, Brenig,' put in Basso Morgan. 'That takes courage, doesn't it?'

'He was different sailing. More confident. Because he was handy at it, probably. Better than some of the others, anyway, including Ranker. And that Michael Chard.'

'Mr Chard doesn't live in Pentre Beach, does he?' asked Basso. 'That's where his company office is.'

'He lives inland. St Asaph way.' It was Mrs Davies who answered.

'You'd know him through the sailing, of course, Brenig,' the old man observed. 'It's chummier at the sailing club than in the factory, I expect? More democratic.'

'A bit more, yes. Mark you, Joshua was the only one of the nobs who sailed from Llanegwen right through the season.' As a highly qualified department manager Brenig Jones rated as a 'nob' himself, except for various reasons he'd never quite identified himself or registered with others in that guise. 'Joshua kept his boat at the club, of course,' he continued. 'The others use those old club boats when it suits. When they can't be bothered to drive to Beaumaris.'

Beaumaris is a celebrated sailing resort – over the bridges of the narrow Menai Straits on Anglesey, and more than twenty miles west of Llanegwen.

'That's where they keep their own boats?' This was Basso again.

'Most of them. Expensive boats, better than Joshua's. He had a nice little craft all the same. Knew how to handle it too.' It seemed the dead Joshua only earned compliments from Brenig Jones for his sailing prowess.

'Except he was drowned doing it. Sailing can be very dangerous. I'm glad you've got a motor boat Albert. Safer for you,' said Mrs Davies protectively. They all knew Shotover was a non-swimmer.

'Only an outboard,' he responded. 'Always breaking down.'

'Safer though. No mast to hit you over the head.'

'It was the boom that hit Joshua, not the mast,' offered Brenig Jones the expert. 'Sail must have gybed when he wasn't paying attention. Boom knocked him out and he fell overboard, losing his life-jacket. That's what the coroner said. Everything was in place when they found the boat, washed ashore in Penrhyn Bay. Miles from where the body was found.'

'The boat was capsized, though,' said Shotover, unaware that the women at least were finding the subject distasteful.

'Yes. Terrible blow that must have been. They say his face was—'

'Oh, change the subject, Brenig, for God's sake,' Marian broke in.

A stony silence followed, broken only by the beat of the engine and the hiss of the tyres.

'That's where I kicked him. In the face,' young Gwyneth uttered suddenly and very loudly.

'Not Mr Evan, love,' said her mother leaning over the seat to her.

Gwyneth burst into tears.

'Then I'll be happy to accept your helicopter and your hospitality,' said Treasure into the telephone. 'Until tomorrow evening then. And thank you again . . . Lewis. Goodbye.' He replaced the receiver, looked at it for a moment with eyebrows raised, then left his study and joined his wife in the drawing room across the first-floor landing of the house in Cheyne Walk.

'Your friends Lewis and Constance Bude are desolate you won't be coming too,' he commented.

'I know. Constance said so when she rang.' Molly looked up from the sofa opposite the Adam fireplace. She had been reading a play script. 'And they're as much friends of yours as mine, darling.'

'Except I never warmed to him. Also I had the distinct impression the feeling was mutual. I quite liked her.'

'So, they're casual acquaintances met at other people's dinner parties to be exact.'

'And once at Ascot, as I remember.'

'That's right. Year before last. In the Lagden's box. I saw

45

Constance for lunch once after that, with Elizabeth Lagden. And we do exchange Christmas cards. That's why I was certain this morning we knew somebody with a Llanegwen address. Actually it's *near* Llanegwen. I looked it up. Still, it's good of the Budes to have offered. Especially if he loathes you.'

'I didn't say that.'

'I wouldn't believe it anyway,' Molly smirked. 'You ready for coffee?' The tray was in front of her.

'Please.' He took the filled cup, eschewed the sugar, and moved over to the long bow window overlooking the garden, though at nine thirty there was scarcely enough light to see anything. 'I'm still staggered at how fast news travels to North Wales.'

The couple had just finished dinner. When Treasure had got home earlier, Molly reported that the Budes had heard he was attending the G. L. Evan meeting on Saturday morning. Constance Bude had telephoned with an invitation for the Treasures to stay with them for the weekend. Molly had declined for herself because the play she was appearing in, part of the National Theatre repertory, was running for the following two nights. After thinking it over during dinner, Treasure had decided to accept – at least for Friday night.

'I was never quite clear about what Lewis Bude does,' said Molly.

'Ah, you have that in common with a lot of people,' Treasure commented drily. 'I imagine he'd like to be known as an international financier and public benefactor. He's a lone operator, since he sold Bude Electronics to a multinational company. He did well on that deal. I believe he's now mostly involved in property. Also noted for large and well-publicised gifts to charity.' He sniffed over the last remark.

'He doesn't work from London?'

'No, Liverpool. And from Plas Gwyn, this house in North Wales, which sounds very grand.'

'And he owns helicopters? Constance said . . .'

'One helicopter, I should think. From what he told me. Owned through an air-taxi company he's set up. It's used to get

46

the Budes about the country, him mostly, but hired out when they're not using it. Good idea. It's meeting me off the shuttle at Manchester Airport tomorrow afternoon.'

'So now you're properly committed to going.'

'I was in any case. The involvement's doing me good.' He wandered across to sit in the leather wing chair beside the fireplace.

Molly frowned, took off her glasses, and put the script to one side. 'I understand about paint strippers and night-club strippers. Tell me more about pension-fund strippers.'

'In the main they're neither useful nor entertaining like the others you mentioned. The motives of some bear examination, but I don't believe Segam Holdings's will. Sharp operators on reports so far.'

'So you think Marian Roberts was right about them?'

'Probably.' His lips pursed. 'Pension-fund stripping's caught on because company pension funds have got too rich for their needs over more than a decade, while the value of their investments has kept on soaring. As a result, most companies, but not all, have organised increased pensioner benefits in one form or another. That usually sops up a respectable part of the surpluses.'

'But if money's still left over?'

'It can legitimately be claimed back by the company on payment of an extra charge to tax.'

'I see. But at G. L. Evan Limited they haven't improved the pensions at all?'

'Afraid not. The directors weren't in favour.'

'Nor were the pension trustees?'

'They appear to have taken the same view.'

'One of the trustees being a director anyway. Wouldn't they normally be different people?'

'They *can* be the same people. It's better that they aren't. A pension trustee should only be concerned with looking after the interests of pensioners.'

'You mean he can't do that if he's a director of the company as well?'

47

'There's a danger. If there's a conflict of interests he might want to put the well-being of the company before that of the pensioners. In the case of G. L. Evan, it's only the one trustee who's also a director. Incidentally, he seems to be acting principally in the interests of himself. The other two are professional advisers to the company.'

'Grenwood, Phipps being one?'

'Actually a chap called Stanley Wigid, the bank's nominated representative.' He grimaced over the fact, while sipping his coffee. 'But yes, the bank's the real trustee.'

'So if it's the pension-fund trustees not the directors who call the tune—'

'In theory,' he interrupted. 'In practice it's usually the directors who decide things. Especially in smaller companies. You see, in bad times, a company pension fund is dependent on the board of directors for providing extra money if it's needed. That doesn't happen to apply at the moment.'

'Because pension-fund investments have been doing so well?'

'That's right.' He paused. 'Pension-fund trustees are also sometimes afraid of their company directors. That's if the trustees are employees, or outsiders in any way dependent for a living on the company, like its lawyer or accountant.'

'This Joshua Evan who was a trustee—'

'And the youngest director. He seems to have done as his elders told him until shortly before he died. When he started to rebel, it was too late.'

'And your Mr Wigid?'

'Was useless. Took the view the other two trustees could always outvote him, so never resisted anything they'd agreed on.'

'Going for the quiet life?'

'That explains Wigid exactly. But it's going to be noisier for him from now on.'

'Why are Miss Roberts and friends pressing for such fast action?'

'Because if the company is going to be wound up by Segam,

they'll need to wind up the pension fund first. That way the surplus in the pension fund could automatically become part of the company assets.'

'Will people lose their pensions?'

'People retired already with pensions can't be done out of them, but their pensions needn't necessarily be improved.'

'And what about people like Mrs Davies and the weird Mr Shotover?'

Treasure's eyebrows knitted. 'Was he weird?'

'I thought so.'

'If the company is closed down, present employees will eventually get what are called deferred pensions. That's when they reach normal retirement age. Actually, they'll be better off than the others in the sense that the law stipulates deferred pensions must be increased by five per cent every year, until they become payable.'

'Aren't there some new laws about pensions?'

'Yes, but only marginally more difficult to screw up than the old ones, given determination.' The banker frowned. 'The biggest complication is when a pension fund is wound up. The second biggest is when the company involved actually ceases to exist. After those two things happen, anyone fighting for pensioners' rights can find he's boxing shadows.'

'And that can happen with G. L. Evan?'

'Very possibly. It really seems Segam are simply after that pension surplus.'

Molly made a face. 'So they'll want to wind up the fund and the company quickly. It all sounds terribly unfair. Yet it could have been stopped. Miss Roberts said Joshua Evan controlled enough shares—'

'After he died, his wife couldn't wait to sell his shares to Segam. The pension trustees sold the ten per cent they controlled just as promptly. They understood – at least two of them did – that Segam were buying the company to inject new life into it.'

'Not to close it down?'

'That's right. The third trustee, the one who replaced Joshua Evan and who's chairman of the company, he convinced the other two. Certainly he convinced Wigid.'

'So what are you intending to do?'

'First, show the G. L. Evan staff that Regal Sun and the bank take their responsibilities seriously. Then put the bite on Segam to improve pensions to the maximum allowed by law, and affordable out of that surplus. Segam have been invited to send someone to the meeting.'

'How will you know what's affordable?'

'The Regal Sun actuary is just about to tell us. That promised report will be ready on Monday.'

'An actuary being a super sort of accountant?'

'In a way. Also a super sort of statistician with a special aptitude for reading crystal balls.' He grinned. 'They really are the oracles of the insurance world. Produce the vital statistics then balance premiums to risks. Predict how long people will live, how much pension they'll need to see them out. All that sort of thing. They're very expert, and their word is practically law.'

'So armed with the actuary's word you'll become Marian Roberts's champion. Good. Lucky Marian. Incidentally, I think you'll find the late Joshua Evan was her lover, and that Brenig Jones is hoping to be.'

'She told you that?'

'Of course not. But I bet I'm right. I'm pretty certain about Joshua Evan. It's why she's so dedicated. Isn't the whole mess the result of his death?'

Treasure pouted. 'Yes,' he replied, before adding thoughtfully, 'and if the circumstances had been different, one way or another it might have been the cause of it too.' Which, as it happened, was to prove an unusually prescient observation.

5

Owen Watkins looked at the time on the kitchen clock before
helping himself to another Shredded Wheat.

'There's an appetite you've got this morning,' said his father.
'You wouldn't believe anyone so skinny would eat so much.'

'You would if you saw the food bills in this house, I can tell
you,' Mrs Watkins countered with feeling. 'And hurry up with
that egg, Catrin. You'll be late for school.'

'Can I see the end, Mam?' begged Catrin, aged seven.

'No, you can't. Square eyes you'll have from breakfast
television. And look where you're putting that spoon. You'll
have boiled egg up your nose next.' Sighing loudly she leaned
over and wiped the child's chin. 'Don't know why we keep that
old TV in here.'

The Watkins family lived in a small terraced house in Terfyn
Street on the east side of Llanegwen – in the older part, below
the High Street. Mr Watkins worked for the district council as a
refuse collector. His wife had a mornings-only job in a
vegetable shop.

The emaciated-looking Owen was still making opportunities.

The kitchen television receiver was a recent acquisition. It
offered pictures in black and white only. It had been 'recycled'
from the Pentre Beach official rubbish tip by Watkins senior.
He was well placed for picking up perquisites of that type, and
adept at getting them back into usable condition; the house was
practically furnished with them.

'You got work today, Owen?' This was his mother again,
over her shoulder, as she carried dirty dishes out to the sink in
the scullery. The cooker was there too. It was why Mrs Watkins

herself never saw much of breakfast television.

'Expect so. At G. L. Evan,' the boy answered with unfounded assurance. He was angling to avoid having to take his sister to school – especially today: the sweet factory was in another direction. In any case Owen considered it was time Catrin saw herself to school. Because she had been very much an 'afterthought', she had been treated like a piece of Dresden china for as long as he could remember – not that the Watkinses had any real pieces of Dresden: choice china figurines didn't get thrown on tips.

The deeper point was that Owen didn't get nearly the amount of attention at home that his winning ways and ascetic features earned for him elsewhere. And since the Gwyneth Davies episode his mother had become even more fixated about protecting little Catrin.

The incidence of seven-year-old girls being molested between Terfyn Street and the close-by St Elfod's Junior Church School was nil – and in Owen's opinion predictably so. But, like a lot of local mothers, Mrs Watkins sensibly chose to treat that fact as less of a comfort than as certain evidence of an oversight on the part of the sex maniac still lurking in the community.

'I'm off, then,' said Mr Watkins getting up from the table in a hurry. He took the bus every day to and from his work depot at Pentre Beach. 'You coming up the road with me, Owen?'

'Not ready, Dad. Haven't had my egg yet.' He was purposely taking his time with the second lot of Shredded Wheat too. Simply, he needed to be here when the post arrived, but he didn't want to admit it. They didn't get many letters, and those that did come his mother was in the habit of opening, whoever they were addressed to. He'd been trying to head her off doing that all week, using a variety of ruses.

'Well, you can clear up and wash the dishes if you won't take Catrin. Like yesterday. Suppose I'll have to take her myself again, on my way to work,' Mrs Watkins announced with pained emphasis on every phrase.

'OK, Mam,' he answered.

'Well, mind you leave the place tidy, then,' she added,

slightly surprised at his continued compliance. 'And Catrin, if you want the bathroom, go now. This instant.'

Owen watched his sister slip down off her chair. She sidled to the door, guided entirely by instinct since her eyes remained fixed on the pop group gyrating on the television screen.

Five minutes later he had the house to himself. He poured himself another cup of tea. There was no rush with the dishes. He knew there would be no early casual work at the sweet factory. It being Friday, some of the senior people might want their cars cleaned for the weekend, but that would be after the dinner hour, when they could be more certain it wasn't going to rain.

The postman was late – or else there was no letter again today. It had been seven days now. Owen moved to the room at the front of the house where he could watch the street through the lace-curtained window.

Whatever happened, he consoled himself, he'd been right to delay doing anything in a hurry about the dinghy episode. The bottles he'd taken that night had fetched more than expected, so there had been no pressing need at the time for extra cash.

The first time he had been interviewed by the police had turned out to be no more than a routine check. It had been early on the morning after the attempted rape of Gwyneth. They had needed confirmation about where and when he and the girl had parted, that was all. It had been a shock when it happened all the same. Up to that point he had heard nothing about the attack. When the detective constable had first introduced himself, Owen was sure it had to be about the theft. It was why he had been on his guard for some time afterwards.

The second interview had been three weeks later. This time the detective – a different one – said he was checking on everyone who had anything to do with that drinks delivery to the sailing club.

Owen's mother had been present at both interviews – insisting on being so. She had been outwardly incensed and inwardly unnerved about her son being questioned on the second occasion – and privately uncertain of his innocence.

It came out then that the drinks robbery had been discovered on the Saturday morning, the day after Owen had done it. You wouldn't have thought it was grounds for a serious CID investigation, and it wasn't if you took into account the time taken to follow it up. It had been one of a bunch of similar burglaries, the detective said, so they were checking on common circumstances. Owen had needed steady nerves over that part. It wasn't the first time he had stolen liquor first delivered by himself; he wouldn't risk doing it again.

The fact that he and Gwyneth had got off the bus that night so close to the sailing club had been touched on again at the second interview. In the end, though, his being with her had worked in his favour. The whole community was in sympathy with the girl – and that included the police. Everyone admired her courage. Nobody would have credited that she could have been involved in stealing six bottles of spirits – or wanted her prosecuted even if she had been.

The police had accepted the first time that Owen had gone straight home after leaving Gwyneth in the High Street. That he deeply regretted having left her like that went without saying – but he said it all the same, whenever opportunity offered. His mother had resolutely confirmed his statement that he had reached home at eleven twenty that night. Really it had been nearer eleven fifty when both she and his father had been sound asleep. Mrs Watkins was a very supportive mother against any outside challenge to a member of the family.

It was only a week since Owen became satisfied that the dust had settled – but enough for him to try profiting out of what he had seen at the sailing club. He'd been short of cash again after buying a new shirt. He'd still had qualms – but after he had made the telephone call he'd reckoned he was onto a good thing.

In some ways he was still very naïve.

He had made the call from a street phone box. The conversation had been a bit one-sided – but he'd expected that.

He'd explained he had a friend who was worried about seeing Mr Joshua Evan's dinghy being taken from the club the night

54

before Mr Evan drowned. Should he have reported it to the police? the friend had wondered – and asked Owen, who'd wondered too. Naturally, the wondering had been on a strictly confidential basis. The matter hadn't been mentioned to anyone else – not yet.

Of course, Owen said, he had pointed out to his friend that the boat must have been brought back. Otherwise, how else could Mr Evan have taken it out himself next morning? The friend had been surprised it hadn't come up at the inquest, about the boat being borrowed just before the tragedy. Again, Owen explained, he had reminded his friend that the boat had been undamaged when found capsized on the beach – so it wasn't as if it had been interfered with when it was borrowed. At least that wasn't likely.

The awkward part was that Owen's friend had recognised the person who'd taken Mr Evan's boat that night. If he went to the police he'd have to admit that. It would be on his conscience otherwise. Probably cause a lot of unnecessary fuss too, which seemed a pity.

Owen went on to explain he was ringing because his friend had worked out a proposition – a compromise, you might say. His friend was too shy to suggest it himself, in case of misunderstanding.

The friend was unemployed, but he'd been promised a job in Scotland, in Dundee, if he could get there. His conscience was one thing, but the job was another – and more important. Now if the person Owen was speaking to would care to let him have the money for his friend's fare to Scotland, plus incidentals, that would end the whole business. The friend would guarantee to forget what he'd seen – or thought he'd seen. There had been no witnesses, Owen was sure of that. There'd be no question either of anyone having to explain why the boat was borrowed and then returned – innocent as the reason must have been.

Exactly where had Owen's friend been that night? the person he was calling had asked calmly – so calmly it should have worried Owen more than it did.

'Underneath the club-house,' the boy had answered promptly. He'd expected the question. The watcher had to have been close enough to identify a face: there was no cover for hiding on the beach itself. He'd been careful not to admit his 'friend' had been inside the building on the night the liquor was stolen.

'How much would your friend need?' the other had asked after a pause.

'A hundred pounds would cover it nicely. Cash. Posted to me at fourteen Terfyn Street. To arrive not later than next Friday. We won't have to meet. The post's very reliable.'

There had been no actual promise made, but at the end of the call Owen had been confident.

And that's where the matter had lain until . . .

"Morning, Owen. Night telegram for you. From London. There's important. Expecting it, were you?' Fred the postman smiled as he handed over the package. Owen had been standing waiting for him at the open front door.

The boy tried not to let the disappointment show, while wondering if you could enclose money with a night telegram. He closed the door and tore at the envelope. On the single piece of paper inside the teleprinted message read: 'Sorry, held up. See you Evan's Yard 11 Friday.' It was signed 'Sailor'.

There was only one Evan's Yard. In the circumstances, it was clear enough to Owen that he wasn't being summoned there for eleven in the morning.

Paul Ranker swept the red Jaguar left off the Llanegwen High Street into the narrow drive fronting the twin-bayed, mid-Victorian house – all gaunt and grey-stuccoed.

He stopped the car sharply, demonstrating its instant reaction to his firm command – and spewing loose chippings on to the pavement over the low, stone street wall on one side, and against the painted, half-glazed front door on the other. So it was about time they had the drive surfaced properly. At his own modern house in Chester he'd had pink tarmac laid, bordered by coloured crazy paving – and his front drive ran sixty feet from road to garage: it wasn't a rutted pull-in like this one.

He got out, crunched his way to the rear door, then lifted the jacket of his brown-check, mohair suit from the back seat and donned it carefully. He was dark, spare, middle height and middle forties. If you referred to him as suave in his presence the epithet would have pleased him – nor would he have suspected any adverse connotation in the description. Suave was precisely the impression he cultivated – image, he would have called it.

After registering the time at eight twenty-nine on his digital wrist-watch, Ranker carefully pulled down the double cuffs of his striped shirt. The journey between Chester and the G. L. Evan factory where he was managing director usually took him thirty-one minutes, sometimes a minute less going home in the evenings. Given the chance, he would tell you – and repeatedly – that less expert drivers took forty minutes. The factory was half a mile further along from George Evan's house where he was now stopped.

Gripping the handle of his black-hide executive briefcase, Ranker went up the steps to the front door, leading with his tight-skinned beak of a nose and sharp, optimistic chin. He jabbed at the old-fashioned bell in the door centre, below the two long, stained-glass panels. The device screeched loudly at both pokes, vibrating through his finger. While he waited for an answer, he fingered both sides of his narrow moustache, then, using both hands, briskly combed back his straight, lank hair. This was why he was holding the briefcase between bent knees when the door came open a moment sooner than expected.

''Morning, George,' said Ranker, diving past the diminutive, elderly George Evan, while deftly fielding the briefcase and pocketing the comb in the same co-ordinating movement. 'In the lounge, are we,' came as a statement not an enquiry.

Ranker entered the first room to the right at the front of the house. It faced north, had a dark and sombre Pre-Raphaelite air – and was distinctly not a 'lounge'. The chairs were upright as pews and the fender brass-railed. The mantelpiece bore ornaments arranged as meticulously as artefacts on an altar – an impression heightened by the fringed moquette surround, like a 'frontal', in a faded liturgical green.

57

'If you'd like some tea, Sybil will . . .' Evan offered tentatively from behind, remaining in the doorway like an uncertain flunkey.

'Coffee'd be nice. If it won't be a trouble,' Ranker snapped, and perfectly aware that it would. He planted his briefcase, hinged open, on the seat of the least uncomfortable armchair, while the host left to tell his sister tea wouldn't do. The visitor meantime arranged himself in a commanding stance before the empty fireplace, gazing approvingly at his car, visible through the window, and because there was nothing inside that pleased him nearly so much, or even at all.

'Won't be long,' apologised George Evan when he returned. He was a bachelor – a plump, energetic little man, nearly bald, with too many chins, sad eyes behind heavy spectacles, and thick lips that he wetted as a preliminary to all speech. 'It's something we can't discuss in the office?' he questioned, hands kneading together the lapels of his clerical grey suit. 'After you telephoned last night, I wondered . . .'

'Can't be too careful. Walls have ears. Oh, yes.' Ranker looked about dramatically for auricular sproutings in the brown flock paper. His voice, in a high register, had a nasal, piercing quality. 'The position's serious. Mind if I smoke?' He lit a cigarette.

'No,' said George Evan, without enthusiasm, but too late to affect the issue. 'I know it's serious, Paul. We all know that.' He lowered himself on to a leather-padded, armless wheel-back chair. The small table next to it was covered in a velvet cloth, tasselled around the edges.

The other narrowed his dark eyes, and not just against the smoke of his cigarette. 'You're quite sure you've understood this two-part share sale we're doing, George?'

Evan's gaze went to the glass paperweight he was fingering on the side table. 'Of course,' he answered, with petulance in the tone.

'You know how it has to work?' Ranker had ignored the short assurance. 'The shares held by the trustees were paid for in full. Twelve pounds each. They're over and done with. No problem. For the others, there's been a first payment of only four pounds a share, which we've had already. The second payment, next year, will be for another eight pounds a share. Provided everything goes according to plan. You've no doubts about any of that? No, er . . . no misgivings?'

'Why should I have? It's perfectly legal.'

'Naturally it's legal. We wouldn't be doing it otherwise. It's also confidential.'

'I haven't told anyone.' Evan wiped his lips with a fresh white linen handkerchief.

'You haven't? That's good. I hope none of the other shareholders have either.' Ranker shook his head to demonstrate the gravity of the expectation. 'We don't want it blabbed to the whole world that it was a conditional deal. That Segam Holdings require to net two and a half million pounds. After the pension surplus is paid over. That's clear of their total costs.'

Evan shifted uncomfortably. 'I suppose that's what we agreed.'

'No suppose about it. We also agreed that if they net less than two and a half million, the difference gets deducted from their second payment for the shares. Under no circumstances should anyone forget that, George.'

'With fifty thousand shares I'm not likely to forget it, am I?'

'Quite right. As the largest shareholder. With a quarter of all the shares, how could you forget?' He paused for the points to bite. Then he added in a louder tone, enunciating as though he were indulging a backward child. 'If the deal goes through as planned, in the end Segam will pay in total twelve pounds each for the shares. But if they should get less than expected out of the pension fund, then it's the shareholders who'll stand the loss. Because the shortfall will be deducted from their second payment.'

'There's no need to repeat it all, Paul. And it's not necessary to shout at me. Really, I understand perfectly well about . . .'

'Good,' Ranker swept over the other's protests. 'So there should be no need for me to stress again that if Segam should get quite a lot less than they require, there won't be any second payment. No further payment at all for the shareholders, George. Think of that. Like in your case, instead of picking up another four hundred thousand pounds to go with the two hundred thousand you've got already, you'd get nothing.'

'The same applies to you, Paul.'

'Exactly. Except I've got a lot less to come. Because I didn't have as many shares as you.'

'You had thirty thousand . . .'

'Which makes my point. And in my case the principle's different too. I'm not a pension-fund trustee. I can't stage-manage things like you. Don't have the authority. And I can't be held responsible for letting down the other shareholders as you can.'

Evan twice wet his lips. 'I don't know what you mean.'

'He means you must harden your heart, George, and see to it the pensioners get nothing extra.' The softly spoken words came from the grey-haired lady who had entered a moment earlier – but soon enough to have heard the last exchange.

''Morning, Miss Evan. I hope you're well? Really you shouldn't have troubled.' Ranker gave an unctuous smile to match the words. He rubbed his palms together in expectation, eyeing the tray of coffee things that Miss Evan was bearing.

Sybil Evan was older than George – sixty-seven to his sixty-five – and as short as her brother, but not nearly so stout. She wore her hair in a bun, cast positive glances through gold-rimmed pince-nez, and was dressed in a high-necked, brown blouse over a darker skirt and no-nonsense brogues. Her legs moved somewhat woodenly, as if efficient articulation ceased below hip level.

'Good morning, Mr Ranker,' she answered shortly. She put down the tray on a table near him, then, drawing away, sniffed and stared with evident disapproval at his cigarette. 'I'm sorry if you didn't think your shareholding was enough. Remember I was one of the family who gave up a lot of her own shares to make some available for you? Well, I'll tell you straight, if I'd thought we'd be selling the company within a year of your coming, I wouldn't have parted with any.'

60

'I did pay for my shares, Miss Evan.'

'On the never-never. And at two pounds each, which gives you a nice profit, even if there isn't a second payment.' She had progressed to the bay window while speaking. Now she undid a catch and threw up the centre sash.

'Two pounds was all the shares were worth when I joined the company.'

'And it's more than they're really worth now, after you've been running it for a year.' Miss Evan turned about sharply to face him. 'That's if you don't count the money in the pension fund which belongs to the pensioners. I'll remind you as well, I never voted in favour of the sale to Segam, not as a director nor as a shareholder. The ten thousand shares I had left were taken over, not voted over. I took poor Joshua's view.'

'Very commendable too, dear lady. Even if we have to guess a bit about Joshua's view, since he never expressed it very clearly.' Ranker screwed up his eyes and sipped the coffee. 'Anyway, you're forty thousand pounds to the good so far, with another eighty thousand pounds to come.'

'If it comes. In any case, I don't need the money. I hope my brother will decide he doesn't either. Our style of living is perfectly well provided for already.'

Her brother made as though to speak, then changed his mind.

Ranker had paused with the cup halfway between saucer and mouth. 'Ah. Mystery solved perhaps. I've called because a little bird's whispered something in my ear. That an important member of the family is contemplating some kind of deal with Miss Roberts and her clique. A deal that would involve telling them everything about the share sale. I'd hoped I could assume that person wasn't you, Miss Evan.'

'You can assume whatever you like.'

George Evan got up suddenly. 'There'll be no deal, Sybil,' he uttered, staring woodenly at his sister. His face had gone an angry red. 'No deal,' he repeated. 'I can't afford such a terrible risk. I'm much too vulnerable, and you know it.'

6

The four-seater Jet Ranger helicopter, flying low, turned inland off the sea.

'Llanegwen,' called Timothy Wells, the tall young pilot, waving a bronzed arm forwards expansively. He adjusted the position of his microphone antenna. 'Looks better from the ground. It's the slate roofs that spoil it from up here. Bit uniform.'

'Still, more attractive than the other towns. Older, too. It's a pre-Tudor foundation,' Mark Treasure answered from the adjacent seat. 'That church is fifteenth century.' He had looked it up before coming – and the rest.

Wells was impressed. 'You can see the way the town's been boxed in on two sides by the expressway,' he said. 'And just look at the traffic on it. It's not five o'clock yet. Glad you're up here?'

Treasure smiled. 'Think I'd prefer to be swimming down there.'

'Sea's too cold yet. Mr Bude has a heated pool at the house.'

There were hardy bathers waving up to them as there had been along the miles of wide beaches they had already overflown. Although the season had scarcely started, the sunshine had brought people to the beaches early for the weekend.

The landscape had been similar all along the North Welsh coast from where they had joined it, just west of the Dee estuary. Modern urban sprawl – including huge, permanent caravan parks – had been hugging the sands, but this was invariably relieved by unspoiled, gently rising green land beyond, backed in turn by majestic, purple hills.

As the pilot indicated, the ribbon of the busy new road here swept up from the interior to make a stark eastern boundary to Llanegwen. It headed towards the shore then swung westward to continue close along the seaboard.

'That sweets factory you asked about? It's that group of buildings ahead, with the old-fashioned smoke stack.' The protuberance in question had SUGS lettered vertically down its length in white paint.

'SUGS?' Treasure questioned.

'Brand name. Sort of near-Welsh for "sucks". Strong cough sweets. Take your breath away. Got some somewhere. Like one?'

'No, thanks.' He felt the machine lift as it breasted the factory with the stack immediately below. 'That must be a flying hazard at night.'

'Not really. Shorter than the church tower, actually.' The pilot brought the craft lower again, searching along the landscape – snout down in the way of helicopters, like a scenting gun-dog. 'Plas Gwyn is the big white house, well ahead. That's what it means in Welsh. White Mansion.'

They were over open country now – empty, narrow roads between hedges, patchworks of big fields, edgy congregations of sheep, and only occasional buildings.

The smaller house, in a direct line before the white one, appeared suddenly from behind a row of trees. The glimpses were fleeting – of a big car and a brightly coloured delivery van in the drive, a sheltered garden full of tulips and two surprised people. A young woman with a shock of blonde hair and a ravishing figure was lying face up on an airbed in the centre of a small swimming pool, arms behind her head. She was wearing dark glasses – and nothing else. A fully clothed man appeared briefly in the act of stepping through French windows from the house to the poolside. Treasure hardly noticed the man who, in any case, went back into the house at the sight of the aircraft. The woman had lifted a hand to shield her view from the sun.

'Natural blonde,' said the pilot, beaming. 'Name of Mrs

Evan. Widow. Her pool's warmed by solar heating – or something. Nice to have the summer sights back with us.' He chuckled: the nude Mrs Evan was evidently part of the seasonal scenic route for helicopter users. 'Our helipad's to port. To the left. Over there.' He banked the aircraft away from the big house before they came quite abreast of it.

Plas Gwyn was a three-storey, nearly square, whitewashed building of mid-Georgian vintage, and more of a gentrified farmhouse than a mansion. Set commandingly into the hillside, it was surrounded by well-tended informal gardens on three sides. To the north, the entrance front faced back down the hill towards Llanegwen. The south aspect was stone terraced, with lawns beyond. To the west Treasure had caught sight of an elaborate swimming-pool arrangement overlooking a huge expanse of rhododendron bushes in riotous bloom.

On the east side of the house there was a cluster of brick outbuildings – stables and garages – around a cobbled court-yard. It was below these that the helicopter landed on a levelled grass area.

'Marvellous to see you again. Comfy flight? Everything go according to plan? Noisy brutes, of course, but they do get one about. How's dear Molly?'

The petite and spirited Constance Bude had made her well-attended entrance down a flight of stone steps and had been waiting close by to greet Treasure as he walked clear of the helicopter. She paid no attention to the pack of four baying black Labradors prancing in front of her. She was wearing a sleeveless flowered dress and trailing a ribboned straw picture hat. At her feet was a flat wicker basket that held secateurs, gardening gloves and some magnificent red and blue rho-dodendron blooms that complemented the colours in her dress. She was a study in genteel domesticity – a country lady disturbed at her not-too-arduous outdoor labours, but judging from her becoming appearance, adequately prepared for the disturbance.

'Delighted to see you, and looking so gorgeous,' rejoined Treasure, confident that the dogs gnashing around his heels wouldn't savage him for responding to their mistress's warm embrace.

He had always liked Constance. The turbulence set up by the now stilling rotor blades hadn't bothered her nor diminished her air of self-possession – a common trait in pretty women with tip-tilted noses, or so Treasure chose to believe. He guessed that Lewis Bude's second wife was in her mid-thirties: her aristocratic voice and bearing were predictable in the daughter of an earl, albeit an Irish and notably impoverished earl.

Constance took her guest's arm, drawing him towards the steps, but giving him little chance to utter in reply to her own commentary. The dogs scattered in front, feverishly scouting the ground as if they were in virgin territory and not simply retracing their outward route.

'I do wish Molly were with you. Would she come tomorrow night? After the theatre? Or Sunday morning perhaps? If we sent the chopper all the way? Oh, that reminds me,' Constance turned, still holding Treasure's arm, to call: 'Timothy, you are coming up to the house? My husband wanted a word. He's vanished suddenly, but he must have heard you arrive.' She nodded brightly at Timothy's own waved acknowledgement; it seemed the *cognoscenti* or the unassertive settled for answering Mrs Bude in sign language. 'Such a sweet boy. So reliable. He—'

'I don't think we can expect Molly,' Treasure interrupted firmly. 'Very kind of you to have me at such short notice.'

'But important. Lewis is deeply concerned with this business you're here to see to. You know?' She waved a slim arm about vaguely as they reached the top of the steps. 'They've just had a meeting. Here.'

'Who?'

'The . . . the G. L. Evan people. Ah, there's Lewis. He'll tell you. Darling, where did you go?'

Lewis Bude, stocky and muscular, was swinging himself down from a Range Rover. He stomped towards them ignoring the dogs who had raced forward in a frenzy of boisterous, noisy greeting. 'Had to run George Evan back. He didn't want to ride

65

with Ranker. God knows why. How are you, Mark? Glad you're here.'

The voice was heavy – like its owner – the eyes unusually dark. The smile in the welcome had been brief, the speaker's features quickly returning to their characteristic mould, which Treasure remembered as one of brooding seriousness – an impression deepened by black bushy eyebrows and the thick mane of hair sprouting from low on the forehead.

The leather suitcase Treasure had brought wasn't particularly heavy, but the nonchalant way Bude grasped it, after the two had shaken hands, made it seem almost weightless.

'You'll need a car while you're here. Use that one over there. Here's the key.' Bude had pointed to a small white BMW just inside the wide, open garage door and standing in line beside a Rolls-Royce and a big Mercedes station-wagon. The Budes evidently didn't stint themselves for transport.

'That's very thoughtful. Thank you.' Treasure pocketed the ignition key. 'I had promised to meet some people at the G. L. Evan factory at six. Actually I'd planned to walk there.'

'Please yourself. It's further than it looks from the air, and bloody steep coming back. That'll be the Workers' Revolutionary Committee you're meeting?'

'They don't really call themselves that, do they?'

'Of course not. Lewis is joking,' put in Constance. 'They're very worthy, and not at all red.'

'I suppose you couldn't blame them if they were,' replied Bude, but the meaningful look he gave his wife seemed to be prompting something more than support for an almost idle comment.

'Well you must sort that out between you. I have to see about dinner,' Constance responded quickly. 'We dine at eight, Mark. Informal. Drinks before by the pool when you get back, all right? Lewis will show you your room.' Without waiting for acknowledgements, she hurried ahead towards the house.

'There's a small dinner party in your honour. I thought it might be helpful for you to meet more of the interested people. I mean G. L. Evan management and shareholders. Exshareholders, that is.' Bude frowned as he spoke, keeping his gaze on the banker as though anxious to gauge reactions. 'Paul Ranker's coming. He's the managing director.'

'Who's been in the job about a year?'

'That's him. Used to be with one of the big confectionery groups. Except he doesn't seem to have learned much from the experience. Hasn't stopped the company from going to the wall. Michael Chard and his wife will be here too. He's the accountant.'

'Who's also a pension trustee?'

'Mm. And I think Constance has asked Barbara Evan. That's Joshua's widow. She was made a director of the company quite recently.'

'To replace her husband?'

'I believe that was the idea. She lives next door. Constance keeps asking her over. Doesn't want her to get lonely.'

From his brief observation of Barbara Evan the banker doubted there was much fear of that. 'You mentioned George Evan just now. He's the chairman?'

Bude nodded. 'I asked him for tonight, but he couldn't accept. Wouldn't, probably. Nothing to do with you. He and his sister don't socialise. Not with us, anyway.'

'I see. There won't be anyone from the . . . the workers' committee?'

'Possibly. Constance left a message inviting Marian Roberts. Don't know whether she's answered. I believe you met her in London. Like a drink? Sorry about the mess.'

Bude had led them to the south terrace. There was no mess to speak of – just a few empty glasses on a white table under a huge, colourful umbrella. Half a dozen elegant, cushioned garden chairs had been pushed back from around the table. To the side was a drinks trolley.

'A tonic water would be fine for the moment. Thank you.' Treasure seated himself in one of the chairs.

'Had a meeting out here this afternoon. Involving the Evan business,' said the host, pouring drinks. 'Broke up not long before you got here. Lasted longer than I expected. It's why I haven't had a chance to change.' He was in a business suit, though he had been carrying the jacket. 'I flew back late from a meeting in Liverpool. George Evan and Ranker were here already, waiting for me. George was looking bloody uncomfortable, because Constance was looking after them probably. Odd chap. As I said, he doesn't come here socially. And, er . . . he doesn't care for women, if you follow me. Chard came along later.'

'That meeting wasn't also because of me?'

'No. Not directly.' Bude came over with the drinks, then also seated himself at the table. 'The meeting was about the future of the sailing club here. I've been a patron of it for the last two years. When G. L. Evan Limited decided they wanted someone to share the cost of the upkeep.'

'It's a company enterprise?'

'Used to be entirely. Not any more. As a keen sailor I felt I should put a penny or two in. For the general good of the community.'

'Do you sail from Llanegwen?'

'Not often. I keep my boat on Anglesey, at Beaumaris. It's only a half-hour's drive on the new road. Anyway, since we talked yesterday I thought I'd try to defuse things here a bit. The sailing club provided the excuse. In a general sort of way.' Bude studied his glass. 'I'm afraid the takeover's upset the local community more than one expected.' He looked up. 'More than I expected, certainly. It's not been well handled. Poor management communication with the staff for a start.'

'According to the delegation that turned up on my doorstep, the late Joshua Evan had the right ideas in that respect.'

Bude shook his head. 'That's largely myth. Joshua was always ineffective. Especially so as a director of the company, which he'd been for a good many years. Had the title of administrative director, whatever that meant. They had to give him a job, as a member of the controlling family with nothing else to do. But no one had any opinion of him. When they needed a new managing director, after his father died, he wasn't even considered.'

68

'But I gather he was leading a spirited opposition to the takeover.'

'Well, I understand he was doing as he was told by Marian Roberts. She'd been a strong influence over him recently. Jogged him out of years of stupor. They were close. Very close . . . Or so I'm told.'

'Just in a business sense? She's very attractive.'

'It possibly went further than that.'

'And where did his wife stand in this?'

Bude hesitated before observing carefully: 'Barbara was never much involved with the company. I don't suppose it'll be any different now she's on the board. The appointment was primarily to recognise she's a large shareholder.'

'Was a large shareholder?' Treasure put in, but as a question not a statement.

'That's right.' Bude loosened his tie. 'Barbara may not have been intimately involved with her husband either, not recently. It was common knowledge in the community that he was a disappointment to her. She married him thinking he was going to head the company eventually. No children, of course, but that could have been by accident not design. I think she saw consolation in this deal. They've always lived quite well.'

'And she was expecting to go on doing so, with the money he'd be getting for his shares? He was the biggest shareholder after the chairman. I calculated he'd have picked up over half a million pounds from Segam Holdings. Presumably his wife has now done just that?'

'Um . . . I expect so.' This time the hesitation had been more marked. It seemed also as though the speaker had been minded to say more, and then decided not to.

'I wish it looked as though more effort had been made by somebody to keep the company afloat,' said Treasure.

The other man shook his head. 'It really had no future. If Joshua, or anyone else, had kept it alive this time, I don't believe it could have lasted. They'd been trying for years to find another company to merge with. Another confectionery manufacturer. But no one was interested.'

'Perhaps they didn't try hard enough.'

'Could be, I suppose. They did import new management, of course.'

'This man Ranker?'

'Just a bad choice. Not what he was cracked up to be.'

'But he hasn't done badly for himself from the takeover. Considering he's a Johnnie-come-lately, hired to put the company back on its feet.'

'You mean what he's got from selling his shares? I understand he insisted on a share option when they employed him.'

'Which at worst might put a doubt over his motives. In view of what's happened. But only at worst,' Treasure reflected, frowning. 'So, we have uninterested family directors, avaricious family shareholders and an incompetent new managing director. But all of them now seem to be well enough off to enjoy a comfortable retirement, or to fund a new career.' He shrugged. 'The only people with nothing to be pleased about are the employees, who'll presumably soon be jobless, and the pensioners, who as yet have been promised nothing.'

'If the company's folded, the workforce will get redundancy payments, of course.'

'In the circumstances they'll get the legal minimum, I expect. Might have been the same for the pensioners.'

'Until you came to their rescue.'

'I hope we can effect something, certainly. So far it all seems to me too simple. Too comfortable for the people who're doing well over this deal, including Segam Holdings. Llanegwen being an industrial backwater, closing up the company could have been done with nobody much noticing. The workforce is non-union—'

'And the pension trustees not very conscientious. Including the one in London, or so I've been led to understand.'

Treasure nodded at the pointed interruption. 'I entirely accept that, and I'm not proud of it. I told you, it's why I felt obliged to come.'

'Does you credit, of course.'

'You know, Joshua Evan seems to have been the only person involved with any decent motives. In the end that is. Even if he'd been ineffective up to that time – or only guided by Marian Roberts. Incidentally, does it strike you that his death was highly convenient for a lot of people?' The banker frowned. 'I suppose it was a pure accident?'

'Good heavens, yes! At least the coroner said so. So did the sailing community. Joshua shouldn't have gone out that morning.'

'It was only a passing thought. On another aspect, I hope Segam Holdings are represented at the meeting in the morning. I've been trying to find out whether they really are determined to close the company.'

'Why?' Bude asked sharply.

'Because I've had some enquiries made. It's just possible we could find another buyer for G. L. Evan, as a going concern. It could involve another of the bank's clients. We've put out a feeler. It's too early for a considered reaction, but the signs are promising. We need a lot more information.'

'The client being another confectionery manufacturer?'

'Something of the kind.'

'You surprise me.'

'If the pension trustees succeed in holding on to that surplus . . .'

'Keeping it for the pensioners?'

'Yes. If that happened, Segam may find they paid too much for the company. I would guess a lot too much.' Treasure had been watching the other carefully as he spoke.

Bude leant forward in his chair, his eyes on his clasped hands. 'My own feeling is you'd have to be right on that. It stands to reason.' His gaze lifted to meet Treasure's. 'In a way, of course, I've been closer to the matter than you.'

'In more than one way, perhaps?'

'I meant living here amongst the people involved,' Bude had come back quickly. 'Could place me in a . . . a very awkward position.'

71

It had seemed the speaker had been about to say something more pertinent than he had managed with the last somewhat stumbling utterance.

Treasure waited for further elucidation, but since none was volunteered he questioned: 'So, do you imagine Segam would be ready to sell the company for the reason I suggest?'

'Selling it cheap to cut their losses, you mean?'

'Probably. And to a company that, on acquiring G. L. Evan, might be happy simply to borrow the pension-fund surplus, and use it as loan capital to help keep the show going for everyone's benefit?'

'That's feasible, I suppose?'

'Perfectly. And legal. If the pension trustees approved. If it was in the interests of the pensioners and the future pensioners – the present employees. It's probably what should have been tried earlier. Before the company was promised to Segam. Before the management and shareholders got the idea it'd be easier to feather their nests than tackle things the hard way.'

Bude's expression became more serious. 'That's something Segam themselves could be interested in pursuing, of course. Perhaps as a joint enterprise with someone else in the confectionery business. Like the other bank client you mentioned.'

'Selling half the Evan company to the other participant? Sounds like a proposition.'

Suddenly Bude sat back in his chair. He nodded. 'Segam Holdings will be represented at the meeting, Mark. That's if it's still necessary to hold one.'

'You know they'll have someone there?'

'Yes. And I think you know why.' He got up, and drained his glass before continuing. 'I think you've guessed I control Segam Holdings, which I do, in a roundabout sort of way.'

The banker nodded. 'I admit, it crossed my mind when you invited me for the weekend. Thank you for telling me. So now perhaps we can get down to cases properly.'

7

'You're staying then, sir?'

Treasure, driving the BMW out of the courtyard, had stopped when he saw Timothy Wells. The pilot had emerged from one of the outhouses, a towel and swimming trunks slung over his shoulder.

'I'll be here overnight certainly,' replied the banker.

'The governor said . . .' the young man stopped, then began again. 'I mean, since no one's flying anywhere, I can take off for home after my swim. You been in the pool yet?'

'No chance, unfortunately.' He was due at the factory by six o'clock, and it was nearly that now. It had been only a few minutes earlier when, their talk concluded, Lewis Bude had shown him up to a comfortable, north-facing guest suite. There had been time only to unpack. 'Where's your home, Timothy?'

'Not far. Chester. Near the airport.'

'Enjoy your swim,' Treasure moved the car off, intrigued that the pilot had obviously been forewarned that he might have been flying his recent passenger back again tonight.

Prior to his admitting he owned Segam Holdings, Bude had evidently been deeply apprehensive about the banker's likely reaction to that fact. Nor was it clear whether the financier would have owned up to his involvement if Treasure hadn't indicated he had guessed it anyway. Up to that point Bude had been angling to gauge the depth of the other's own commitment to the whole affair, and to get a lead on his specific intentions.

Treasure had been ready to humour his host in all this. The discussion which had followed the disclosure had been positive, involving firm promises that entirely satisfied the banker. It was a pity that this result had been marred by Bude's ultimate suggestion that his guest might now decide to plead an urgent call from London and leave immediately – without reference to commitments here, including Constance's dinner party. The idea was that Treasure could thus avoid having to confront the staff committee again. It was why the helicopter had been kept available. The proposal had evidenced a signal failure by Bude to read Treasure's character – even if it exposed a good deal about Bude's own business attitudes.

Treasure had firmly elected to stay and see his business through. The decision had caused him no embarrassment since Bude had insisted the proposal that he leave had been put solely to spare the banker's feelings.

Earlier, Bude had explained that Segam Holdings was one of his smaller business interests. He exercised only the remotest kind of control over it. So long as the management team running the company showed a profit, he let it alone.

He said that when he had first learned Segam were taking over a company on his own doorstep, negotiations had already been well advanced. He hadn't felt justified in interfering. If expropriating a pension-fund surplus had been part of the deal, that was not uncommon these days. Even so, he would naturally have expected arrangements to be made to protect the pensioners – but by the people responsible for their interests. He had discovered that nothing much had been done in that direction only two days before; a direct result of Treasure becoming involved.

'I've told the Segam directors in Liverpool there'll have to be a fair settlement on present and future pensioners' benefits, backdated where appropriate. They're to get the maximum the Revenue will allow. The settlement to be approved by Grenwood, Phipps. By whoever you nominate at the bank, Mark. I can't say fairer than that, can I?' Bude had offered expansively. 'You have my word on it from this moment.'

'Which I accept. Presumably that's going to upset the whole Segam calculation?'

'Yes. Fundamentally, now the pension surplus is virtually out of the picture. It's why we'll have to consider new proposals on the future of G. L. Evan Limited.'

'You did intend to close the company?'

'It seems my people did, yes. Now they'll think again – about winding it up, keeping it going or selling it on to someone who will. They'd certainly consider selling it back to the old shareholders. Segam will look at anything that brings them out with a profit. Even a modest one.'

It had struck Treasure as being an unexpectedly handsome and potentially expensive climb-down, and he was still wondering about the real reason for it.

The banker was not convinced that Bude had been ignorant of the Segam intention to take over G. L. Evan until late on. A less charitable observer might have deduced that the man had been in the perfect position actually to have instigated the deal.

Rattled by the recent turn in events, Bude's astute reaction had been promptly to invite Treasure to Plas Gwyn. There, he had probably figured, he stood the best chance of arranging a gentleman's agreement if it became necessary – swiftly, ahead of anything that teams of accountants and lawyers could hatch in the time, and before the news media ran the wrong story. And that was precisely what had happened.

'And you'll not let it out locally I own Segam?' Bude had pressed, after Treasure had declined the suggestion about leaving.

'Certainly, if that's the way you want it.'

'For the time being. And you'll get them to call off the staff meeting in the morning?'

'I'll do my best.'

'The concessions I'm making—'

'My very best,' Treasure had interrupted to reiterate the intention. Had Bude yielded so much simply to avoid bad personal and corporate publicity? It was beginning to seem so, and yet . . .

In any event, as the banker drove through the outskirts of Llanegwen, he felt his visit had already been more than justified.

He recognised the brick and rubble wall surrounding the factory when he came to it. This eastern boundary of the G. L. Evan domain replaced the bracken hedge on one side of the road that he had followed down from the house. As directed, he turned the car left at the next corner into Dewin Street, then left again through the open factory gates.

The factory yard was broad and cobbled, with an iron weighbridge beyond the gate to the right, in front of a newish, grey-rendered office block with steel-framed windows.

The triple-storey main building with a low-pitched slate roof was thirty yards ahead, facing the gate, and flanked on both sides by flat-roofed sections of different heights. The chimney stack sprouted from the rear, and was slightly, almost perversely, off centre, exuding colourless vapours that made curious turmoils in the air above it.

Most of what Treasure was seeing was older than the century, stone-built and with the kind of ugliness that mere venerability can still dignify in an industrial edifice. Unfortunately, what mean integrity this place might have claimed was spoiled by the entrance, approached by some shallow steps in the centre. It was framed by a cream-plastered lintel and pilasters – late additions, but earlier than the red-painted double doors that should have been disgracing a fire exit in a backstreet cinema.

To the left of the factory was a cluster of circular storage tanks – steel, twenty feet high and served by a Wellsian tangle of pipes in different colours, and connecting with the building.

Set back at the other side of the main block was a low, whitewashed extension fronted by a series of long roller shutters and a continuous van-loading platform. Beyond this were some seemingly abandoned sheds and what was evidently the main carpark, nearly empty. Instead of driving to that, Treasure parked close to the main door in an area marked with a 'Visitors' notice and beside a lone Austin Montego. As he was leaving the car the red factory doors opened, and Marian Roberts came out, wearing a professional-looking white coat and a deeply preoccupied expression. She was in conversation with a short man in a sports jacket and flannels who looked to be in his late thirties.

'Thanks again for your help, Miss Roberts. I'll let you know if we hear anything,' the man was saying as the couple neared Treasure. 'Good evening, sir. Friend of Mr Bude, are you?' Despite the accuracy of the conjecture, the speaker was, even so, waiting for it to be confirmed.

'Yes, I am.' Treasure smiled. 'You know the car, obviously.'

'Mr Treasure. So you're here. Welcome.'

The greeting from the young woman was more reserved than he had expected – or felt he was entitled to expect. It was as though she had found his arrival more surprising than commendable.

'Good to see you again, Miss Roberts.' He smiled and nodded.

'This is Detective Inspector Alwyn Thomas,' she offered. 'He's always well informed.'

The two men shook hands.

'It's just I know the numbers of the cars belonging to the chairman of the local bench, sir,' said the policeman with a grin. 'He's got quite a lot of them, too.'

'Mr Bude's a magistrate? I didn't realise.' He glanced from one to the other. 'Am I interrupting anything?'

'Certainly not, and I'm just off.' The inspector went to unlock a door to the Montego. He was well built and stocky, with humorous eyes, and a squashed nose on a ruddy face.

'Whatever happens, Mr Thomas, I don't want Owen Watkins charged on my account.' This was Marian. She turned towards Treasure. 'A boy who does odd jobs here is accused of selling stolen goods.'

'And allegedly stealing them in the first place, too.' Thomas sighed.

'What sort of goods?' asked Treasure.

'Spirits, mostly. Nicked from the local sailing club. And a silver-plated drinks measure belonging to Miss Roberts.'

'Which had my postal code on it in invisible ink. It's not

77

worth anything really. I wouldn't have lent it to the club otherwise.'

The policeman sighed again. 'Still stealing, I'm afraid. Anyway, it's academic till we've found him. He's disappeared.' He shrugged. 'Goodbye for now, then. Nice to have met you, Mr Treasure.' He got into the car.

Marian and Treasure turned back towards the factory door. 'The boy was expected here today. To clean cars.'

'Must have been a big haul for a police inspector to be looking for him.'

'Oh, Alwyn Thomas was here unofficially. He used to help with the local youth club. He knows Owen. I'm sorry, this can't be of any interest to you.'

'I'm interested to know why you don't want to prosecute.'

'Because he's really a decent kid from a decent home. But he's out of work. No prospect of a job when he left school, and none to date. Not to speak of. He's short of money, so he's taken to petty thieving.' The sentiments and acerbic tone were reminiscent of her attitude at their first meeting in Cheyne Walk.

'It doesn't follow that was the only alternative, surely?'

'Have you ever been out of work, Mr Treasure?'

'No, but I doubt I'd have turned to crime if I had.'

'Well, let's hope the one hundred and ninety-four employees of this factory don't either. When they're all laid off.' She thrust both hands into the pockets of her coat as she entered through the door Treasure was holding open.

'Perhaps they won't be laid off.'

'You've got some good news?' Eager-eyed, she swung round in the huge tiled vestibule they had entered.

The place had more the atmosphere of a Victorian public library than a factory, except that there was clocking-in equipment fixed to the wall on the far left in front of closed, half-glazed double doors. Straight across from the entrance was a pair of oak, panelled doors, while some way to the right, wide stone steps with an ornamental iron balustrade led to the upper floors.

Treasure was looking about him with interest as he said: 'The firm information I have affects pensioners. And it's good news. I've been in touch with . . . with Segam management.' Briefly he told her what had been promised without disclosing who the spokesman had been. 'I also see some possibility of keeping the company going,' he ended. 'But that's theory at the moment. Incidentally, I'd like to look over the plant while I'm here.'

'After what you've achieved to date, you deserve to be carried through it shoulder high.'

'A brisk walk round will do, I assure you,' but he was pleased at the enthusiastic response. 'From now on I'm looking to generate some goodwill on all sides. On that score, can I persuade your committee to postpone the meeting in the morning? If they'll accept my word, it's quite the wrong time to be holding it.'

'Bit short notice. But if you say it's important, we'll do it.' The respectful look matched the compliance in her voice. 'The others are waiting upstairs in my office, except for Brenig Jones, and he should be back soon. Would you like to see round before we go up? It won't take long.'

'Why not? What's through there?' He pointed at the doors in the centre.

'That's the rock room. Not important nowadays. Where we make sticks of seaside rock. It's only seasonal business.'

He smiled. 'I've always wanted to know how the lettering's put in.'

'In this factory in the old-fashioned way, by hand.' She took a bunch of keys from her pocket and unlocked the doors.

The room they entered was narrow, but around sixty feet long. Running almost the length of it was a wooden table with a worn top scarcely three feet wide.

'To start with we make a stiff, round core out of a mix of sugar and edible fats. Looks like a big white drum, five feet high and about eight feet around.'

'Eight feet? In circumference?'

'Yes. It's enormous. Then we take thick strips of the same ingredient, this time some red, some white, and build them round the outside, making up the letters that spell out the name of the town. Then we bind them in with a blanket wrapping of more white sugar and another of red for the outside.'

'As simple as that?'

'Simple but cumbersome, and only disastrous if you make a spelling error.'

'So you end up . . .'

'With a mammoth, squat seaside rock, which is trolleyed onto that big press in the corner.'

'Looks like the boiler of a steam locomotive with a cut along the middle?'

'It's hydraulic. Divides in half like this.' They were now beside the press, which was eight feet long. The top half of the cylinder hinged back silently in response to a pull on a lever. 'It's used to elongate the rock, in sections. To about twenty feet. Compressing it in the process, of course. Afterwards the whole thing is manhandled onto the table. Women sitting on both sides then roll it with their forearms till it's down to the required size. After that it's hardened, cut up into individual lengths, wrapped and boxed for shipment. And that's it.'

'With their bare forearms?'

She smirked. 'I thought that might bother you. There's a machine now for making rock. It puts the lettering across the middle not round the side. It'd be murder trying to do that by our method. But we've never been able to justify the capital for mechanising. Local housewife labour is cheap. They do have immaculately clean arms.'

'I should hope so. Don't think I'll bother with seaside rock again.'

'Lots of foodstuffs are processed by hand. Look in on the kitchen of the next five-star restaurant you lunch in.'

'I shall do nothing of the kind. It might wholly destroy the mystery as well as my appetite.'

'Anyway, the hygiene arrangements in this factory are exemplary. Our only problem is we've lost most of our rock orders to companies that have mechanised.'

'So it could pay you to do the same?'

80

'Only if we could rely on having the volume of orders to justify it. It's a chicken-and-egg situation. If we don't mechanise we should probably drop the rock business altogether and convert that space to some other use.' They had returned to the vestibule and she was locking the doors again as she spoke. 'Incidentally, this morning the management suddenly agreed the staff meeting could be held on the premises tomorrow, and in there. It's the handiest room and suits the numbers best. Still, if we're calling it off.' She shrugged.

'I'm glad they were being so co-operative,' Treasure commented, not surprised at the so-recent change of attitude.

'Nobody's working in the main factory now, I'm afraid. We close at four thirty.' She was leading him past the clocking-in area and unlocking the doors beyond. 'After checking in, all employees go through here, change into special working gear and shake out round the building to the various departments – manufacturing, packaging, stores, despatch . . .'

It was a cursory tour, but adequate for Treasure's purpose. The main plant was modestly impressive, including the modern locker rooms which his guide insisted on displaying to justify her earlier point about cleanliness.

Most of the manufacture was done in a lofty, open area rising through three storeys without conventional flooring. Instead, the space was divided by a gantry system – wide metal gangways and staircases criss-crossing around clusters of feeder shafts and hoppers. These were arranged to deliver raw materials to big stainless-steel vessels for mixing and cooking. The vessels, in turn, fed the cooling and lozenge-stamping equipment at ground level. Conveyor belts then took the bare product – boiled sweets of different types – to be wrapped in the next section of the building, except for SUGS which, Marian explained, were made, then individually wrapped, assembled into tubes and boxed for shipment in a continuous vertical process.

The SUGS cooking vessel was still in operation. It was covered with a hood, but Marian raised this electrically to show the dark bubbling liquid that close to gave off a strongly medicinal odour.

81

'Mm, what a healthy smell,' Treasure remarked, looking down into the huge vat from the second-level gantry. He was leaning over a removable guard rail, which his guide had put in place before opening the hood.

'Don't want too much of it though, or you might become an addict. A sniffer. It's been known. It's why the extractors and the cooling system are still on,' said Marian over the humming of the ventilating fans, then she nodded towards the vessel. 'That's part of an export order. Should have been processed this afternoon, but there was a breakdown. On the packaging line. Brenig Jones fixed it, but too late.'

'So it'll go on simmering for the weekend?'

She smiled. 'Musn't let it cool off, not once it's in this state.'

'Because it would seize up into one gigantic cough drop?'

'Mm. That's fairly accurate.'

Some minutes later, the tour ended, he remarked: 'For a specialist, you have an impressive familiarity with the complete set-up.'

She had led them back into the entrance area and was locking the doors behind them. She grinned. 'A good deal of it's pretty elementary – like the storage and despatch sections at the end. And it's a small outfit. Everybody mucks in.'

'And as chief chemist, of course, you're part of management,' he offered tentatively.

'So why do I identify with the workers, you mean? Demonstrate outside the homes of unsuspecting merchant bankers?'

'That had occurred to me, too.'

'Management and workers here never used to be adversaries. It was a good place to work. That's why I came here three years ago. Why I stayed. That and because I got to run a whole department. The "us and them" problem only started last year. When Paul Ranker came. He was supposed to increase sales, but all he's done is sour staff relations. Anyway, that's why I've chosen to side with the wage earners.'

'I see. The company's not been profitable for some time, of course.'

'Agreed. The products are good, though. And they have potential. Especially SUGS. We needed a marketing dynamo. Ranker isn't that.'

'And Joshua Evan?'

'Didn't think he was, but he could have been.' Her tone was thoughtful. She had motioned him towards the stairway at the end of the hall. They paused there. 'Joshua had an inferiority complex. Because he was family he never believed he deserved his job.'

'You thought differently?'

'Sure. He was a late developer, but potentially good, and getting better. He actually believed in the company too. George Evan, his uncle, had lost the faith. Ranker never had it. Trouble was, the high-ups never believed in Joshua.'

'You did.'

'So did quite a few others lower down in the pecking order.'

'But he didn't effect anything?'

'Yes, he did,' she answered quite sharply. 'Export orders were up. That was his doing. And sales in North Wales and the north of England were moving up as well. It needed time, that's all. It was Joshua who wanted us to concentrate our selling in regions close to the factory, instead of trying to do it nationally. Ranker was against that. He didn't understand because his background was in international brands. He also killed off our "own name" brands of sweets for local chains.'

'For supermarket chains, you mean?'

'Mostly. We were very well placed for increasing that kind of business. Joshua was proving it. If only all the people he respected had backed him. It would have given him confidence. Whatever happened, he was set on stopping the sale to Segam.'

'I imagine he respected you. And you seem to have been pretty intimately involved with his plans.'

'I helped him a bit. But I couldn't do anything about finding extra capital for more machines, like the one that makes and wraps SUGS. We need them, even if they do sometimes break down.' She looked at her watch. 'We'd better go up. My office and lab are on the next floor. Converted out of the old board

83

room, I think when all the executive offices were moved to the new building by the gate.'

'New building?'

'Not that new. Built twenty years ago. No lift here, I'm afraid.' She hurried on ahead up the stone steps, energetically, with a straight back. He had forgotten what good legs she had until they had started climbing gantries; now he was reminded again.

'Just one other thing.' He stopped her on the wide landing. 'I believe you're invited to dinner at the Budes' tonight.'

'I got the message just before you arrived. It's very short notice.'

'It had to be, of course. Are you coming?'

'I hadn't decided. I hardly know them.'

'In a way it's for my benefit. More to the point, Paul Ranker and Michael Chard will be there. Chance to demonstrate the old non-adversarial attitude perhaps?'

She hesitated, pulling a face. 'OK, I'll ring now to say I'm coming. Means getting through here quickly.'

Her small office was separated by half-glazed partitioning from what seemed an impressively equipped laboratory beyond it. Three people, all known to Treasure, were grouped around the desk when he entered behind Marian.

'We're very glad to see you again, Mr Treasure. And grateful, yes.' It was the elderly Basso Morgan who stood up and spoke first.

'Hear, hear,' called Mrs Blodwyn Davies in strong support. Albert Shotover, in a white coat similar to Marian's, had half-risen but was prevented from completing the gesture because he and his chair were tightly jammed between desk-end, wall and Mrs Davies. He made enthusiastic throat-clearing noises.

'I did promise to come.' The banker smiled at the three, then laughed out loud at the small, neatly lettered showcard in the centre of the desk and facing him. The message on it ran: WE TREASURE MARK TREASURE.

8

'Well, you'll have to go before I leave to meet my Mam. You promised. And you don't have to stare at me like that, Owen. You said you wouldn't. Spoils it.'

Gwyneth Davies was sorry as soon as she had uttered the last words. The whole point was not to be self-conscious at all, and he'd been very good. She had been topless in front of boys before, plenty of times, and nothing special implied or allowed. It was supposed to be the same now. She had just come back from taking a shower and wearing only her panties. Now she was putting on a bra in front of the wardrobe in her study-bedroom as nonchalantly as she could manage.

It was just that this was the first time she'd been alone with a boy since the attack. She'd been testing herself – using the chance to prove she hadn't developed what she'd overheard her mother darkly call a complex. If she'd had a complex she'd never have made herself come in from the bathroom like that. But it hadn't been easy all the same, even with Owen Watkins agreeing to co-operate – and behave. She was certain it was important for her acting career that she didn't get hang-ups.

Really, Gwyneth was recovering very well from her nasty experience. All she had to contend with now were the after effects people seemed to think she *ought* to be suffering.

'But if you're meeting her for supper at Basso Morgan's, I could stay up here till ten, say. You won't be back before that?' pleaded Owen. For once the pathetic, hard-done-by expression was genuine. The tight, pale-coloured cotton shirt and faded jeans accentuated his pallor and spindly frame. 'Your Mam won't need to know. I'd be safe here till dark.' Then came as an afterthought: 'And I wasn't staring. At least I didn't mean to.'

5

It was true that to this point he'd been feeling worried not lascivious, and ever since she had let him in. He was sitting dejectedly on the studio bed in the corner of the prettily decorated room, leaning forward to avoid denting the cushions on the wall behind him.

It was after six. He had been waiting in the coal shed next to the back door of the house in Sheep Street when Gwyneth had come home from school earlier.

'But if the police are after you?' She took down the skirt she intended wearing, but she didn't step into it, just carried it across to the desk-cum-dressing table in front of the net-curtained window.

'It's all a mistake. I told you that.'

'Why not tell them, then, instead of hiding?'

'Because they're not going to believe me. Not straight away. I decided that at our house. When they came looking for me.'

When a police constable had called there at lunch-time, Owen had been coming in at the back door. He had waited to hear what was said to his mother at the front, snatched up a few essentials from his room, then slipped quietly out the way he had come. He had left a note saying he'd be away for a few weeks.

'Well, you can't be running away forever.'

'Won't have to. They'll find out the truth after a bit.' What he meant was he hoped the police would lose interest in time. It wasn't as though he'd robbed a bank, and they had to be working on suspicion not fact. 'By tonight I'll have the money to get to Dundee. I can get work there through the summer.'

'You promise you'll go at ten?' She was finding things to do, rearranging what was on the desk top, putting clothes in drawers. She crossed the room several times, running her hands through her hair, striking poses on purpose – making believe she was in front of an auditorium full of people.

Owen got up from the bed. 'Thanks, Gwyneth.' He moved close to her, putting his arms around her from behind. His hands went to cup her young breasts.

She stayed still. 'You weren't supposed . . .'

86

'I know. I can't help it, though. I'll be back in September at the latest. You won't forget me by then?'

Gwyneth felt him unhook her bra. 'Call me Gwendolene.' Was she still willing herself into giving a performance?

'Gwendolene,' he whispered dutifully, in a good cause. 'What time they expecting you at Basso Morgan's?'

'Not till seven,' she breathed back. 'But I've got my homework to do first.'

'It's Friday. Do it tomorrow.' He turned her about and kissed her, then backed her down onto the bed. The last movement was awkward, not suavely executed as he'd intended, but Gwyneth hadn't resisted.

'What you doing, Owen?' she asked, when it was patently evident that he was rolling down her panties. More than just knowing what he was doing, she was passively willing to allow what he'd be doing next. Her eyes only appeared closed as she watched him fumbling with his clothes, then take out the contraceptive packet.

'Fancy having that with you,' she murmured.

'Never without.'

She might have found the implication of earlier sexual experience unsettling if she'd believed it. What mattered to her now was that she wanted him to go on. She hadn't told him the protection wasn't necessary: the woman doctor she'd seen in London had recommended Gwyneth go on the pill for a bit – as a sort of reassurance. Her mother had agreed, but only just. So in that way the girl was prepared for the event, only she needed to know if she could cope mentally.

Later the little groan she gave marked the start of the new and altogether agreeable experience. And no part of it was painful as she'd been told it could be.

When it was over the first time, she held on to him tightly.

He watched while tears welled in her eyes. 'Why you crying?'

'Because I'm happy.'

'That's all right, then.'

'Love me, do you, Owen?'

'Of course.'

87

She could have done with more heartfelt confirmation than that, but still.

When he was ready, she drew him into her again. Now there was nothing passive about the part she played. She felt uneasy after that second time, aware that it had proved nothing – except that it was better than the first time. But the real conscience-stirring by genes inherited from her Welsh Noncon-formist forebears had still to be properly awakened by events.

For the time being, Gwyneth consoled herself that her stage career had not been blighted, nor her normal appetites ruined by what had happened that night in Garth Lane – and she had needed to be certain.

Owen suspected Gwyneth had succumbed because she needed to know whether she could – but he didn't allow that to detract from his sense of conquest. Despite impressions, it had been a first experience for him too. He'd been carrying those sheaths about for so long he had only been worried that they might have rotted.

So what happened later was to add poignancy to the initiations in the Sheep Street bedroom – to the proof that genuine adversity hadn't hurt Gwyneth's life very much, nor poor Owen's either, not up to then.

'Mark, I don't believe you've met Michael and Megan Chard,' Constance Bude enthused, trailing them out to him on the terrace. 'Michael is auditor to G. L. Evan Limited and he's Lewis's private accountant.' She didn't trouble to expound about Megan, who was coming in a poor third.

The Chards were both in their early forties. He was thin with receding hair, a seriously undeveloped beard and a nearly permanent querulous expression. She was mousy, earnest, and unsuitably dressed in a too-enveloping pink taffeta dress and clashing shoes.

It seemed from Chard's fleeting facial reaction that he hadn't expected the mention of his second professional function.

'And you're also a trustee to the Evan pension-fund, of course,' said Treasure, with pronounced affability because he was anxious not to sound accusing in the matter.

'An office that attracts little profit and less thanks. Still, one does one's best,' was the other man's wholly unexpected response.

Mrs Chard gave Treasure only one brief, uncertain glance. Her gaze had otherwise been concentrated dependently on her husband's face. She stood very close to him, and since he was somewhat taller than she, her status seemed more that of supplicant than spouse.

'Are you all going to be warm enough out here?' Constance enquired as part of a soliloquy that encompassed several questions to which she wasn't expecting answers. She was in a sleeveless silk dress and more likely to feel the cold than anyone else. 'It's so good to be out by the pool again in the evening, don't you think? Such a long winter this year. Ah, here's Effy with the drinks. Champagne all right for everyone?'

An aged maid, angular, diminutive and with a long loose strand of hair over one eye was advancing on the group, slowly and unsteadily. She bore filled tulip-shaped glasses on a silver tray, at a precipitous, gravity-defying angle. Lewis Bude appeared some way behind her with Paul Ranker, who had just arrived.

'Nectar, as usual, dear lady,' lyricised the managing director of G. L. Evan after he had been introduced to Treasure. 'Always vintage champagne in this house, Mark. I may call you Mark? Well, here's to all of us. Sorry my lady wife couldn't make it.' He had whisked a glass from the tray and brought it to his lips with so much enthusiasm he dribbled some of the contents down one of his lapels. He glared reproachfully at the blameless Effy.

'I gather you're going to the G. L. Evan staff meeting in the morning, Mr Treasure.' This was Chard while Ranker was mopping at his suit.

Treasure watched Constance glide back into the house as he answered. 'If it's still on. The staff committee has agreed to a postponement. That's if they can head everybody off. I still have a date with the chairman of the company at nine. I believe that's to be in the factory.' He was studying his questioner and debating whether as Lewis Bude's personal accountant the man could have failed to know his client had owned Segam Holdings. Really that possibility seemed highly improbable – a conclusion that invited several other pertinent questions.

'I'll ring George Evan in a minute about your meeting, Mark. Fix where you're to see him,' offered Bude.

Chard frowned. 'If you're seeing George about pension-trustee matters, would you like me there too?'

'Thank you for the offer, but I think probably not. As you know, I'm not formally a trustee.'

'Naturally, you're much more important than that.' The tone was matter-of-fact, not fawning. 'I only meant—'

'See him in the factory. Don't go to his house. George Evan's, I mean,' Ranker had thrust himself back into the conversation, and was now holding his glass with the base in the flat of his palm, his thumb at the bottom of the stem. 'Confidentially, their coffee's poisonous, and his sister's worse.' He screwed up his eyes, wrinkled his face, and thrust out his sharp chin defiantly to underline his resolution in the maligning of old ladies.

Bude coughed. 'I hardly know Miss Evan. I believe she's harmless enough,' he added, a touch reprovingly.

'Better avoided, take my word for it,' returned Ranker, unabashed. 'Factory's best for you, Mark. At nine, you say?' The eyes narrowed again. 'I shall be in myself by then. Great deal on at the moment. If there's anything . . .' He brought the glass to his lips in a theatrical gesture, forearm in parallel with the flattened palm. He sipped like a caricature connoisseur before continuing, '. . . anything at all I can do for you there, don't hesitate to say so.' His elbow then descended sharply on the head of Effy, the maid, who happened to be passing.

'Miss Evan is very well meaning. She gave a lot to the sailing club. Her own money.' Mrs Chard had made a surprise intervention, and immediately reddened. Her head retracted between taffeta puff sleeves, which gave it a gift-wrapped appearance.

'You sail, Mrs Chard?' asked Treasure.

She shook her head, making the taffeta rustle. 'I help with tea sometimes. At the Llanegwen club. On Sundays. In the summer,' she pumped out each phrase with effort and a strong Welsh accent.

'But you do sail sometimes, Megan,' reproved her husband.

'Not any more. Not after Joshua.'

Ranker made a deprecating sound, and not just over the fresh spill of champagne he'd been wiping off his shirt-cuff and sleeve. 'Oh, come, Megan. You can't let one sad accident sour your view on sailing. Joshua copped it for going out at a daft time of day, at the wrong time of year, in appalling weather.'

'He wasn't the only one,' Mrs Chard answered quietly, and showing a great deal more spirit than before.

'Other people were sailing that morning?' Treasure enquired.

'Not from Llanegwen, and not that early,' said Bude promptly. 'You're so dependent on the tide if you sail from the open beach here, or an open beach anywhere else for that matter. That's why he was off so early.'

'And he was by himself, of course,' the banker affirmed.

'The three of us sailed from Beaumaris later the same day.' Bude hadn't answered the question directly. He had indicated with a glance that the companions referred to were Ranker and Chard. 'As I remember, we started around one thirty. Conditions had improved a lot by then.'

'That's on Anglesey. To the west,' Ranker filled in, as though the location of that prominent island might be unknown to Treasure. 'Lewis moors a sailing cruiser there, don't you, squire? Superb craft. Michael and I keep dinghies at the same club, but we crewed for Lewis that day.'

'It's generally more sheltered there. In the Menai Straits,' offered the accountant.

'Joshua should have come with us. He knew he was always welcome,' said Bude.

'He didn't . . .'

'He was always a loner when it came to sailing.' Chard seemed pointedly to have talked down his wife. 'And in some other ways too.'

'Took a separate line, you mean?' This was Treasure, when it was clear Mrs Chard was not going to try again.

'You could say that, yes.' Ranker made a pained face. 'Or that he just preferred his own company. Take that night. He didn't sleep in his own house. Dossed at his mother's flat instead . . .'

'It's closer to the beach,' put in Mrs Chard looking down into the glass she had just emptied for the second time. 'They said that at the inquest. His mother was away. She usually is. He often slept there before an early start. So as not to disturb Barbara. That's his wife. He was always very thoughtful.' Her voice had trailed off wistfully.

Ranker scowled at his interrupter. 'Yes, Megan, but my point is he didn't need to do his sailing from a tatty company club in Llanegwen.' He paused, perhaps to reflect that as managing director of the company he might have some responsibility for the tattiness of its sailing club. 'I mean it's not really company any more. Not a club either, not in the proper sense. All right for a snatched outing late on a weekday, in a beaten-up club dinghy. But Joshua could perfectly well have afforded to join us for the serious weekend stuff. Much nicer crowd at Beaumaris, and it's a hell of a lot more convenient. As well as safer.'

'He wasn't very expert?'

It was Bude who answered the banker. 'Competent enough. Or not quite enough, perhaps.' He gave a disconsolate grunt. 'I think what Paul's getting at is Joshua wasn't at all a gregarious type. If he had been he'd most probably have been sailing with us that day. Nobody went out in a dinghy, or anything else, till after lunch. Too many people around advising against it.' Silence followed the last remark.

'Joshua was against selling the company,' said Megan Chard unexpectedly and almost to herself.

'Weren't we all? Weren't we all, dear lady?' repeated Ranker. 'Yet it had to be. This is the age of the big battalions. I came from one of those myself. Thought we could buck the system here. Show initiative. Beat Mars, Cadbury's and the others at their own games. But it didn't come off. We failed. And why did we fail?'

'Because you weren't bloody good enough, Paul, love.' The sensuous female voice belonged to the statuesque blonde, who was still several paces away and walking across the terrace with some deliberation. The white sheath dress was moulded so tightly to her well-shaped figure that it seemed impossible she could be wearing anything else – save the long earrings, the white high heels and the very sheer tights. The slit skirt was revealing a remarkable length of thigh as she moved. Her main anatomical features may have been marginally overdeveloped for perfection, but, judging from the expressions, none of the men present would have protested the point.

Lewis Bude kissed the newcomer on the cheek. 'Barbara, welcome. I'd like you to meet . . .'

'Mark Treasure, the glamorous banker. I'm Barbara Evan. Joshua's widow. I've heard about you.' She gazed hard into his eyes, mostly, he thought, because she seemed to be having trouble focusing her own. 'Were you in the 'copter this afternoon?'

'Yes, I was.'

'Then in a way we've met already.' She grinned. 'That bastard Timothy's always catching me in the raw.'

'I don't think it was intentional.'

'There's charity for you. But who cares? I bet you didn't.' And it was obvious from her playfully wicked tone that she hadn't minded either. She turned her head languidly from side to side, then ran her tongue over her lips before asking, 'Lewis, I badly need a . . .'

'There's champagne.'

'There always is, lover. I've been drinking Scotch. I hope it doesn't show, because I'm having another. Effy knows. I hope she's bringing it.' She turned in Ranker's direction. He was some distance away so she blew him a kiss. 'Am I forgiven for saying you weren't bloody good enough, Paul?' she called.

'Mm, provisionally. Since you didn't mean it.' He blew a kiss back. 'There'll be a heavy forfeit exacted later.'

She sucked in air sharply through her mouth. 'Ooh, I can't wait for that.' Then, before switching her gaze, she said under

93

her breath to Treasure, 'I bloody did mean it, though. Hello, Megan,' followed quite loudly. 'Still beating up Michael, are you? That's the way.' She purposely brushed against the banker as she went to embrace the uncertain Mrs Chard, and before turning next to the lady's husband. 'Hello, Michael. How's the money business?' She wrapped her arms around his neck and kissed him full on the mouth. 'God, that sexy beard could drive me crazy. Don't know how you contain yourself, Megan, love. But where's the gorgeous Constance?'

'Small crisis in the kitchen. She'll be here in a moment,' offered Bude handing her the whisky Effy had just brought. The maid was also balancing a bottle of champagne on her tray and counter-moving Ranker, who she was watching with the trepidity of a cautious hamster.

'Thanks, darling,' said Mrs Evan, squeezing her host's hand. 'Is this the whole party? With the men outnumbering the women? That's the way we like it. Isn't that right, Megan?' Now she was in front of Treasure again, clasping her glass with both hands and holding it close to her half-open mouth. Her body was swaying a little. 'Oh, yes, we've heard a lot about you,' she said.

To this point Treasure considered the woman's entrance to have been as noteworthy as her appearance – and not a little unexpected in a widow of about six weeks. It was difficult to estimate how drunk she was. Idly he went on to wonder if one of the men present might have been the shy visitor at her poolside – the figure he had briefly glimpsed from the helicopter. She was evidently on close terms with all of them. They had all been nearby, here at Plas Gwyn, just before his arrival.

'Did you say Marian Roberts was coming?' Ranker asked Bude but keeping his eyes on Mrs Evan.

'She is, yes. Her car's broken down. I had to send someone to fetch her. I think I heard a car drive up a moment ago.'

'You didn't tell me, Lewis,' commented Mrs Evan, over-sweetly.

'Didn't I? I thought I had. Constance felt it'd be right . . .'

'If you gave the gallant little loser an airing? Oh, I'm sure it would.' Barbara Evan moved closer to Treasure as she spoke, putting an arm through his. 'Did you hear about the girl who lost on a technicality, Mark? Her lover died before she could get him to the altar. Or the divorce court, rather. Not before she got him into bed, of course. Bad timing, though, wouldn't you say?'

'It doesn't sound as if the lady had much option,' said Treasure diplomatically.

'Oh, she's no lady . . .'

'Barbara, I don't think you should talk about . . .' Megan Chard began.

'About her? Or her lover I suppose?' Mrs Evan interrupted insistently and loudly. 'He was drowned. In a sailing accident. So whose husband is the poor cow after now, I wonder? Anyone here? She'd fancy you all right, Mark. She goes for the rich, good-looking ones.' Unsteadily the speaker swung herself about, and Treasure with her.

Marian Roberts and Constance Bude were only a few steps away and well within earshot.

9

'Sure you won't have another beer before you go, Brenig?'
Basso Morgan enquired, but only out of politeness. The young
engineer shook his head. He was already on his feet ready to
leave.

Morgan turned to Mrs Davies. 'I think you had a coat, didn't
you, Blodwyn?' She was sitting on the sofa beside Albert
Shotover and repairing her lipstick prior to departure.

They were in the front living room of the Morgan bungalow
in Brynteg Avenue off Sea Road. It was just on ten o'clock.

Mrs Davies puckered her lips into a kissing shape, smiled at
her reflection in the little mirror, and then at Shotover, before
putting things back in her handbag. 'Don't bother with my coat,
Basso. Gwyneth knows where it is. Don't you, my lovely?'

Her daughter nodded. 'I'll get it, Mam.' She had been
perched cross-legged on a cushion on the floor next to Basso
Morgan's chair. There had only been proper seats for five. They
had all eaten the buffet meal from plates on their laps.

Gwyneth got up with extra gracefulness, conscious that
people would be studying her. It wasn't so much that she felt a
physical difference since she stopped being a virgin – three
hours and forty-six minutes earlier (she'd just checked again). It
was more that she sensed she'd acquired a different aura: more
worldly it had to be, more experienced. People were bound to
notice that – men especially. Even Mr Morgan had been eyeing
her in a new way. And Brenig Jones had hardly taken his eyes
off her all evening. Mr Shotover had been looking at her a lot as
well – more than usual, though in his case it meant less since he
was her mother's boyfriend.

'And thank you for a lovely supper, Nan,' Mrs Davies said to the hostess, rising from the sofa, and silently noting that the moquette covers had worn a good deal since her last visit.

'Always a pleasure to see you, Blodwyn.' Grey-haired Mrs Morgan meant it, but she wasn't sorry the party was breaking up. It had been a long day and she wasn't sleeping too well. 'It was Basso's idea. To have all the committee members tonight. And Gwyneth as well, naturally. Nice, anyway, that it turned into a celebration. Pity Marian Roberts couldn't come.'

'She'd love to have,' Mrs Davies answered quickly. 'Only it was best she was at Mr Bude's dinner. Representing us, like. Support for Mr Treasure. We all agreed that.'

'I didn't,' said Brenig Jones promptly, and for the record. If he'd known about Marian he wouldn't have been here either.

'Only because you missed the meeting, Brenig. Fair do's, you'd have agreed right enough if you'd been present to hear the reasons,' admonished Mrs Davies. 'Anyway, when all's said and done, it was up to Marian, wasn't it?'

The young man shrugged but said nothing.

'Can I do the rest of the washing up, Mrs Morgan?' This was Gwyneth.

'You've done it all already, except for the cups. I'll leave them till tomorrow. You're a very good girl,' said the hostess, touched that Gwyneth immediately flushed pink at the description. Such an old-fashioned child with proper values – not flighty like some, and not altered by that nasty experience, either.

'Good thing the meeting's cancelled in the morning,' Morgan remarked.

'*Sunday Mirror* will be disappointed,' Shotover said abruptly: it had been some time since he'd last spoken. He was already on his feet, and appeared to be contemplating the gas fire and its 'simulated coal effect'.

Blodwyn Davies, watching him, thought she had guessed what was in his mind. He'd had a fire like this one in his own lounge, which his late wife had considered old-fashioned. It had been taken out when they'd had central heating installed, just

97

before she'd died. Tonight, though, people had said how cosy the fire had made things here, when the evening had cooled.

There was a gas fire in the front room in Mrs Davies's house in Sheep Street. She and Albert had never seriously discussed which house they would live in – his or hers – when they got married. Her place was bigger, but a lot older and not so up to date. And there was always Gwyneth to consider.

It was Gwyneth not gas fires that Albert Shotover was actually thinking about: currently he was thinking about very little else – about how he could come to terms with her. She'd been looking at him in a funny way all evening, probably because it was the weekend again. No doubt she guessed what he and her mother got up to on Sunday afternoons at his house – and the rest. His shoulders started to rise as he tried to dismiss the obsession. 'Yes, better be off,' he blurted out, and again because he couldn't help himself – because he'd been compelled to say or do something or burst.

'The *Sunday Mirror* won't be disappointed because they weren't coming,' said Brenig Jones firmly. 'I rang the Manchester office before I came.'

'Wonder why they cancelled? They seemed ever so keen, didn't they?' queried Mrs Davies, fluffing her hair.

'Their Manchester people knew nothing about it,' answered Jones. 'Anyway I told them the protest's off. So they won't have the excuse to exploit Marian's body,' he finished stiffly.

'Nor mine,' said Gwyneth quietly in a sad voice: she'd been looking forward to being exploited.

'Not enough human interest in the story,' remarked Shotover in a tentative way.

'Get away, that's nonsense,' Mrs Davies returned, but without rancour as he helped her on with the coat her daughter had fetched. 'And what if Mr Treasure keeps the factory open? What about that for human interest?'

'He didn't promise that. Not in so many words. Only that Segam would increase pensions, with back payments from the date of retirement,' Basso Morgan affirmed.

'By five per cent a year for all, for ever and ever,' Mrs Davies rejoined headily, like a triumphant evangelist. 'Worth our trip to London, that was.'

'Better still if Segam or somebody else did keep the company going, of course,' said Morgan, filling his pipe.

'Not if it isn't permanent,' Jones followed up darkly. 'We've had good intentions before. Remember what they said when Mr High-and-Mighty Ranker arrived.'

People were now making for the hall. 'Coming back to our house for something, Albert? It's not too late,' Mrs Davies whispered to Shotover: she had kept him back to ask.

'Not tonight.' He gave no reason.

'Well, I can't very well come to you. Can't leave Gwyneth on her own at night. Not yet.'

'Anyone want a lift? Mrs Davies? Gwyneth? Van's in the road,' Brenig Jones was offering from where he was standing in the little front garden, his eyes following Gwyneth when she emerged.

The girl and her mother got into the Ford Transit; Shotover refused the offer. He lived fairly close by, but in the opposite direction to the others.

After they had watched the party disperse, Basso Morgan lit his pipe on the doorstep and spoke over his shoulder to his wife. 'Think I'll get some air before I turn in, Nan. Don't you wait up.'

She smiled. 'Please yourself, love. Put a jacket on, though.' She assumed he was going out because he knew she didn't care for his smoke in the house, not so late at night.

'Well, I think you handled the whole thing very well,' said Treasure to Marian Roberts as he got into the BMW beside her. 'That dress is enchanting, by the way.' It was a simple black dress, backless, with a halter neck and a straight skirt. He approved the scent she was wearing, too. Her only jewellery was a gold watch and bracelet. She was altogether an agreeable contrast to the loud – in every sense – Barbara Evan who had been placed next to him at dinner, on the other side from the hostess.

99

'I still feel I was invited on sufferance. Never mind, and thank you for the compliments. This dress wasn't meant for an early summer evening in North Wales. It was just the handiest at short notice.' She had turned to smile at him, distinctly more relaxed in his company than she had been before this evening. 'Surprisingly early for a dinner party to break up by your standards, I expect,' she went on – about a gathering that had somehow lost its reason for being around the coffee stage.

'But not early by Llanegwen standards, it seems. Mrs Chard must have left half an hour ago. Her husband wasn't far behind her either. Why did they come in separate cars?'

'He hadn't been home all day. His office is one way from here, their home the other. At St Asaph. Only fifteen miles between them, though. You'd have thought he'd have made the effort to collect her. She left because she was worried about her baby-sitter.'

'She has a baby?'

'A ten-year-old child. A late and unexpected blessing, I'm told. But she's not that old. Anyway, it was nice of you to insist on driving me home. Michael Chard is pretty stuffy. I never know what to say to him.'

'I think Paul Ranker would have offered.'

'No. Otherwise engaged. By Barbara Evan.'

'For the hundred-yard drive to her house?' He moved the car off as he spoke.

Marian grimaced. 'Good thing, anyway. Mr Ranker is not to be trusted at close quarters. Case of arrested development.'

'Really? Which left only me. And the host, of course.'

'Who's very nice. With all those Labradors dying to be walked. Did you see? His wife says he takes them walking at this time every night when they're here.'

Although he hesitated to say as much, for his part Treasure had sensed Lewis Bude had been uneasy for most of the evening. 'So, I got you by default?' he joked.

'I think you know that's not true,' she answered quietly. 'And I've never been driven home by a merchant banker before.'

'Where to?' The car had reached the gates.

'Just follow this road down to the factory, and on to the centre of town. Can I find us some background music?' She leaned forward to switch on the radio. The lights of the dashboard softly illuminated the sweep of her hollowed bare back - as well as an intriguing amount of bare front under the outstretched arm.

'Push the second button on the right. You should get some Mozart.'

She pressed it and listened for a moment. 'I did too. God, you even have the BBC working for you.'

'Nothing so romantic. I heard an announcement earlier. You warm enough?'

She dropped back into the seat again with a sigh. 'One can tell you're married. I'm warm enough, thank you, and damned if I'm going to spoil the effect my dress is having by covering it with a woolly.' She paused, crossing her legs, and smoothing the skirt over her knees with both hands. 'Why do I have to be so frank with you? And do I sound as if I've drunk too much?'

'I imagine rather less than Barbara Evan consumed before she arrived. She was tending to frankness all evening.'

'Poor Barbara.'

'You're very charitable.'

'You mean even though she was bitchy to me? I'm used to that. We used to be friends. Now I'm just sorry for her. She's lost her husband who she didn't much care about, and who didn't much care about her.' Marian took a deep breath slowly, then let it out fast. 'Trouble is, she figures I'd stolen Joshua from her before she'd made fresh arrangements for herself. Fresh permanent arrangements, that is. It rankles with her.'

'And had you?'

'Stolen him from her? Not the way Barbara thinks. Look ahead. Isn't that heavenly?' The sea, shimmering in the moonlight, was making a dramatic horizon at the end of the valley they were following. The sky was traced by delicate sweeps of unmoving, mackerel cloud.

'I have a similar view from my bedroom, over trees,' Treasure commented. 'You'd never guess there was a town between here and the water.'

'Quite a small town. And we're nearly into it now.' A minute later the wall of the G. L. Evan factory appeared to the left, then they were dropping down between a pattern of streets more compressed than the one on the northern, seaward side of the town, but just as deserted at this time of night.

'High Street coming up at the next crossroads,' warned Marian a little later. 'If you turn left there, our flat's along a bit, up a turning on the left. Will you come in for a nightcap? My flatmate . . .'

'Male or female?'

'Oh, Olive is unquestionably female. Teaches biology at the local comprehensive.' She paused. 'Or . . . it's such a lovely night we could take a walk on the beach?'

'I'd like that.'

The beach she directed him to was not the local one but a less-developed stretch called Hafod Bay. It was a mile or so west of Llanegwen, reached by a rough side road that tunnelled narrowly under the expressway and railway line, disgorging almost straight onto the shingle. They left the car there and began walking along the strand, back in the direction of the town.

'That used to be a lifeboat station. Till the turn of the century.' Marian stopped to point behind them at a low building running back from a sloping stone breakwater at the far end of the beach. 'Pretty dilapidated now. What's usable is let off by the council for boat storage. To Albert Shotover. It's his private domain.'

Treasure nodded, while taking in the scene, but his mind was on other matters. 'D'you mind telling me something? If you and Joshua weren't . . .'

'Having an affair, what were we having?'

'Really, that wasn't what I intended asking.'

'It doesn't matter. I was just advising him. I suppose, keeping him up to a sense of responsibility.' She stooped to take a handful of dry sand, then, as they walked, let the grains trickle through her fingers. She was carrying her shoes.

'You advised him about the business?'

'That's right. On a plan to turn it round, in spite of Paul Ranker.'

'So you weren't emotionally involved at all?'

'We weren't sleeping together, no. I think he'd have liked to. I was . . . committed to someone else, for most of that time.' She looked up at him. 'Not any more, as it happens. Joshua and I were emotionally involved in trying to save the company.'

'Was the plan Joshua's, or yours, or someone else's?'

She frowned. 'Officially Joshua's. It was all fairly straightforward. Copy-book marketing tied into an achievable production schedule, and realistic budgets. We'd got too sophisticated since Ranker came. But we're not that kind of a company, even though Ranker couldn't see it. Still can't. Are you interested to hear more? Ouch!' She had stumbled over a large pebble.

'Very interested. And why don't you take my arm?'

They moved off together, and for the next half-mile Marian expanded on the plan.

Treasure was impressed, as much by the young woman's enthusiasm as by the ideas and the way she expressed them.

'Well, amongst other things, you've answered one of my earlier questions,' he said at the end. 'It seems the grand design was actually yours not Joshua's.'

'I'm not sure. And how can you be so certain?'

'Because Joshua had years as a director of the firm and presumably never came up with anything usable. Otherwise he'd have got the managing directorship vacancy last year. Did you ever get that whole proposition down on paper?'

'Yes. Several times. The last draft is locked in my desk. I wish you'd look at it. I could give it you tomorrow.'

'I'd rather read it tonight.'

'OK. We can pick it up later.' She shook her head. 'It's not true that Joshua might have been made MD last year. His uncle, the chairman, wouldn't have agreed. Not at the time. I think he was altering his attitude, though. You know, Joshua's

103

own wife didn't believe he had it in him. To pull the place around, I mean. And, for what it's worth, Michael Chard thought the same way.'

'For what it's worth? You mean Chard is only the outside accountant, so shouldn't have had that much influence?'

'I think that's how it should have been. But it was Chard who really recruited Ranker. They didn't use proper job consultants. Chard ran some advertisements about the vacancy and did all the preliminary interviewing. Then he put up a short list of three suitable candidates to the directors. Joshua told me the other two were much worse than Ranker.'

'Much worse? He said that?'

'Not exactly. At the time he'd probably have said they weren't as good as Ranker. He was quite impressed with Ranker at the start. With his track record. His experience in the industry. We were all impressed.'

'So Joshua was definitely party to Ranker's appointment.'

'He'd had to accept he wasn't going to get the job himself, yes. So he did his best to get the right man in.'

'Chard and Ranker seemed very close tonight. Almost like old friends.'

She murmured agreement. 'I'm sure they knew each other before Ranker applied for the job. Eventually Joshua thought so too.'

'If the company survives as a going concern, will you want to go on with it?'

'I'm not sure. I wouldn't want to go on doing my present job. Not for much longer. I'm not a committed scientist. More interested in management, I suppose. Except . . .' she hesitated.

'Except so far you've felt safer working within your own academic discipline?'

'Something like that.' She pulled a face. 'Otherwise known as lacking the guts to apply for anything outside it.'

'There's also that touching inclination to identify with the workers.'

'That's only partly true. And anyway, it's not always a

104

misguided inclination. For instance, here at the moment—'

'It's misguided if it clouds a capacity to be a good manager,' he interrupted. 'Good management benefits the workforce more immediately than it does the shareholders. Or should do. Anyway, you're quite young still. Presumably you came here for experience. Judging by your grasp of the G. L. Evan problems I'd say you're quite ready to move onwards and upwards.'

'Am I being interviewed for a new job?'

'Certainly not.'

'That's good. I hoped we were here because we fancied each other.' She bit her lip. 'I shouldn't have said that, should I? Altogether too frank.'

'But perfectly true, and I promise I shan't try to seduce you on the strength of it.'

'Shame.' She tightened her hold on his arm and lengthened her step so that it matched his own. 'You're very nice. Everyone's saying so. To have put yourself out as you have . . .'

'In the circumstances it was the only thing I could do.'

'When did you talk to the Segam people? Was it before you got here?'

'Does it matter?' he hedged, not wanting to give Lewis Bude away, nor to lie to Marian.

She smiled. 'Not if you don't want to tell me, and it's none of my business, anyway. Can I ask, will you be involved in the company in future? Long term?'

'It's a possibility. That the bank might be, for one of its customers. It's sometimes part of our job to bring companies together. Compatible ones.'

'And you have a marriage in mind for us? One that cuts out Segam and doesn't involve our old shareholders either?'

'That's looking too far ahead for the moment. Let's say I have to talk to people after the weekend. I wouldn't write out Segam either. Not yet.'

'And what about our present lousy management?'

'That could be rectified. What's that building?' They had reached the centre of the Llanegwen beach.

105

'It's our uncelebrated sailing club.'

'I thought it might be. Just remind me. Joshua sailed from there that morning alone, in the dark . . .'

'Around dawn. Or so it's assumed. When the tide was highest.'

Treasure stopped then and turned to look at the water. The tide had been coming in and was now only about twenty yards from where they were standing on the edge of the sand. 'And there was some kind of gale a blowing?'

'Not at the time he started. It'd been fine the night before. Just a stiff breeze. It got squally after he'd been out.'

'For how long?'

'Nobody knows. I mean, nobody knows for certain what time he started.'

'That's what I thought. Who saw him that morning?'

'Nobody. He slept at his mother's empty flat. That's not far away.'

'How far?'

'Half a mile. Opposite the church.'

'And no one saw him between there and here? So how are they certain he sailed from here?'

'Because the dinghy was kept here. Oh, and someone thought they saw his car pass. It was in the carpark at the front.' Her forehead wrinkled. 'You sound suspicious. You think he didn't sail from here?'

'I think there are a lot of insufficiently explained events surrounding G. L. Evan Limited, and Joshua Evan's death is one of them, that's all. I also think you should have brought that woolly, ravishing as you look without it. So you can put this over your shoulders right now.' He had taken off his jacket and was firmly draping it around her. 'Let's go back to the car, then drop by the factory for that report . . .'

'Then go to my place for a warming brandy? It's Spanish, but quite nice.'

'A Spanish brandy with biological Olive.'

Marian linked her arm through his again. 'Actually, I started

106

to say earlier, Olive's away for the weekend.'

'Hm. Then we'll have to make do with each other,' he answered solemnly, but not with the air of someone contemplating a genuine sacrifice.

10

Owen Watkins sprinted into Dewin Street from the lower side of the intersection, avoiding the pool of light from the corner lamp. It was ten thirty-three. Crossing the road to the shadow of the mossy factory wall, he quickly covered the short distance to the G. L. Evan yard, ducking in through the permanently open gates.

He wasn't due here until eleven. Since leaving Gwyneth's house he had been lurking in the fields behind the factory. He had come down from there now on the chance the person he was meeting might be early too. He decided to wait in the unlit porchway of the office building just beyond the gate. He could watch arrivals from there – and leave again quickly if necessary. His plan was to collect his hundred pounds, then hitch-hike to Scotland.

The place was empty: he'd expected that. It was why he hadn't thought to question the time and place of the rendez-vous. Evan's yard would be more abandoned than even the Llanegwen churchyard at this time on a Friday night – and it was certainly less overlooked. He couldn't see the vehicles parked at the back of the warehouse section, but, even if he had been able to, their identities would not have surprised or alerted him. There were two lone exterior lights burning in the cobbled yard – one over the main factory door and the other, to the right, above the loading bay. There was a corridor light reflecting from a window inside the offices behind him, but that was always left on, winter and summer. He'd be safe enough until . . .

'Hello. It's Owen, isn't it? What you doing here? Oh, sorry, boy, I didn't mean to frighten you.'

He had literally jumped in the air at the sound of the voice. Mr George Evan, the chairman, was standing behind him in the doorway which had yawned open silently and without warning. There was no point in running away. Mr Evan had identified him instantly with the corridor light shining full on him. They knew each other well. Owen sometimes cleaned Mr Evan's car, and he'd often run errands for Miss Evan.

'Nothing else to do, Mr Evan, not really,' Owen answered uncertainly, while desperately looking for reasons to account for his being there. 'It's . . . it's boring at home. Been for a run.' He started doing jogging steps on the spot to embellish the claim. 'Dropped by here for a minute. In case there was anyone working late. Anyone wanting anything done, like. Never miss an opportunity.' He was now warming to the invention. Mr Evan didn't seem at all suspicious – more pleased to see him, really. Owen continued the standing steps, knees well up.

'Good exercise,' said Evan approvingly. He seemed actually to be taking a vicarious pleasure in the other's actions, even savouring the leg movements. 'Well, as it happens, I have been working late. Don't believe there's anything I want doing.' But the tone was far from certain and the smile was positively indulgent.

'That's all right, Mr Evan. Didn't think there'd be anything really. It's just . . . Well, I haven't got money to do anything else. Not the pictures, or anything.' He stopped the running movements and concentrated on deepening his dejected look. 'And I don't drink,' he added for good measure.

Evan twice ran his tongue around his lips. 'And you don't go out with girls. Owen?' he asked, adding a nervous little laugh and jerkily rubbing a hand back and forth across his stomach.

'Specially not girls, Mr Evan. Too expensive if you're unemployed.'

'Handsome chap like you, though. I should have thought . . . but you were with Gwyneth Davies the night she was attacked.'

'Before she was attacked, Mr Evan. Yes. That was the last time I was out with a girl.'

Evan put a hand on the boy's bony shoulder. 'Well, perhaps you can take them or leave them for the moment, is that it?'

'Expect so, Mr Evan.'

'Tell you what,' said the tubby chairman, his hand running down the other's thin arm, and stopping to squeeze the muscle lightly. 'There *is* something you can do for me. Help me lock up, over in the factory. I was checking some things there earlier. I can't remember if I left any doors open.'

It sounded to Owen like a tactful, gentlemanly lead-up to offering him payment for a non-job. Well, if it was, he wasn't too proud to accept a contribution, deserved or otherwise. Going around the factory wouldn't take long, and anyway he still had time in hand. And if the person he was meeting saw him with Mr Evan the situation would explain itself.

'D'you always have to work so late, Mr Evan?'

'Not always, Owen. I've just been replacing things I'd got ready for a staff meeting tomorrow, now it's cancelled.' Evan kept a friendly hold on the other as they crossed the yard, quickening the step as they went. 'Your parents well, are they? That's right. There we are, then,' Evan nodded and continued speaking before there was a chance for the boy to reply. 'You go first.' He'd had to unlock the main door for them.

Owen went in quickly, concerned not to loiter under the light outside. It would be just his luck to be spotted if a patrolling policeman looked in at the gate from the street and recognised him.

Unseen by either Evan or the boy, the corridor door on the left of the vestibule closed softly after they appeared. The surprised figure on the other side of it had been in the act of stepping through, but had gone back swiftly to watch on hearing the movements from the main entrance.

'Pity we can't find you a regular job here, Owen. Smart boy like you.' Evan shook his head, though his expression seemed to register more of keen anticipation than regret. His little eyes were roving ceaselessly, busy behind the glasses, making fresh assessments of the face and the slim frame of his companion. 'It's the times, you see? Very difficult, yes,' he ended vaguely,

110

and failing to keep the impatience out of his voice.

'You do your best for the town, Mr Evan. Everyone knows that. You can't subsidise everybody for ever,' said Owen dutifully, the conviction growing in him that some of the largesse referred to should shortly be spreading in his direction.

'Thank you, Owen.' Evan hurried them left towards the door that had only just been gently closed. He was beginning to breathe quite heavily, but it seemed not from exertion. He took out his handkerchief to wipe the beads of sweat from his face. 'Hot in here, isn't it? Very hot, yes,' he answered his own question, then ran his tongue around his lips again. 'Ah, thought I hadn't locked that door.' They went through to the far corridor. Evan moved his open hand to press it into the small of Owen's back. 'Seen our men's locker room, have you? Along here on the right. Have a look.'

'It's very nice, Mr Evan. Very modern.' He'd seen it many times before.

'Cost a lot. Come and see the showers at the end.' He was practically propelling the boy ahead of him. He cleared his throat noisily, swallowing hard before he spoke again. 'Uh, tell you what. We're both all sticky, let's . . . let's take a shower. Save on the hot water when we get home.'

Even as he spoke, Evan was throwing off his jacket, purposely ignoring the boy's uncertainty. His tie and shirt went next in a frenzy of activity. He sat down on a long bench to pull off his shoes. 'Come on, Owen,' he urged, unzipping his trousers. 'I'm ahead of you.' He stood up and appeared to be trembling. 'Here, let me give you a hand.'

'I've said it once, and I'll say it again, you make the best cup of tea in the principality.' Detective Inspector Alwyn Thomas beamed at his wife Maureen over the top of his cup.

'Go on. But it's nice to be appreciated,' she said, sitting down beside him on the sofa facing the television set. They were in the living room of their semi-detached house in Pentre Beach. She was dark-haired, small and jolly, the same age as her husband, proud of her two teenage children, and noted in local choral circles for her rich mezzo-soprano voice.

'You should taste the stuff that's coming out of that beverage machine at the station.' He shook his head in disgust, after applying emphatic disdain to the word beverage.

'You've said before. And I keep telling you to take a Thermos. Sure you don't fancy the bit of pie I kept you?'

'No, thanks.' He'd eaten in the station canteen. 'Fancy the bit next to me on the sofa, though.'

'Well, that's nice.' She squeezed his hand. 'No news on the promotion?' she added casually, as if it weren't currently the biggest subject in their lives.

'Not yet. Not till next week most likely.' He remembered he had said the same thing last Friday; so did Maureen, but she was too tactful to remark on it.

'When's the film starting?' she asked.

'In five minutes.' He'd turned off the television sound for the time being. It was nearly eleven. He'd only just got home, but except for emergencies, he wasn't on duty again until after lunch on Monday. He was looking forward to watching the late movie and getting up in the morning when he felt like it. Both children were already in bed.

'Why'd you have to do overtime today, love?' He should have been home in time for supper at eight.

'Because one chief detective inspector's off sick, and two DIs are on leave. And there's too much crime and too much paperwork.' He sipped the tea she'd poured.

'Have you found Owen Watkins?'

'Not yet. We're still looking. I had a private word with Marian Roberts.'

'That was good of you.'

'She doesn't want him charged on her account.'

'I thought she wouldn't.' The two women were members of the same local choral group. 'So why are you so keen to catch him? What he's done doesn't sound so terrible.'

'It isn't, but he might be able to help on something else.'

'I was right. He *was* in the same class as Barry, as well as in

112

your youth club.' Barry was their seventeen-year-old younger son. 'He's left school now.' Barry was still there, studying for university entrance. 'Barry knows him well. They still meet at football. He doesn't think he's a thief.'

Thomas frowned. 'You shouldn't have said he was. Not to Barry. Or anyone else. A person's not guilty till proved.' It sounded trite, but with him the axiom was sacred.

'Barry won't mention it to anyone.' She shook off her shoes and drew her legs up under her. 'He says Owen's a big spender. You know he was the one involved with that Davies girl who was nearly raped?'

'I did know that. About the girl, not the spending. The family's not well off. Respectable, though. Another one in the pot, is there?' He passed her his empty cup. 'Barry doesn't say where the Watkins boy got his money?'

'Odd jobbing.'

'Who for?'

'That cut-price drink shop in Llanegwen . . . And some of the local ladies who he says he obliges.' She articulated the last word slowly.

'How d'you mean obliges?'

'Bit of a gigolo, Barry says. But you know how kids exaggerate.'

'Owen Watkins cleans cars for people, that's all.'

'Not according to the boy himself. He'd have you know he's a spinsters' and widows' delight.'

Thomas thoughtfully rubbed the end of his squashed nose, twice injured when he'd been an amateur boxer, and a lot younger and measurably lighter than he was now. 'Any particular widows or spinsters mentioned?'

'Miss Sybil Evan of Afon House.'

'George Evan's sister? Well, there's imagination for you! She's not the type for romantic dalliance with young boys. Too old and too proper.'

'Owen claims she dotes on him.'

'In a motherly way, I expect. Older women feel sorry for him.

That's what his own mother says.'

'Does she? So would that apply to Mrs Barbara Evan as well?'

The inspector looked up sharply, but the telephone had started ringing before he had a chance to answer the last question.

'You'll catch me yet . . . Do terrible things . . . Oh, terrible things to me!' squealed plump little George Evan joyously. He was stark naked, except for the glasses, breathless, and making a slow ascent of a metal gantry stairs, embellishing his progress with flowery movements. He lay back now at a perilous angle from the steps in brief tableau – like a trapeze artist – one arm raised, the other clutching the handrail, an arch expression suffusing the downward-peering face. 'How I long to be caught by a lusty boy!' he uttered. 'Whoops!' One bare foot had slipped as he threw himself back into the climb.

Owen Watkins felt foolish and embarrassed. He had heard of kinky old men but this one took the biscuit.

It had all started in the locker room. Mr Evan had tried to help him off with his clothes – and partly succeeded, after Owen had watched him coyly slip two ten-pound notes into his shirt pocket. Then the old fool had skipped away from him, clamouring about a chase – a chase, he'd explained, to work up a glow for the promised shower.

So, naked as well, Owen had dutifully padded after Mr Evan, who had gone romping and shouting, like a superannuated cherub, into the corridor, then on through the empty factory.

The episode was incongruous, even ludicrous, but hardly obscene. Mr Evan had so far failed to exhibit the obvious physical sign that he was being sexually stimulated. Owen had taken great comfort from that clear fact.

Simply, the chairman of G. L. Evan Ltd seemed to be getting a huge kick out of what they were doing. Owen supposed he thought it was daring – which it would have been in the daytime with the factory full of workers, most of them women. Perhaps that was Mr Evan's special fantasy. Owen had read about such

114

things – only he had the uneasy feeling that women probably didn't feature much in Mr Evan's fantasies.

'You're . . . getting . . . closer . . . I'll have to . . . put on a spurt . . . in a minute,' Evan forced out the words delightedly between great heaving breaths as, purple-faced, he pulled himself onto the second tier gantry walk and began clawing his way along it between pipes and big steel vessels. Suddenly, he halted with a 'whoop' and turned to do one of his more elaborate poses. One fat arm was clasped behind the uplifted head. The plump stomach was thrust outwards. A podgy leg was bent upwards and inwards, primly covering the Evan genitalia – objects so small as to make the act of coy modesty pointless as well as ridiculous.

'Come and get me!' Evan simpered. Then he dropped the pose with a giggle and moved on, pausing shortly after to leer again over his shoulder at Owen, who was still taking his time on the steps.

'I'll get you all right, you . . . you naughty man,' the boy called self-consciously, but trying to enjoin the spirit of the thing.

Mr Evan shrieked with delight and hurried ahead.

It had been made clear to the pursuer that, really, Mr Evan had no wish to be caught. That had been at the start when Owen had quickly overtaken his quarry. Then Mr Evan had turned on him and in a sober, petulant whisper admonished: 'It's only pretend, you know?' before hurrying on again, out of reach.

Recalling playful chases after his little sister when she was very small, Owen had now taken to using the same sort of fatuous threats he'd shouted at her – because they were producing similar rapturous reactions.

The more the boy came to realise he was helping to indulge a harmless fantasy and not something sinister or depraved, the more interested he became. He was bearing in mind he had already been paid something for his co-operation. He confidently expected to be able to extract more from the same source – if not immediately, then on an enduring, regular basis in the future. After all, the ridiculous figure prancing naked before him was one of Llanegwen's most prominent citizens, a pillar of the church and the business community. Mr Evan had even given away the speech-day prizes at Owen's old school, and you couldn't do anything more respectable than that.

All in all, Mr Evan must surely expect to have to pay dearly to have his curious whims satisfied, kept secret and perhaps satisfied again before long? The effort required of a participant appeared not to be onerous, whereas Mr Evan's ability to pay for it had to be more than adequate. The only problem was timing.

As he had demonstrated in the matter of the modest hundred pounds he had first come here to collect, Owen was naturally more practical than greedy when it came to compensation. Perhaps he was both untutored and unwise in this, but that would be a separate consideration.

The fact remained that since the boy was determined to quit the town within the hour for an undecided period, and since Mr Evan might not be prepared to contribute more money tonight than he'd done already, the picking up of the certain hundred pounds was now becoming a primary consideration. The longer the present performance continued, the less likely it was that Owen could meet with his other benefactor in the yard outside.

'We're here at the witches' cauldron. Now for the treat!' Evan called clearly from somewhere ahead on the catwalk, interrupting Owen's train of thought. Because of a right-angle turn in the gantry around a steel hopper, Evan had gone out of the boy's sight, though not out of his hearing.

There was a resolution in the shouted words that made Owen suddenly uneasy – that along with the sound of a chain running through an electric hoist. So there had after all been a goal in this purposeless forage, and one that seemed to have been reached. Was it here that depravity would rear its nasty head?

Owen hesitated. He could turn now, unseen, and belt back to his clothes and the yard, possibly before Mr Evan even realised what had happened, let alone came lumbering after him. It must be close to eleven already.

116

The boy had been more than half resolved to quit when the unnerving cry came from ahead. It had started as another triumphant 'whoop' but finished as a strangled shriek. Impelled by its urgency, Owen raced forward around the gantry angle, keeping his balance and momentum with a thrust at the metal handrail.

Because he was quick he was in time to see the end of Evan's plunge, the ghastly finish to the escapade – the ghoulish, total immersion that drowned that last bloodcurdling cry. Paralysed with horror, he stood uncertainly in the unprotected gap above the open vat, a helpless witness to the nightmare end of the figure that after one heave ceased movement of any kind.

It was then that the watcher stepped forward from behind him on the gantry, placing one gloved hand on his shoulder. 'Did you do that?'

The boy spun around. 'Of course not. You know I didn't. Quick, how do we get him out?'

'You serious? He's dead. Terrible accident. His own fault, of course. Larking about. Hope they don't say you did it.'

'I wasn't anywhere near. I . . .'

'Playing games were you? In the nude? Kinky. You'll have to explain. Difficult that. Better to get away. Fast. The way you came.'

'What about Mr Evan?'

'I told you, he's had it. Take my word for it. Slipped, I should think, when he opened the vat. What was he up to?'

'I don't know.' He was nearly weeping.

'Police will expect you to, though. And they're after you already, too. Well, nobody need know you're here. Except your friend, of course. He'll know, I suppose? Pity. I can't help you if . . .'

'There's no friend. Honestly. It was only me all the time,' he blurted out, desperate to avoid trouble.

'I see. Come on, then, you'll need to be quick. It's for your own good. No difference to me.'

The petrified Owen allowed himself to be bundled down the steps.

'Go through the rock room. It's quicker.'

The boy continued to obey mindlessly. He didn't see when the figure behind withdrew the wrench from under the coat.

The heavy tool was brought down with merciless force. It split the boy's thin skull, killing him instantly.

11

'Sorry I'm later than promised, Susan,' said a worried looking Megan Chard when she reached home at ten twenty-five.

'That's all right, Mrs Chard. Only ten minutes later,' answered the attractive, seventeen-year-old baby-sitter, closing her textbook. She was a tall girl with long golden hair, a freckled face and a slight figure. She had been a pupil of Mrs Chard's years before in junior school, and was now studying for university.

'Well, it's not good enough, letting people down. But I couldn't get away,' Mrs Chard went on chiding herself. 'Billy behaved all right, did he?' Disconsolately she dropped her evening bag onto a chair and went to study her appearance in the mirror above the fireplace.

'Like an angel. Went to bed at nine thirty like you said.'

'That's good,' but Billy always behaved himself, so his mother hardly registered the answer. She sighed. 'Oh dear, this dress was wrong for tonight. I felt it all evening.' She pulled at the neckline and glowered at the sleeves.

'It's lovely, Mrs Chard. Too formal, was it?'

Inwardly Susan agreed about the dress. It didn't help with Mrs Chard being overweight either. Someone should advise her on clothes – and a diet. She was a gauche as ever. Yet she had been such a good teacher, confident enough in the classroom, with no problem about keeping order. The children had loved her.

'My husband will be back soon. He'll drive you home.' Mrs Chard had turned to look at Susan who was dressed in a loose cotton blouse and very tight, bleached jeans.

'That's really not necessary. It's only ten minutes' walk.'

'Fifteen more like, and it's late. I'm sure your mother wouldn't want you out alone. Pretty girl like you.' She smiled approvingly as she spoke. There was no envy in her mind about the good looks, only a sadness about the condition the girl coped with so stoically, even though it must restrict her lifestyle. 'The streets are so dangerous these days,' she went on. 'Remember there was a girl attacked in Llanegwen only last month?'

'Mm. Doesn't happen often, though. Not round here. They don't think that was a local man either. Someone driving through on the new road probably. It doesn't worry me.'

Mrs Chard wasn't so easily assuaged. 'Well, let's have a cup of tea while we're waiting. I could do with one.'

Fifteen minutes later there was still no sign of Michael Chard.

'I think I ought to be getting home if you don't mind,' said Susan, standing up and gathering the chemistry books she'd brought to work on. 'Thanks for the extra money, Mrs Chard. You shouldn't have.'

'Oh dear, I'm sure Mr Chard will be here any second. Can't imagine what's keeping him.' This wasn't strictly true: her imagination had been hyperactive in that regard for some time. 'I could run you home myself . . . '

'And leave Billy alone in the house? Certainly not.' Susan knew that would have been anathema to Mrs Chard: it showed in her face at the mere suggestion – and in the relief at the refusal. 'I'll be perfectly all right. Honestly. I often get home on my own later than this. I'll stick to the main streets.'

'Let me pay for a taxi then.' She was already dialling the number. 'Tch. Engaged, of course.'

'Always is this time of night. I think they take the phone off when they're busy. Never mind. I'm off. Don't worry, Mrs Chard. I'll be OK. Promise.' And so she left, with reassurances ringing – and Megan Chard feeling uncomfortable as well as let down by her husband. He had promised faithfully to be home right behind her.

The man had been hidden in the shadows on the other side of

120

the road as Susan emerged. Until then he had been undetermined on what to do next.

The Chards' home was on the hillside to the south-west of St Asaph – in a tree-lined avenue of modern houses. Susan's safest way home was by Denbigh Road, a straight, well-lit, main thoroughfare, some minutes' walk east of where she was. Following this northwards would take her to the centre of town, to the cathedral, and just half a mile from where she lived, to the right, in Chester Street. That was her most sensible route – also the longest and the steepest.

This was why, despite her promise to Mrs Chard, the girl set off on a quicker, diagonal course ending on a short farm track that led up to the back of the cathedral precinct: it first involved her following a succession of now ·mpty avenues.

The pavement trees provided ·lenty of cover for the man silently following Susan. Shortly he guessed the pattern of the route, and where it was leading. Abandoning a plan to grab her where any screaming might be heard, seizing a chance, he raced down a road parallel to one she was in, got ahead of her, and pressed on to wait in the perfect place for his purpose.

St Asaph has the smallest of all the cathedrals in England and Wales, but there is a large open precinct surrounding it. The heavy, squat cathedral tower was casting deep shadows in the moonlight as Susan entered that empty precinct from the west, on the path that ended near the junction of Denbigh Road and Chester Street, passing the building first on its western side.

The assailant sprang from behind her, from the darkened west doorway. Clamping his left hand over her mouth, he took her off balance, dragging her backwards under the arch of the doorway. His right upper arm was tight across her chest, the bent elbow lodged between her breasts. The heel of the upraised hand was pressed against her chin: in that hand was the carpet knife, with the blade nearly touching her cheek.

She went limp at the sight of the open knife, dropping her books, and not attempting to struggle. He forced her down with her back on the flagstones, and his body astride her, one hand still tight over her mouth. The raincoat he was wearing was open. Part of it seemed to flap against her face as he leaned over her.

Even though her eyes were accustomed to the night, with the light behind him she could see only his outline. There seemed to be something covering his head.

He brought his face close to hers. 'Scream and I'll cut you,' he whispered hoarsely. Now he was pressing the cold knife flat against her throat. Slowly he took his hand from her mouth. She stayed quite still and silent.

He pulled open her blouse, greedily pawing the naked flesh beneath but ignoring the engraved disc about her neck. Then, abruptly, he shifted from his position over her to kneel at her right side, moving the knife again so that she could feel it lying against the rise of her breast. 'Stay flat. Strip off the rest,' came the husky command. 'Everything.'

She did as she was told, kicking away the shoes, then peeling down the jeans and briefs, keeping her shoulders on the stone. Afterwards she lay still again.

His following quick demands were unspoken but more intimate, made by the forcing explorations of his free hand. Now the slaverings and noisy breathing were suddenly displaced by rabidly impatient, pulsing grunts. Roughly he moved on top of her again, lowering himself onto her body, his hardness against her softness.

As she felt him prepare to thrust into her, she spoke for the first time – coolly, distinctly and with total conviction: 'I've got AIDS. From a blood transfusion. If you don't believe me, read what's on the disc.'

The words took a moment to register. 'No!' With a shudder he threw himself away from her. 'No!' he repeated, kneeling below her, panicked, wiping at his groin in a frenzy of short movements, not passionate, only scared. The knife was still in his right hand.

She sat up, holding the disc like a talisman. He was smaller than he'd seemed to her before. There was a woman's stocking over his head. Again she spoke: 'Read it. You'll see.' She was praying he wouldn't.

122

But he was already scrambling to his feet, moving away, the way she had come, stumbling, running scared.

Quickly she pulled on her clothes, willing the shaking in her stomach not to take control of her whole being. She told herself that there was no point in her screaming her head off here. The main road and the police station were close. She needed to be fast and then coherent if they were to catch him.

She found her shoes, gathered the books, and started to run, going over his appearance in her mind, occupying it to stop herself succumbing to hysteria.

The medical disc stated she had Von Willebrand's disease – a condition similar to haemophilia. She didn't have AIDS, but a scare over some possibly contaminated blood used in a transfusion years before had suggested the ruse she'd just used. She knew it might have failed on a rapist who was more determined, or crazier, or even informed. She had realised that before taking the risk – to avoid the other risk.

If her assailant had read the disc would he have known that her condition wasn't a form of AIDS, or even contagious? But would he have then known that if he'd cut her she could have bled to death? The answer to the first question might have been yes, but to the second it could just as likely have been no.

It was why she hadn't dared resist.

Paul Ranker focused again briefly on the dashboard clock. He was going to beat his own night record on the empty expressway back to Chester – and he needed to.

He kept his hands moving where they were placed, high on the steering wheel, the fingers tightening then loosening in conscious spasms. He liked to imagine his beautiful car was responding to him like an obedient woman: it was an analogy that frequently occurred to Ranker on a fast drive – when the adrenaline was flowing, when he'd been drinking, when he needed to feel totally in charge. Expectantly he moved his foot down a fraction more on the accelerator. The surge of power registered within him as a deeply sensual response.

Ranker was in an excited and fanciful condition.

As the speedometer reading went to ninety, his mouth expanded in a satisfied smile. He was ending the day with almost total victory – a contrast to the crushing defeat that had threatened at the start of it.

Now it would take more than a smart London banker to reverse the deal he had created to benefit himself and all the other G. L. Evan shareholders, deserving and undeserving, grateful and ungrateful, alive and dead.

With a majority of the pension trustees again ready to do the right thing with the surplus money, no law could stop them. He'd allow they might have to make a few cosmetic concessions. But that would be the extent of it. The main position had been saved because, in the morning, he would formally replace George Evan as the trustee nominated by the board of directors. And if two out of three trustees wasn't a majority, then people who thought otherwise should learn arithmetic.

So the effect of the afternoon's meeting at Bude's swimming pool would be wiped out. Chard had been carefully neutral then, a regular Pontius Pilate – crafty devil – fixing it so any new decision would be up to George Evan.

And George had been the weak sister all along. It was why he'd had to go. Ranker's hands squeezed the wheel even harder.

Michael Chard would support the new arrangement, now there was safety in numbers again. Earlier he'd been losing his nerve. With George ready to capitulate, Chard would have given in with him, without a fight.

Ranker watched the traffic flashing by on the other carriageway: on this empty eastbound side he must be closing on the fastest cars over there at combined speeds of more than 160 miles an hour. Gently he increased the pressure on the accelerator. On the road, as everywhere else, he needed the assurance that it was he who was setting the pace.

His only purpose in applying for the managing directorship in the first place had been to have G. L. Evan bought out and closed down. All right, it was Chard who had first alerted him to the huge opportunity. That had been more than a year ago. But it was Paul Ranker who had carried through their plan. The accountant had been scared stiff of risking his precious neck for fear of becoming traceably involved in a conspiracy.

But the sanctimonious Chard was still getting half whatever profit Ranker made on his shares: not bad for a sleeping partner.

There had never been a future for the company. Only the pension fund had rated. And if Treasure did find some other outfit to buy what was left from Segam, there would still be no future for it. In any case, he, Paul Ranker, would be out of it by then – in a far better job. He had used the Evan company as a career stepping stone as well as the way to make a fortune. Last month he had accepted a top job with a firm in Sydney, Australia – on the strength of his recently widened experience. Naturally, he'd timed things so the Australians wouldn't find out that G. L. Evan was folding – nor that his previous important employers had been glad to get rid of him.

He looked at the clock again. He'd made up for some of the time he couldn't account for, but it was well over an hour since he had left Bude's house. His right foot exerted just a fraction more pressure on the pedal; the response was as exhilarating as before. The drive was nearly making up for the irritating disappointment he had just endured.

He had no regrets about what he'd done, but he wasn't aiming to be found out either. Daphne, his wife, was a very jealous woman – only one of the reasons she was being excluded from his Australian plans. She didn't know that yet. He'd lied to her already about tonight, to stop her coming to the Bude dinner. It had been essential she wasn't around when it was over. He'd said it would be a solid business event – the kind she hated.

He had expected the party would break up early – but what had happened afterwards had taken longer than he'd allowed. It would be after eleven thirty before he was home. He couldn't afford to have Daphne asking any of the others later about the

125

time he'd left – exactly the question she would ask if she suspected anything. If she found out he'd left with Barbara before ten thirty . . .

The police patrol car was flashing and sounding a siren abreast of him before he'd even noticed its existence.

'. . . at an average ninety-eight miles an hour, sir. Now if you'd please blow into the tube in the way I asked.'

'I suppose this is really necessary?' Ranker had got out of the car and was standing, jacketless, between the two uniformed officers. 'I've had very little to drink. Been dining with Mr Bude. Mr Lewis Bude in Llanegwen. You know him I expect?' he added carefully, waiting for a response before he did anything with the contraption in his hand.

'That's Mr Bude the magistrate, I expect, sir? No, we don't know him socially,' replied the policeman, who so far had been doing all the talking. 'If you'd just blow into the tube, sir. Done a breathalyser test before, have you?'

'Certainly not.'

'Ah, well, it's quite straightforward . . .'

'Excuse me, sir,' the second policeman, the driver, interrupted. 'Can you tell us how you came by that stain on your shirt-cuff?'

'What stain? Oh, that one. Yes, it a . . . looks like blood, doesn't it? Ah, of course, I remember now. I had a small accident earlier. Opening a friend's front door. Nothing serious . . . '

'Well, I never expected to see you again tonight, Albert,' said Basso Morgan, and not looking overpleased about it either.

Albert Shotover also seemed uncomfortable at the encounter. 'I'm not sleeping well at the moment,' he responded, as though that would totally account for his being this far from his bed at eleven twenty.

They had run into each other at the junction of Dewin Street and a side road, less than fifty yards along from the entrance to the G. L. Evan factory. The place was nearly a mile

126

uphill from the Roberts's bungalow, and a little more than that from Shotover's.

'Indigestion, is it?' asked Morgan.

'Probably.' Shotover gave an embarrassed cough. He put on his steel-rimmed spectacles – a fraction lop-sidedly, which they needed to be when properly adjusted for looking through. 'No indigestion tonight, of course. I mean it was a nice party, Basso. Nice supper. Thank you again,' he added, partly because the compliment would be expected but mostly because it provided something to say.

He was wearing a raincoat which he hadn't had with him when he left the others earlier, so he'd been home – or else to his locker in the factory. Basso wondered which it had been and questioned: 'Been inside, have you?' indicating the factory gate across the road.

'No,' came the over-prompt, over-sharp reply. Shotover blinked, several times, quickly. 'Have you?'

'No. I'm the same. With the sleep,' Basso offered. He pulled on his pipe, then exhaled with a loud belch. 'Sorry. Better out than in, as they say. Yes, with not sleeping, it's age with me, I'm afraid. Not enough to occupy the mind in the day. Goes on working at night.' He looked about him. 'Which way you going now, Albert?'

The other hesitated. 'Home.'

'Me too, I suppose.' They moved off together: there was no real alternative without risking offence.

After a bit, Basso said: 'Funny how all roads lead to the old factory for me. When I'm out going nowhere in particular. Walking. It's like a magnet. Just old habits, I suppose. Retirement doesn't break them.'

'Well, I'm not retired,' answered the other defensively. 'I came this way because it's the shortest route to the country air above the town. That's where I've been. You er . . . you get tired of walking along that seashore.'

'I read somewhere that ozone's poisonous.' Unwarily, Basso inhaled even more deeply on his pipe.

127

'Is that right?' Shotover looked politely disturbed at the intelligence.

'Don't suppose so. We're healthy enough living here, after all.'

The two proceeded in silence for some way, with Basso's leathered footfalls echoing on the pavements of the empty streets. Each man was wondering if the other believed the reason he had given for being outside the factory.

'Have you used your outboard this season yet?' Basso enquired eventually.

The other swallowed. 'Not really. It's being repaired.'

Again nothing else was said for a while. Basso tried to reduce his step to match his companion's. Shotover tried, equally unsuccessfully, to swing his arms in co-ordinated military fashion like Basso.

'Blodwyn's a fine woman,' said Basso as they paused before crossing the High Street – out of habit not necessity: there was no traffic.

Shotover nodded, and made a short embarrassed gurgle without actually speaking.

'Well rid of that husband of hers,' the other continued, stepping into the road. 'Divorce is a lot easier these days, of course. Good thing too.' He belched again. 'Excuse me. Must have had her work cut out bringing up two daughters. By herself. Still needs a man about the place, my good lady says.' He waited, but there was still no response from his companion. 'You seem to get on well enough with young Gwyneth.'

Shotover stiffened. 'Why shouldn't I?'

'No reason at all. I was only saying as much.'

'Sorry, Basso. She is a problem. If Boldwyn and I get married,' he concluded, without the caution everybody else applied to that subject in his presence.

Basso's thick eyebrows lifted. 'Gwyneth still too attached to her father, you think?'

'That's it,' Shotover answered, but it wasn't really.

12

'Aren't those gates ever closed?' asked Treasure as he drove into the factory yard. He headed the car for the front of the main building where he had parked before.

'Too heavy and too neglected,' answered Marian Roberts. 'They're cast iron. Probably welded themselves open by now. Anyway, they're ornate not burglar proof.'

'And the factory's the opposite?'

'Ugly but fairly secure. We do have alarms fitted.'

Treasure watched as she searched in her black evening bag, eventually producing a key ring. They both got out and walked towards the main door. 'Which people have keys?'

'Only directors and department managers. Big deal. Actually, I only have them for this building, not the office block.' At the door she took longer than she should have done finding the keyhole. She gave a small chuckle. 'And I'm still heady from the booze at dinner.'

'Then it becomes you. You've been fascinating company.'

'And boringly loquacious, I expect,' she answered, going inside. 'This won't take me a minute. You don't need to come up.'

'I think I can manage the stairs. Even race you to the top in your thoroughly inebriated condition.'

'Winner take all? OK?' she joked as she opened a wall box just inside the door. 'Hm. Last one out forgot to set the alarms. Unless there's someone here still.'

He looked at his watch. 'At eleven twenty-six at night?'

'Could be someone from production checking on that working vat.'

'Would that be necessary?'

'Only for the conscientious. You haven't met our production manager. He's very dedicated and lives just round the corner.'

'On second thoughts, I'll leave you to it while I drop into the men's room. All right?'

'Sure – you may need a key, though.' She waited till he tried the corridor door. It was unlocked.

Treasure noticed the two sets of clothes as he was returning through the shower area. They were not piled neatly but strewn over opposite benches and the floor. He was sure they hadn't been there when Marian had shown him around earlier. A good-quality leather wallet had been left protruding from an inside pocket of the grey suit jacket. Almost as a reflex action he went to stuff the wallet out of sight but couldn't resist thumbing it open first. The papers poking haphazardly from it were the corners of bank notes. The compartment for credit cards showed the owner was George Evan.

'It seems your chairman is the conscientious visitor,' the banker remarked to Marian as they met again in the hall. He explained about the clothes, adding, 'Presumably he's changed into overalls. There seems to be someone with him.'

Marian shrugged. 'They must be in the factory, or maybe they've since gone over to the office block.'

'There was no other car outside.'

'Mr Evan usually walks here from his house.' She had just noticed the door to the rock room opposite was slightly ajar. 'That door's supposed to be kept locked. I can't imagine why the chairman or anyone else should want to go in there tonight.'

'Except as part of a conducted tour, like the one you gave me. They've left the lights on.' Mildly curious he went over to the door and looked inside.

The long table was empty as before. Only the big press near the far right-hand corner was differently arranged. Earlier, its two semi-circular halves had been separated, the upper one hinged upright against the wall, and at ninety degrees from the lower. Now the halves were together, making one long cylinder. As Treasure moved closer to it his curiosity turned suddenly to alarm.

'How d'you open this thing?' he shouted, but he was already spinning the butterfly nuts around the edges that secured the side clamps. He had levered back the top before Marian reached his side.

'Oh my God!' she whimpered, stiffened, then seemed ready to faint.

The thin naked body of a young man lay face upwards in the centre of the press. The head was bloody but the rest of him was white and unmarked except for the letters daubed across the hairless chest. The capitals 'GE' had been roughly smeared there in what looked like dried blood. The whole human frame had been stretched by the press – not by much, but enough significantly to have increased its macabre appearance.

Treasure had taken Marian by the shoulders and turned her away. 'Sorry, I didn't know what was in there. Only what looked like blood at the join.'

'I'll be all right.' She had relaxed in his arms, then took several deep breaths. 'It's Owen Watkins. The boy the inspector was looking for. I'll go and phone for an ambulance.'

'For the police. He's very dead. Where's the nearest connected telephone?'

'In my office. They'll still need to take the body away, won't they?'

'In a while. You sure you're OK?' On her nod he released her and looked about the room. 'Where does this other door lead?'

'Into the factory. It's never locked.'

He took her arm as they went back to the hall, then up the stairs to her locked office door. After checking inside that the office and the laboratory behind it were empty he asked: 'Anyone else have a key to this door?'

'Only Jane, my assistant.'

'Right. I'm going back to look in the factory. Lock the door behind me, then call the police. If I'm through before they arrive I'll shout from the landing. Don't let anyone else in.

Nobody, whoever it is. Understood?'

'Yes, but who . . .?'

'Please, just do as I say.'

He made for the manufacturing area. In contrast to his first visit, the place was deathly quiet because the extractors had stopped working. Despite that, though, the smell of menthol was less noticeable than before.

'Anybody here?' he called loudly, his voice echoing through the high building. He climbed the gantry steps to the first level, looking down on the floor below. There was too much equipment impeding the view to make a search from there very practicable. In any case he had it in mind to reach the still-functioning piece of plant – the logical destination for any interested visitor. He scaled to the next level, moving along the metal walkway, casting about on both sides as he went.

He distinctly remembered the volume of heat that had been generated earlier when he had approached the working vat. This time there was no big temperature change as he turned the same corner on the gantry.

The vat itself was certainly still warm, but the syrupy contents, far from bubbling, were cooling and well into the process of coagulation.

And lying nearly submerged in the glutinous substance was the apparently naked body of a fat, elderly man. His spectacles were still attached to one ear, their presence seeming to heighten the incongruous look of placidity on the half-exposed, upturned face.

'. . . with Mr Evan ending up as the soft centre in the biggest cough drop ever made. No disrespect intended. Terrible thing,' Detective Inspector Thomas concluded, shaking his head.

'D'you believe he did himself in?' asked Treasure.

'Your guess is as good as mine, sir. If he was alive when he went into that vat, it would have been a very painful end.'

It was just short of one a.m. The two men were standing beside the BMW in the factory yard. Marian Roberts was already seated inside the car. She and Treasure had been kept

132

waiting earlier, and then occupied making lengthy statements to the police.

There were more than a dozen official vehicles in the yard already, and more arriving. An empty ambulance was parked beyond the BMW. A police incident van, nearly the size of a bus, was being manoeuvred into a position on the further side of the factory main door.

'I suppose the obvious assumption has to be it was a piece of horse-play that went badly wrong. One reads about such things.' The banker frowned to indicate he wished his own experience had remained that remote. 'George Evan did for Watkins in passion and error, was stricken by remorse, put his initials on the body to advertise his guilt, and then plunged in.'

'After switching off the cooling to the factory, and the heating to the vat. It's what my sergeant thinks too, sir,' remarked Thomas. 'It's a point of view.'

'But not one you're supporting?'

'Why would Mr Evan chuck himself into a boiling cauldron? He could have jumped off the top gantry and got the same result.'

'Not guaranteed. People have been known to survive that kind of fall.'

'Not many of Mr Evan's weight and age, sir. Submerging in that stuff must have been excruciating. And he'd have known it better than most.'

'Instant, though. But you reckon he wouldn't have contemplated it? Even as a penitential death?'

'Possible, sir. It's also possible he got high inhaling that vapour, passed out, and fell in.' The tone was sceptical.

'But you're not favouring either possibility. Or rather you have to keep an open mind, Inspector. But if he didn't take his own life, and it wasn't an accident, it's equally certain young Watkins couldn't have done in Evan, then coshed himself and laid himself out like that. Which suggests there had to be a third party involved, who did in one or both of them?'

'A third, fourth or more parties, sir.'

'You mean there may have been some kind of orgy here

133

tonight?' The banker glanced up at the building. 'Incongruous place for an orgy, I must say.'

Thomas's cheeks stretched into a weary smile. 'We'll know more when we get the forensic evidence. It's early days yet, sir.'

'And nights, Inspector. I gather you weren't technically on duty.'

'On call for emergencies. And we'd had rather a lot in the division tonight, before this. Having to muster a murder squad on top has stretched things, like. At the start, anyway. We'll have a hundred people working on it by first light.'

'Meaning it's certainly not an open and shut case.'

'Meaning we have to be thorough, Mr Treasure. In the public interest.'

Treasure turned to open the driver's door. 'Miss Roberts mentioned you knew the dead boy.'

'Well enough to know he had no real reason for that stealing we were investigating.'

'Or for indulging the sexual aberrations of elderly bachelors for money?'

'We don't know for certain he did that, sir.' The speaker paused. 'We don't know Mr Evan was that way inclined either.'

'Well, I wouldn't count on his not being, Inspector,' Treasure answered, ignoring the reproof in the last comment. 'I saw the ten-pound notes stuffed into Watkins's shirt pocket. I'll bet they came from Evan.' He shook his head. 'What a damned shame you didn't catch the lad earlier today. For his own protection. Miss Roberts sensed you were personally more concerned to reform him than arrest him.'

'I might have been, at that. But there was another reason I wanted to get hold of him.'

'To do with the sailing club? I gather Watkins could have been there the night before Joshua Evan was drowned?'

The inspector hesitated before offering: 'Or early on the same morning, yes.'

'So he might have seen Evan?'

'He didn't come forward to say so. Not at the time of the inquest. Of course, he couldn't have said he was there without

134

incriminating himself. And perhaps he wasn't there. I was only working on circumstantial evidence. It'll stay that way now, too. Yes, I'd like to have asked him about it.'

'Just as I wish I could have met Joshua Evan. From everything I've been told about him, he sounds too sensible to have gone sailing alone that morning.'

Once more Thomas considered for a moment before replying heavily: 'The coroner took a different view, didn't he?'

'I hope he was right. Joshua's death had a huge bearing on the business I'm here about.'

'I understand, sir. Well, I must get back. Thank you for your help. You too, Miss Roberts.' He leaned down to speak to Marian through the open driver's door. 'Sorry we kept you so long.'

'You couldn't help that,' she called back. 'Oh, Mr Thomas, one of the sergeants told me he'd come off a police hunt for a rapist. In St Asaph. Is it the same one? The one who attacked Gwyneth Davies?'

'Certain similarities reported, I gather,' was the guarded answer. 'Good night then, what's left of it. Perhaps I'll see you again in the day.' He turned about and moved towards the now open doorway of the incident van. Before he got there he was joined by two other plainclothes officers who had obviously been waiting to speak to him.

'He's asked me to stay here for tomorrow at least. To help the enquiry along,' said Treasure, starting the engine. 'Made it sound like a favour, but it may have been an order. This'll teach me to visit harmless-looking factories in the middle of the night.'

'At the instigation of interfering females?'

'I wasn't complaining about that. Did I tell you, the Budes are devastated about what's happened. When I rang to explain where we were, Lewis offered to come down, of course. I said there was no point. At least they're prepared for their house guest to extend his stay.'

'Will they still be up now?'

'I don't imagine so. I rang around midnight. Said we'd probably be here for hours. I have a house key. Lewis thinks of

135

everything. Like this car.' He slowly threaded the BMW between the other vehicles parked in the yard, before being stopped at the gate. The uniformed constable standing there spoke into his hand set, then signalled them through. 'Strange that Paul Ranker didn't decide to come back tonight,' the banker observed as they drove away.

'Should he have done? He lives thirty miles away.'

'He didn't have to. But I was there when Thomas telephoned him. It was left open for him to come if he wanted. As managing director of a factory where all kinds of mayhem had happened, in Ranker's place I think I'd have come. In fact, I know I would. Even out of simple curiosity. He didn't, though. He rang that production manager instead. Got him out of bed. Ordered him to fall to. Serious sort of chap.'

'Name's Gwylam Idris. I told you he was conscientious.'

'It was he who supervised the . . . the extraction of George Evan. Ghoulish business, that must have been.'

'Gwylam had fallen out with Mr Evan. Since the takeover.'

'He wouldn't have done him in, though?'

'Not a chance. But it partly explains why he was so anxious to get Mr Evan out. So he could start on the cleaning up.'

'Very concerned to see if the equipment had been damaged, he said to me. I thought he sounded a bit heartless. Anyway, the inspector wouldn't let him do it. I mean, drain away the goo.' He looked in her lap. 'Do you still have the marketing plan with you?'

'In this envelope. It was checked out just now in case it was evidence.'

'Which in terms of a grand design it probably is.'

'That's too profound for me.' She frowned. 'Unless you mean the deaths of the two Evans could be related? Not coincidence?'

'I certainly believe Inspector Thomas's mind is moving that way. He obviously doesn't buy tonight's awful event as merely the culmination of a male lovers' tiff.' They had reached the centre of the town. He turned the car left into the High Street.

'Except Joshua's death has to have been an accident, surely?' She put the question slowly.

136

'So it has seemed to date. Tell me, was it generally known that George Evan was actively homosexual?'

'No. I mean tonight's the first time I've realised he wasn't just a harmless, ageing bachelor.'

'But perhaps he was. The scene tonight could have been stage managed so you'd believe the opposite.'

'I see. Yes, I suppose so. Except . . .'

'Except what?'

'It fits. His being gay. I mean he's been a lifelong bachelor . . .'

'So's my wife's Uncle Arthur, but he's a terror with the women.'

'Well, George Evan wasn't. And I didn't mean his just being unmarried. It was his general habits, and being so circumspect about his private life. Secretive. He was away a lot. In London. I think he has a flat there. But even his secretary doesn't know exactly where. She's a friend of mine. Oh, left again at the next turning, please.'

Treasure slowed and turned the car. 'For close relatives, Joshua and George don't seem to have had a great deal in common.' He mused for a moment. 'Except, of course, the uncle followed the nephew as the director nominated to be pension trustee by the board, and before he also met a sudden death. I wonder who'll get that job now? Oh, what a delightful spot.'

The short approach road had disgorged into Pembroke Square, a partly cobbled quadrangle of semi-detached, two-storey houses built of red brick, with high-pitched slate roofs and dormer windows. Illumination was by old-fashioned gas lamps, and the houses were fronted by trim strips of grass. The buildings were new but had the mannerisms of small Edwardian town houses, with outside staircases on both sides leading to the rear of the upper floors.

'Each building is four flats,' explained Marian. 'Olive and I share an upper one over there, at the corner. Our entrance is at the back. There's a parking space there too. We're . . . we're not overlooked like some of the others.' She paused. 'That

Spanish brandy's still on offer.'

He stopped the car behind the building and turned to her smiling. 'No, thanks.' He switched off the engine. 'But I'd adore some tea.'

13

'Don't you think it's what someone intends them to believe, Mr Treasure? That my brother committed suicide? Well, you can take it from me, he did nothing of the kind,' Sybil Evan asserted with vigour. 'He'd been under great business pressure. Very great pressure indeed. Oh, yes.' As part of the emphasis, one hand went abruptly to tweak the bun at the back of her head. 'But he wouldn't have taken his own life.'

'For religious reasons, perhaps?'

The elderly woman's surprised reaction dissolved in a brief, indulgent smile. 'No, Mr Treasure, for selfish reasons. And he couldn't abide pain. Not in any form. He couldn't have killed the boy either. As a matter of fact, he was quite fond of him. Genuinely fond.' The chin lifted perceptibly. 'Not in any unnatural way, you understand? We were both fond of Owen Watkins.'

So the inference was tabled that deviant tendencies could no more be ascribed to the late George Evan than they could be to his sister – in whom moral slippage of any kind would plainly be inconceivable.

The banker and Miss Evan were seated opposite each other in the Evan parlour before the fireplace, its emptiness screened by a tapestry in a glazed wooden frame. It was just after nine a.m. Treasure had called at the lady's invitation, as it happened, at the time he had contracted the day before to meet her late brother.

Miss Evan had telephoned Treasure while he had been taking breakfast at the Budes'. She had declared that she very much wanted to hear his account of how he had come upon her brother's body.

On arrival, Treasure had embarked on the last charge with both diffidence and embarrassment – until it had become clear that his instincts were being misapplied. Miss Evan had registered little reaction to the morbid aspects of the account, but was closely concerned to weigh all details accurately in her mind.

'You sure you won't have some tea, Mr Treasure? Or coffee?' she now put in, repeating an earlier offer.

'Really, no, thank you.'

She nodded. 'He was worried. Worried that he'd done the wrong thing about the company.' Earnestly Miss Evan returned to the main subject, eyes very alert, the corseted trunk upright, not touching the straight leather back of the chair. Her hands were folded on her knees, lightly clasping the gold pince-nez.

She was wearing a white blouse over a dark grey skirt and black shoes. The blouse had a small black bow at the neck. Treasure had taken the costume to be an expression in half-mourning. Already he wondered whether there were reservations in Miss Evan's regard for her brother: whether her concern was more to protect his moral reputation than it was with the fact of her bereavement – a diluted concern like the half-mourning, and perhaps as consciously considered.

'You think your brother had done the wrong thing? About agreeing to the sale of the company?'

'Oh, without question. He knew it too. Someone brought up to a sense of responsibility to others, especially to employees. Well, he should have known better than to sell out like that.'

'You didn't do the same?'

'Only when I had no option,' was delivered swiftly, the lips closing tight afterwards, and before she added: 'After a majority of the shares had been pledged to that Segam company.'

'I understand.'

'Not really, you can't. Not without knowing George. And me for that matter. We were very alike in some respects. Conventional, you might say. Neither of us prepared to shock anyone. Not in the ordinary way.' She paused to make sure the point had registered – again. 'Yes, very normal.'

'You mean people were shocked about the sale?'

'They were. But it wasn't instigated by my brother, Mr Treasure. Nor put through by him.'

'Could it have gone through without his approval? Without his shareholding?'

'In a sense, no. But he was manipulated. Made to be the tool of others.'

'But not, it seems, an unwilling tool.'

'At that late stage, perhaps. But there's an explanation. George had this consuming fear of being reduced to poverty.'

Treasure looked about the room. 'An unlikely eventuality, surely?'

'Not to George. He had this fixation about dentist power.'

'I'm sorry?'

'About the anti-sugar lobby ruining the business. The sugar confectionery business, Mr Treasure. George was convinced that dentists would do to boiled sweets what doctors have done to cigarettes.'

'Reducing him to penury in the process?'

'It's why he was presuaded to sell. After Paul Ranker failed to improve things.'

'And you feel that having sold for a large sum, having become financially secure himself—'

'He was always that, Mr Treasure,' Miss Evan interrupted. 'We both were. I've explained, it was only irrational concern that made him think otherwise. Well, mostly irrational.' But it seemed she was less intent on giving credit to the dental threat than to softening the careless implication that her brother was dotty.

'But deep down he must have known he had nothing to worry about. Except you said he was under pressure. Had he moved on to worrying about the effects of his action on others? On the employees, for instance?'

'Precisely, Mr Treasure.'

'And this couldn't have driven him to suicide?' He purposely left out the perpetration also of murder.

141

'Certainly not. Not when there was a much better way out.'

'You mean buying back the company from Segam?'

Miss Evan seemed disconcerted. 'I didn't say that. If that's a possibility, I knew nothing of it. I don't believe George did either.'

'Sorry, it was only a supposition on my part.'

'I see. I meant it was up to the old shareholders to give up the second payment for the shares. On certain conditions.'

'There's a second payment? On top of the twelve pounds a share?'

She shook her head. 'A second payment of eight pounds on top of the first payment of four pounds, Mr Treasure. So far shareholders have only received four pounds a share. If you didn't know that I suppose I shouldn't have told you. But I have now, and I'm not sorry.' Her lips were tightly pursed during the ensuing pause. 'The second payment is dependent on the company getting most of the surplus money in the pension fund for its own use. It may not be clear to you why . . .'

'Oh, it's abundantly clear, Miss Evan,' Treasure put in sharply, but marking the subject as one that required a great deal of further explanation from Lewis Bude. He recalled, also, that one shareholder had certainly already been paid twelve pounds a share, in full. So there were clearly two classes of shareholder, Miss Evan being in the second class. 'And you're suggesting that the shareholders might give up the second payment if Segam agree the pension money should be devoted to the pensioners?'

'It was what had been put in George's mind. As an honourable solution.'

'Had he done anything about implementing it?'

'I said it had only been put in his mind. As a matter of fact, only in the last few days. By me. At first he was against it, but he let me think later he was coming round to my view.'

Treasure detected less solid conviction in the voicing and framing of the last claim than there had been in her previous ones. 'You'd been a substantial shareholder, of course? As well as your brother?'

'Not nearly as substantial as George. But we didn't need the money. Either of us.'

'But the two of you backing down, over this second payment . . .?'

'Wouldn't have made a majority in favour, if that's what you mean. But I was sure we could have brought over a few other family shareholders. Small ones.'

'But there'd have been opposition from some of the remaining big ones?'

'Embarrassing position for them, of course,' Miss Evan observed in a calculating tone. 'Once it became public we'd only be getting the money for the shares at the expense of the pensioners. That's been secret up to now.'

Treasure pouted. 'It might embarrass, but it wouldn't necessarily stop the arrangement.'

'I thought it might if it made the directors of the Segam company uncomfortable. In public,' the lady added shrewdly. 'Especially if the holders of nearly half the shares said they'd had second thoughts. I was suggesting we tell Marian Roberts. Have her committee confront Segam. That's if the other shareholders said they wouldn't agree.'

'How very astute of you, Miss Evan.' The banker smiled wryly at his quite undevious-seeming companion. Then, human nature being what it is, he fleetingly savoured the thought that a thorn lately removed from his own flesh had been poised for sticking in someone else's – and a body much more nearly deserving of the workers committee's wrath than ever he had been.

Aloud he continued: 'So it seems the shareholders made what's termed a two-part sale agreement with Segam Holdings. In which case it's just possible that title to the shares may technically still lie with the original shareholders.'

'I'm not very good in such matters,' Miss Evan replied, although so far she had demonstrated the opposite. 'You mean, we could still own the shares in some way?'

'The right to reacquire them, perhaps. It would depend on the terms of the sale agreement. There are any number of

143

possible permutations. I wouldn't count on anything, but if you do still have buy-back rights, it could simplify things.' He thought for a moment before adding: 'Of course, any such interest in your brother's shares would now pass to his heir, if he's named one. Perhaps that would be you, Miss Evan?'

'Oh. I don't think so. I . . . I can't remember. I . . . I'd have to check.' Her reply to the question was confused and somehow unconvincing. She made as if to say something more, but finally remained silent.

'I'm sorry,' said the banker. 'I've upset you.'

'Not at all. I'm a little tired. I didn't sleep much last night. Not after the police had been.'

'I understand.' He stood up. 'And I've been here too long already.'

'If he didn't commit suicide, and I've told you he didn't, that leaves accident and murder, Mr Treasure. Accident is not likely, is it? But I ask you, whoever would have a reason to kill my brother – and the boy? Then dress it all up to look different from what it was? As if he was some kind of . . . well . . . pervert is the only word for it. Dear, dear.' She was staring at the embroidered daffodils in the fireplace screen as she spoke, not at her visitor. 'I can't think of anyone . . . unless it was one of the other shareholders, do you think? Someone wanting to be certain of that second payment?' Now she lifted her gaze slowly to focus on his. 'Surely not?' she added, but with an inflexion that suggested something quite different.

'I sincerely hope not,' Treasure replied, and now uncomfortably alerted to Miss Evan's possible underlying purpose. 'Of course, such a person would need to have known about the plan you and your brother had in mind.'

'Oh, I'm afraid at least one of them did,' came very promptly. 'He'd guessed. Put two and two together. From something George had said to someone else. He was here yesterday, threatening us over it. Threatening,' she repeated darkly. 'Not very nice, was it?' She breathed in and out heavily before disclosing: 'That was Mr Ranker.'

'What kind of threats?'

'Moral. They're the worst.'

The lady now sat silently tight-lipped. She was evidently not intending to enlarge on the last equivocal opinion.

'Did you mention this to the police?'

'No reason to. I didn't have the full facts then.'

'I see. And who'd told Ranker about your plan?'

'Michael Chard, the accountant. But as I said, he'd done it without knowing, really. Anyway, it came out again when all three were together yesterday for a meeting at Mr Bude's. That was in the afternoon.'

'And Chard knew about the two-part sale?'

'By then. I'm not sure he knew when it was first arranged.'

And as a pension trustee that would be as well, Treasure concluded to himself. 'Do you know whether Lewis Bude was also involved in this discussion yesterday?' he asked.

'Not so far as I know. He's not a shareholder. They were meeting at his house to talk about the sailing club. Mr Bude is involved in that.'

And Mr Bude's secret about owning Segam had been well kept it seemed. 'Did Ranker threaten your brother again then?'

'He challenged him about changing his mind over the second payment. Said he was calling an emergency meeting of directors for nine thirty this morning.'

'Before the intended staff meeting?'

She nodded. 'George refused to attend any directors' meeting. I told him I wouldn't go either. That only left Barbara Evan.'

'Was she going?'

'I think Mr Ranker was hoping to persuade her. Two would be enough for his purpose. He wanted George replaced as a pension trustee. Immediately.'

'By whom?'

'By himself.' She was suddenly animated. 'And there's another thing. I've remembered about George's shares. Who he left them to. That would be the one who'd get the second payment, if it's ever made?'

'I should think so. And it isn't you?'

'I've told you, neither my brother nor I needed money. It wouldn't exactly be what George intended, when he made his

145

will, but I suppose the money will now go to Joshua's widow, Barbara Evan. She and Mr Ranker are very close, of course.'

Treasure elected to walk to the Watkins' house in Terfyn Street. Miss Evan had given him directions and he had left the car in her drive. He wasn't sure whether he would be welcome, but as the one who had found the boy's dead body he felt obliged to call on the parents, to offer condolences and to give them the opportunity to ask him questions. They were not on the telephone.

A walk would also allow him to order his thoughts before returning to Plas Gwyn and what promised to be a difficult confrontation with his host.

He crossed the High Street, which was not yet over busy with Saturday-morning traffic and shoppers. Then, after passing two building-society offices, a betting shop, an off-licence and a grocery store, as instructed, he turned right at the estate agents' into the narrower, and slightly downhill Sea Road.

There was no doubt in his mind that Miss Evan had summoned him specifically so that she could direct an accusation against Ranker. She had obviously drawn a good deal of satisfaction from this, though the charge may have illustrated no more than her hatred of Ranker. Her pleasure at having fortuitously implicated Barbara Evan in her design had been equally clear – like her distaste for that lady.

Altogether it had been a successful foray for Miss Evan, but the banker was far from sure that he wanted to be her runner to the police.

Miss Evan had certainly exposed a reason why several people might have wanted to take her brother's life, but none for why anyone should have killed Owen Watkins. Curiously, she seemed to have been more moved by the boy's death than her brother's.

She had gone on to explain that in the last will George Evan had made, he had left his G. L. Evan Ltd shares to Joshua – because he had suffered a fit of conscience over his nephew. George had felt he had unjustly underestimated Joshua's

146

commercial capacity, particularly after Ranker had failed to revive the company.

Miss Evan had been sure her brother hadn't made a later will, though he had talked a good deal about the need to. Thus, although the shares had since passed to Segam, and although Joshua had died, it seemed that any second payment for them would now legally go to Joshua's widow.

Sybil Evan had been sure that Barbara would have known she would benefit through George's will. Barbara could also very well have been told by Ranker that George and Sybil were planning to reject the second payment on the shares. Miss Evan had vouchsafed both these confidences with some delicacy.

On his own account, Treasure had reluctantly concluded that Barbara had probably acquired Joshua's factory keys along with his directorship, but he hadn't asked Sybil for confirmation of this potentially damaging fact.

Almost involuntarily he interrupted his stride, and his train of thought, to stop and take in the southern aspect of the parish church now apparent in the middle distance – a castellated and heavily buttressed stone tower at the west end, an oversized, wooden framed Tudor porch on the south aisle. These dominant features were visible beyond a gently curving lane, off Sea Road, that passed the pretty lychgate, and bordered the low church wall with the rising grassy sward beyond.

Treasure knew St Elfod's was the oldest as well as the most impressive building for some distance around, deserving more than the scant attention he was ready to give it this morning. This didn't prevent several oncomers stopping just after passing him, looking back, and trying to spot what the tall, distinguished stranger was studying. But since the object was less than obvious – the church was much too familiar and distant to qualify – the curiosity of most remained unsated. Oblivious, the banker returned to his walk and his earlier preoccupation.

It was the share deal that had stuck in his throat. So payment to ordinary shareholders was to be in two parts – the second and larger one dependent on the fulfilment of a condition he found as questionable as it was repugnant.

A two-part sale of shares in a private company was not an uncommon device in Treasure's experience – nor an unethical one. Usually it meant that the purchaser was not ready to pay in full until certain conditions had been met that couldn't be when the deal was first struck. Perhaps an important and pending order had to be landed before the total offer price could be justified. Perhaps the old owner's estimate of company profits for the year – or several future years – needed to be proved to the buyer's satisfaction.

It was often an arrangement that the parties to it did not wish outsiders to know about, for the simple reason that it was none of anybody else's business.

But in the case of the G.L. Evan sale, the details had been kept secret solely because the deal was dependent on money being stripped out of the pension fund for the benefit of the new owners, Segam Holdings.

Worse than this, one shareholder had certainly not been sworn to secrecy, being unaware there was anything to be secretive about – though since this was a shareholder who in one sense had no contact with any of the others, it was unlikely 'he' would ever have given the game away.

The shareholder in question had already received payment in full at twelve pounds a share. And this shareholder was not technically a person, of course: it was the pension fund itself, corporately represented by its three trustees.

It would have upset the plan completely if the trustee Stanley Wigid at Grenwood, Phipps had known that the shares held by the pension fund were being treated differently from the others. Wigid would certainly have wanted to know why the remaining ninety per cent of the shares were only fetching four pounds each.

Yet at least one of the other trustees, George Evan, must have been privy to the conspiracy. On reflection, it also seemed to Treasure more than likely that Michael Chard had been in on it too.

The other shareholders had been sworn to secrecy possibly on pain of their forfeiting the second payment if word of it leaked out.

148

The pensioners stood to lose millions. The arrangement, though probably legal, was, in the circumstances, morally indefensible. Lewis Bude, for one, should be ashamed to be party to it, and should have come clean when he'd had the chance the night before.

This was not a case for the deal being nobody else's business. It was very much the business of the trustees and the pensioners, and they should all have been told.

Treasure was fast building a fine head of blind fury – so that he was completely unnerved when the sepulchral voice challenged from the inner darkness, 'It's the rood you're after, then, is it?'

14

'Didn't mean to frighten you,' the rotund clergyman offered further in an attractive Welsh cadence. He stepped from behind the threshold into the daylight of the porch, blinking enquiringly over half-spectacles.

'My fault entirely,' answered Treasure, recovering his composure. Instead of passing by the churchyard as he had intended, without knowing it, he had gravitated where his predilections had directed, which was along the path leading to the church door. By an almost uncanny coincidence the door had opened before him. 'My mind was elsewhere. I wasn't coming here at all. Supposed to be on my way to Terfyn Street,' he concluded with an apologetic grin.

'Quite so,' said the other in a humouring sort of way, as though mindless visitations were all part of the pastoral round, and properly to be encouraged. He was short, elderly, and comfortably overweight with a cherubic countenance, and cheeks as red as the apple he was absently rubbing on a not-very-clean cassock. The biretta was set so far back on his head it looked certain to fall off.

'I was intending to look at the church later,' Treasure offered by way of compensation. 'Of course I've read about your rood screen. I gather it's magnificent.'

'Fifteenth century and very well preserved, yes. Better come in now though. The place is locked up when I'm not here. Vandals, d'you see?' The cleric's face was thrust forward as he spoke, the prelude to a closer scrutiny of the visitor over the spectacles. 'Yes, vandals. Mark Treasure, is it?'

'It is. Do we know each other?'

'I shouldn't think so. But that's an Oxford tie you've got on. Jesus College. I was there too. Before you, of course. You've been expected in Llanegwen. For the meeting this morning.'

'I'm still surprised . . .'

'Small town. Word gets about. I looked you up. In *Who's Who*. We have a very fine public library. Mind the step. Oh, my name's Handel Hughes. I was invited to the meeting as well. Not as a main participant. Just as well it's cancelled. Bad business last night.' He saw Treasure in, then peered outside again, with an air of suspicion, before letting the heavy oak door swing closed with a reassuring, echoing clank from its monstrous iron latch.

It was cool inside the broad, low building, and quiet as well, the strong aura of sanctity augmented by a sweet residual aroma of incense laced with furniture polish, the twinkling of many burnished brasses and the flicker of three half-burned candles in a stand by the chancel steps. The background sound that Treasure at first nostalgically defined as heaving organ bellows sadly turned out to be the asthmatic breathing of the Reverend Handel Hughes at his side.

'You're the vicar, of course.'

'No. Honorary curate. Vicar's younger than me. Almost everybody is,' he completed ruefully, sighed at the apple, then put it away in his cassock pocket.

'If that's your breakfast, don't mind me.'

'Elevenses. Present from one of the communicants just now. Service is just finished. Too ambitious, though.'

'Not enough communicants on a Saturday?'

The older man looked perplexed. 'No, no. I meant the apple not the service. I don't have the bite any more, d'you see?' He puffed out his cheeks. 'I'm retired. From a living in South Wales. It's healthier for me up here. I rented the curate's flat next door some years ago. There isn't a proper curate. Not now. The vicar's off sick at the moment too. Small operation. Nothing serious. For piles,' he vouchsafed in a lowered tone. As they moved to the centre of the building his hands parted in an expansive gesture that ended palms outward as in a pontifical salutation. 'So there you have it. Unusual double-aisled nave, fifteenth century but heavily restored. The stone font by the door is earlier. Lady chapel up there on the left was reinstated in nineteen fifty-one. The Victorians had put an organ there instead.' He tutted. 'No accounting, is there?'

'And here's the famous rood screen,' observed Treasure moving towards the chancel arch whose upper half was filled by the rood or crucifix screen. This warranted close examination, like other features the two were to come upon in the chancel and sanctuary.

It was ten minutes later when the banker insisted he should be on his way again.

'If you're still here tomorrow there's communion at eight, parish communion at ten thirty and evensong at six, but that's in Welsh,' warned the priest as they were making their way to the door. 'Calling on Mr and Mrs Watkins now, are you? Owen's parents?'

'Yes, how did you . . . ?'

'You said Terfyn Street. That's where they live. Number twenty-three. It was you found his body, I'm told. Naked. Poor boy.'

'You knew him?'

'He did odd jobs for me. The family isn't churchgoing, but they're very decent people. I knew George Evan, of course.' The last comment called for more than acknowledgement.

'I found his body as well.' Treasure obliged.

'So I understand. Dreadful experience for you. Mr Evan naked too. They weren't in the same place, though?'

'No. In separate parts of the factory.'

'But there'll be the assumption they were up to something together. I've heard that already. Up to something not very nice. I doubt that's true though.'

'George Evan was . . .'

'A burnt-out old queen, if you want my opinion, Mr Treasure,' came with unexpected acerbity. 'And his habits weren't so secret as you'll be led to believe either. Not amongst the older members of the parish. People who grew up with him.'

'But he was harmless, you think?'

'Not a serious corrupter of youth. An old fool when it came to indulging a fleshy impulse, perhaps, but physically incapable of rising to the occasion. Rising properly, if you follow me? Did you see signs of an orgy?'

'No, but I saw evidence of murder.'

'Ah, well, that wouldn't have been done by George Evan.'

'The Watkins boy couldn't have killed himself. George Evan's initials were lettered on his chest.'

The cleric made a painful swallow. Clearly the last piece of information was new to him. He stopped near the font, effectively barring the visitor's further progress towards the door. 'The initials could have been meant as a red herring.'

'Of course. They could also have stood for General Electric.' Treasure gave an amiable grunt. 'If you think Evan incapable of murder I'd accept that as a kind of character reference.'

'But not worth more, I see that. If I'm right, there has to have been someone else there. Someone who killed both of them. In this little town. Doesn't bear thinking about. What had they done to warrant such treatment?'

'Watkins was wanted by the police.'

'You don't say?' the cleric wheezed slowly, then brought the biretta further forward, but only slightly.

'Something to do with what he was up to the night Joshua Evan was drowned.'

'I remember that well. Very windy. He and Gwyneth Davies went past my bachelor pad.' He grinned puckishly. 'Well, that's what the girls in the choir call it. Compliment, I suppose. Anyway, these two were coming up from the beach. The girl was attacked later.'

'The boy had gone home by then.'

'Oh, no.' The Reverend Hughes frowned. 'He passed me again going back down Sea Road a few minutes after.'

'You were outside?'

'No, no. My little living room has a bay window. It's on the upper floor. Gives me a distant view of the sea. Very distant, I'm afraid. But I sit there late with the curtains open and the lights out. That's when my eyes are too tired to read or watch the telly. I don't sleep much.'

'And you saw Watkins go down to the beach again?'

'And come back twenty minutes later. Then he was going home. Or in the right direction, anyway. Bit loaded down, too. Had things under his jacket.'

Treasure hesitated. 'The police think he'd been burgling the sailing club.'

'Dear, dear.'

'And if he'd done it around dawn he might have come across Joshua Evan who went sailing very early.'

'Well, he didn't do it then. Owen, I mean.'

'Did you know Joshua?'

'Very well. His mother's a devout member of the congregation when she's here. She has a flat in a house opposite mine. Ground floor.'

'Joshua used it the night before he died.'

'I don't think so.'

'How d'you mean?'

'No lights there late or early. I always notice.'

'But at the inquest on Joshua I'm told it was reported he stayed there to avoid disturbing his wife.'

'That's as may be. It doesn't mean it happened that way. Joshua could have been staying elsewhere. With . . .' There was the gentlest of indulgent frowns to mark the pause, 'With a friend, perhaps?'

'You didn't go to the inquest to say so?'

'Why should I? Not my business to interfere.'

'All right. But no friend turned up to say so either.'

'So perhaps Joshua was at home after all, and it was his wife who stayed with a friend. Tell me, Mr Treasure, why are you so interested in Joshua?'

'I suppose indirectly it was his death that brought me here.'

'And now there are two more deaths keeping you here.'

Treasure looked at his watch. 'I'm afraid I really must . . .'

'I saw Owen Watkins from my window just after lunch yesterday. He was in a hurry to get somewhere.'

'Home?'

'Wrong direction. More likely coming from there and on his way to . . . at a guess, Gwyneth Davies's house. If he was already on the run. Those two were very sweet on each other.'

'You haven't told the police any of this?'

'What's to tell? As I say, it's not my business to interfere. Certainly not to spread unsupported supposition about people in the parish.' The cleric paused and the bland smile reappeared. 'Not to officials, that is. Different between friends, of course. Friends, and members of the same college.' He nodded at Treasure before seeing him to the door.

'I should have told you about the two-part sale of those shares.' Lewis Bude shook his head. 'You obviously think it indefensible not to have. I just wish you'd believe I've been in an impossible position from the start. More coffee?'

Treasure looked at his cup. 'No, thanks.'

The two were seated at a table on the swimming pool terrace. It was mid-morning. Unbidden, Constance Bude had brought a tray of coffee things, then, sensing the uneasy atmosphere, she had left the men together.

The banker had returned to Plas Gwyn shortly before, following a trying interview with the parents of Owen Watkins. The one he was having now with his host was proving no more palatable.

'I really didn't know Segam were buying G. L. Evan until the deal was well forward,' Bude went on, sternfaced. 'Because I own the company people will find that difficult to credit, but it's the truth. When I did find out, I still didn't take a lot of interest in the detail, but because we live here a good deal of the time, it seemed best not to let on I was behind Segam. Since you entered the picture, I've been trying to dismember the whole arrangement, without upsetting any of the parties. I owed that to all of them.'

'Including the pensioners?'

'Certainly including them. What we discussed yesterday involved a lot of work behind the scenes. I couldn't possibly have tabled a working plan to you without for instance squaring the old shareholders.'

'You mean George Evan and Paul Ranker?'

'Principally. George more than Ranker who I don't really have much time for.'

Treasure made no comment on the last point. Ranker had been welcome as a dinner guest the night before, and, it seemed, as Bude's erstwhile sailing companion. Had he been suffered because he did Bude's dirty work for him – for example, in pressuring George Evan and his sister into keeping the two-part share sale under wraps?

'Barbara Evan was a major consideration too?'

Bude's gaze lifted. 'Certainly she was. But come to that, all shareholders had rights in the matter.'

'Rights to that second payment? Something Segam intended funding with part of the pension surplus?' The banker had put the question stonily.

The other folded his short arms across his chest. 'The shares held by the G. L. Evan pension fund itself were paid for in full. At twelve pounds a share. Segam coughed up for the whole of that.'

'But if you're suggesting that reflects well on Segam, I disagree. It was done as a subterfuge. To fool the trustees. Or the key trustee, Stanley Wigid, at Grenwood, Phipps. If the two-part sale had applied to those shares he'd have figured what you were up to immediately. I'm sorry, it reads like sharp practice.'

'It may seem so.' Bude got up, paced the short distance to the pool, then turned about again. 'All right, I'll agree it's entirely what you say. Sharp. Look, Mark, I'll admit I didn't make my pile without stepping on the competition now and again. Without applying some aggression along the way. But I've always played by rules of fair conduct.' He breathed out sharply. 'Conning pension trustees, or pensioners for that matter, it isn't on in my book, and that's the truth. I told you I've been trying to unravel this mess since the middle of the week. I'm flying to Liverpool this afternoon to meet the managing director of Segam again, with our lawyer. Didn't want them here. And I've had Chard working on the thing in confidence full time.'

'In any case, all very difficult, I'd have thought, without disclosing your interest in Segam.'

'Which is why I decided yesterday that where necessary I'd come clean on that. Chard knew already. I told Ranker and George Evan in the afternoon. Up here after that meeting. Of course, George was key. With him co-operating, we might have been able to reverse the whole deal. He and his sister, and two female cousins in Bournemouth, they'd owned more than half the shares between them. The cousins would have done anything George said, apparently.'

'I'm not clear about the terms of the sale. If the second payment isn't made, are the old shareholders entitled to . . .?'

'Buy back the shares for four pounds each? Yes, they are. Frankly, Segam weren't interested in anything but getting hold of the pension surplus. If we couldn't do that there was no percentage. No profit. We'd be glad to get back to square one.'

'Or to keep some of the shares if the original owners don't want them back? Yesterday we discussed a joint effort to make G. L. Evan viable again.'

'I'll hold to that. We'll play our part.' It seemed Bude had joined the angels with a vengeance.

'Pity George Evan is dead,' the banker remarked quietly.

'He must have been round the twist. Killing himself and taking that lad with him. And if details of the deal come out in public, they'll say that's what unhinged him. Leaves me in a hell of a spot.'

'And I'm afraid it could get a lot worse. If someone else killed both of them. Specifically someone who didn't want that deal reversed.'

'But surely nobody who . . .?'

157

'I'm sorry . . . sorry to interrupt, but this really can't wait.' It was Ranker who had appeared, expostulating loudly from around the side of the house. He was slightly ahead of a protesting Constance, and gaining. In one hand she was holding a potted bedding plant at arm's length. Her other hand, though already grasping a trowel, was clamped on the top of her head keeping the picture hat in place.

'Well, it's not at all convenient, Paul,' Bude responded roughly.

'And it's not at all convenient having Marian Roberts foisted on us as a pension trustee either.'

'Who told you that?'

'Barbara Evan. Ten minutes ago. Says Sybil Evan is proposing Marian Roberts, with a majority of directors in favour. Well, someone can't add. There are only three directors left. Miss Evan, Barbara and me. And Barbara and I are against, which makes a majority. And anyway, Marian Roberts isn't . . .'

'Segam are creating new directors. They hold all the shares. They can appoint whom they like, and they're appointing Marian Roberts and me.' This was Bude again, very angry. The two men were standing facing each other like pugilists just beyond sparring distance.

'I see. So you've chosen to show your hand?' Ranker snapped back, but with a sidelong glance at Treasure.

'Certainly I have. And there'll be no more covering up. Not in any connection.'

'So Mark Treasure knows you own Segam? Knows about the two-part sale?'

'Yes, I do,' the banker himself put in. He had risen and went to stand beside Constance who was looking bemused and unprotected. 'And what you've just heard seems to answer the other question you were about to put. As a director, Miss Roberts will also be qualified to be the pension trustee appointed by the board. That's in place of the late George Evan.'

'Who'd invited me to take over from him yesterday. Barbara

158

agreed last night. We . . . Barbara and I . . . we . . . we absolutely protest.' Confused, Ranker flung out the words. He was shaking with rage.

'If you're hoping to save the deal, you're too late.' This was Bude. 'If you want, we'll arrange for you to have your shares back for four pounds each.'

'Oh no you won't! I don't want my bloody shares back. I want another eight pounds each for them! That was the deal! And the deal's still on because a majority of old shareholders says so. Barbara and I have more than fifty per cent between us.'

'Because Barbara comes into George's entitlement? Doesn't make any difference.' Bude was now much cooler as he went on. 'Segam agreed to the second payment if the surplus was transferred out of the pension fund and into G. L. Evan Limited. It's not going to be. Neither the directors nor the trustees will approve.'

'That's so you can pretend to be Mr Clean? Is that it? Now everyone's under suspicion?' Ranker continued to seethe. 'But George didn't agree to dropping the deal.'

'George is dead, and he did agree to it.'

'Prove it.'

'I can. Efforts were made to stop him, of course.'

'Whose efforts?'

'Yours. You threatened him.'

'Threatened him? You must be mad. I killed him too, I suppose?'

'I didn't say that.'

'You'd better not, Bude. You've got some explaining to do yourself.'

'Rather less than some others.'

'You bastard.' Ranker swung his clenched right fist inexpertly at Bude who side-stepped, closed on Ranker while he was off balance, and made to thrust him past.

Bude's movement would have been quite sufficient defence without the sterner support. This came when Ranker's onward passage was accelerated by a sudden supplement of dog power.

The four Labradors had come headlong to the scene, spotted

the fun, and joined it. Two of them collided with the back of Ranker's knees. The others tangled just ahead of him ready for him to fall over as he was now unstoppably propelled, arms flailing, straight into the swimming pool.

The episode was over in seconds, when the outraged Ranker surfaced, spitting and floundering in chest high water – this to the unconfined delight of the chorusing dogs who were lolloping ecstatically along the pool edge.

Constance Bude had given a little scream and dropped the bedding plant.

Her husband regarded his miserable assailant's plight with surprise but no sympathy.

Nobody went to help Ranker as he lunged towards some steps, glowering at the dogs assembling there above him, and ready for the next game.

Only Treasure turned at the discreet, embarrassed cough from behind.

'Good morning, everybody. Couldn't get a reply at the door. Sorry if I let the dogs out. Swimming party, is it?' Detective Inspector Thomas enquired brightly.

15

The closer Albert Shotover got to the factory gate the more determination it took to go on. At the corner of Dewin Street he very nearly turned around and fled, but by then the uniformed policeman on the gate was watching him – or so it seemed to Shotover.

His arrival was certainly being marked by some members of the bored-looking group of reporters and sightseers that the constable had shepherded on one side. A few of the curious locals were company employees known to the approaching figure. Some of these had come for the staff meeting, not knowing it had been cancelled, then stayed to observe.

Shotover kept going, telling himself he would have felt just as threatened if he'd gone to the Llanegwen police station. And a visit there would have caused talk if anyone had seen him. The factory was his place of work.

'You can't go in,' said the constable. He was young and not a local man – drafted in from another part of the division. Shotover didn't impress him except as a middle-aged runt – an artisan dressed for Saturday-morning shopping in open-necked shirt, grey trousers and sandals, and carrying a plastic bag.

'I'm a manager here,' Shotover half-whispered, anxious not to share his business with anyone who didn't know it already.

'Still can't go in, I'm afraid. Sir.' The claim to management status, even though unsupported by his appearance, had now grudgingly earned Shotover the appellation usually afforded respectable male citizens. It did nothing to increase his confidence.

'I'd like to see whoever's in charge.' He swallowed. 'Of the investigation.' He'd practised this part, but his unease was still growing. He hadn't expected so much activity. The factory yard had more vehicles in it than it had on a weekday, except now they all belonged to the police.

'I see, sir. Could I have your name, then?'

Shotover's shoulders rose uncontrollably. 'Albert Shotover,' he whispered.

'I'm sorry, could you repeat that?' The constable looked up, pencil still poised.

'Albert Shotover,' came out this time in a strangled falsetto. He looked behind at the motley assembly, but no one was showing any interest in him now, except for a girl from packaging who was giving him a little wave as he forced out: 'I'm the manager of the despatch department.'

Which in the constable's estimation didn't exactly make Shotover a captain of industry: still. 'Got something to report have you, Mr Shotover? Something relevant to the investigation?'

Shotover nodded, then took off his spectacles and wiped them.

'Half a minute then.' The policeman eyed him again with what could very well have been taken for suspicion, then said things into his clipped-on transmitter that Shotover couldn't hear, or more likely wasn't supposed to hear. 'All right, sir. Go through the yard to the incident van, that's the big one parked by the main door. Ask there for Detective Sergeant Jago.'

Twice Shotover had glanced back while crossing the yard. Both times the policeman on the gate had been watching him still, making signs that he should carry on to the van. Other people were watching him, too. There was nothing else he could do but go exactly where he'd been sent.

Five minutes later Shotover had said what he'd planned to say, seated on one side of a narrow desk flap across from the sergeant. Jago, an immense man, thirtyish, balding and in shirt-sleeves, was settled midships in the mobile police station, squeezed in between electronic gadgetry. Shotover had counted eight other male and female officers who seemed to be

162

permanently engaged aboard. Others came and went but few spared even a glance his way – for which he was grateful.

His statement had been in his own words, with little prompting. The sergeant had interrupted only twice. A young, cupid-lipped woman police constable had made notes on the keyboard of a small computer attached to the open end of the desk flap. She had just torn a typed sheet from her printer and handed it to Jago who was studying it gravely.

'Do you usually check out delivery vans at ten thirty at night, Mr Shotover?'

'As I said, it was just this once. The vehicle had been giving trouble all week. It's our smallest van. Used for local routes. I'd meant to give it a run when the driver came back last evening, with half his load undelivered. He was late. He said because of a breakdown. I was in a meeting by then.'

'This staff committee meeting?'

'That's right. Then afterwards I was due at Basso Morgan's. I needed to go home and change for that. There wasn't time for anything else.'

'But you came round after the supper at Mr Morgan's?'

'It was more convenient than leaving it for today.' He wondered why he was having to repeat some things he'd said already.

The sergeant had started to make a pencil note, then stopped. 'Than leaving it for Monday morning, you mean? Would you usually come in on a Saturday?'

'Oh, I would have today. If necessary. For this particular vehicle. It was when the engine was hot the driver said it's been giving trouble. That's when I needed to check it.'

'But the driver brought it back at six twenty. You didn't take it out till ten thirty.'

'More like ten forty when I actually drove it away. Still better than leaving it to cool off completely over night.'

'You in charge of transport as well as despatch of goods, Mr Shotover?'

Shotover shuffled in the shaped plastic seat. 'No. The transport manager's on holiday. He's our mechanic really.

163

Normally looks after simple repairs himself. We only have six vans. And company cars, of course. While he's away the work's being done by one of the local garages.'

'And you know about van engines?'

'No, but I know about van drivers.'

'I see. The breakdown could have been invention?'

'I'm not saying that, but with four breakdowns during the week . . . Well, I didn't know whom to blame. The garage or the driver.'

'You're very conscientious, Mr Shotover.' The younger man smiled.

'I know. I can't help it. I'd have been back this morning in any case to check the undelivered merchandise. It's still locked in the van.'

'The driver didn't do that?'

'He's not allowed to. Not unsupervised. I have to be present. Company rule. As I said, I wasn't available when he got back.'

'You didn't do the checking later last night?'

'Couldn't. Didn't have the manifest handy. It was in my office.'

'You don't have keys to the buildings?'

'I do, but I didn't have them with me. I'd like to check the merchandise now. Otherwise there's unnecessary time wasted on Monday first thing.'

'I see. Anyway, you came to tell us you were in the yard at approximately ten thirty, and again at approximately eleven fifteen, and you saw nothing suspicious on either occasion.'

'That's right.'

'And you took the van out.'

'For a short run. After I'd checked it over. It was the starter that was supposed to be at fault.'

'Where d'you take it exactly?'

'Not far. To Pentre Beach. I stopped there for more starter checks. Then back past Llanegwen, nearly to St Asaph, then back again here. No problems.'

'On the expressway?'

'That's right. I turned round at the St Asaph exit road.' He hadn't driven right into the town. The route he'd described wasn't accurate, but it accounted for the length of time he was out, and for places where he might have been seen – as well as a few where he couldn't. He hadn't been to Pentre Beach, or anywhere west of Llanegwen.

'There was no trouble with the van, you say?'

'None. Which is what I'd expected.'

The sergeant scratched absently at the front of his shirt. 'And there were no strange vehicles in the yard?'

'No vehicles at all except the company vans. They're parked at the back.'

'You didn't see Mr George Evan's car? It's a blue Rover.'

'I know his car. It wasn't here. He usually walks from his house.'

'So we've been told.' Jago consulted the typed sheet again. 'You say there were lights on in the buildings?'

'Only in the office block that I remember. I didn't notice any in the factory, but I probably wouldn't have seen any. Not from this side. Lights are always left on in the offices. They work on time switches.'

'I see. And you didn't meet anyone while you were here?' He handed the sheet back to the girl.

'Nobody.'

'Nor after you left?'

Shotover cleared his throat. 'I bumped into Basso Morgan across the road outside.'

'The company pensioner who gave the supper?'

'That's right. We both said it was quite a coincidence. He'd been out for a walk. I . . . I said that's what I'd been doing too. Walking.'

The policeman's brow creased. 'You didn't say you'd been checking out a van? Why was that, sir?'

Shotover's shoulders rose involuntarily. 'At supper . . .' he began, almost whispering again, knowing he was losing his nerve.

'Yes, sir?' Jago encouraged.

'At supper they'd all been joking about me living for the job.

165

Being too keen. Conscientious, like you said. They were kidding me about it. I didn't want to let on to Basso I'd been working. Sounds daft, I expect.' His voice was trailing away again.

The sergeant had been watching the speaker carefully. 'I think I understand, sir. Let's see. You've already given us Mr Morgan's address.' He paused. 'Well, thank you very much for coming to see us. Very public spirited. We shan't need the statement formally signed. Not for now, but if we do later, we know where to find you. That's all then, sir. Won't keep you any longer.'

Shotover's spirits rose. They were accepting his explanation. Not wanting him to sign must show they thought he'd wasted their time. It was obvious no one had seen him with the van. He'd been right to tell the truth about Basso. He'd thought they'd check on that. He was halfway safe. Now all he needed was to get into the van. He produced the ring of ignition keys from his pocket. 'Is it all right for me to get that manifest and check it now? To check the merchandise in the van?'

'Ah, afraid we can't let you do that, sir. Not yet. That section of the yard hasn't been cleared.'

'But it'll not take but a minute.'

'And the office block's closed off too. Till we're done with it.'

'But I must check that merchandise. It's part of my job. It's a valuable load. Please.' Shotover leaned forward over the desk flap. The apprehension he was trying to keep out of his voice showed in his eyes.

'We'll be through in both areas by mid-afternoon, sir. All being well you can come back then, and welcome.'

'I see, but . . .'

'Meantime, if you'd be good enough to let me have those keys? Fit all the vans in the yard, do they?'

'Yes, but . . . Oh, I suppose so.'

Impassively Jago noted the hardly disguised despair. 'Fine, sir. We've been wanting to examine them. We'll give you a receipt, of course. And the stuff in the small van, that'll be safe, don't worry.' He took rather than accepted the key ring from

166

the other's limp grasp. 'WPC Slocombe here will give you the receipt, and see you safely out of the yard.' He nodded pointedly to the uniformed girl.

A minute after a miserable Shotover had been seen off the premises, Sergeant Jago sent two detective constables to search the locked vans drawn up at the rear of the factory. The officers' instructions were to deal with the smallest vehicle first.

'What are we looking for, Sergeant?'

'Anything interesting, suspicious or incriminating. Probably just interesting. Whatever it is, the owner's bloody anxious to get it back. I don't believe it's packets of sweets, but you'll find some of those in the back.' And in reply to two still questioning looks he added, 'You'll know you've found it when you see it, boys.'

They did too – but it took them some time. It was under the driver's seat.

'Quite simply, I thought you ought to know what's happening,' said Treasure, completing his account. 'Paul Ranker left fairly soon after in his car, wet, furious but still claiming your total support. Lewis Bude's still closeted with Inspector Thomas. I think Constance is having the vapours.'

Barbara Evan swept the long blonde hair off her forehead. 'And you need to know where I really stand on all this? If I intend to . . . co-operate?'

Her stare was more sensually provocative than questioning – but he deduced this to be part of Mrs Evan's standard reaction to all healthy males past the age of puberty.

She was dressed in brief, white tennis shorts, a loose, revealing, red silk shirt and open sandals. She had suggested a drink, and that he stay to share the meal she'd been preparing when he'd arrived, but he had declined both offers – the first because it was too early, and the second because he already had a lunch appointment.

They were seated together on a covered swing chair on the pool patio. It was where she had directed him to sit when he arrived. Her shapely bronzed legs were curled under her, knees brushing his thigh when she moved, which was quite often.

'No one's going to pressure you,' he said. 'Inevitably there'll be a vote by the new G. L. Evan board against the company trying to take back the pension-fund surplus.'

'So there'll be no second payment to the old shareholders?'

'I'm afraid that's so.'

'No, you're not, you're bloody glad. It's what you came up for,' she replied, but smiling. She opened a packet of cigarettes and offered it to him.

'I'm glad for the pensioners.' He shook his head at the cigarettes.

'I never believed we'd get that second payment, but I'm not a bad loser like Paul. He doesn't have my backing. Not any more. If Lewis chucked him in the pool, that only makes him slightly wetter than he was before. Can you reach those matches?' The box was on a table beside him.

'He seemed to think you'd want to resist the decision, come what may.'

'That's bilge, and he knows it. The only thing I'll go on resisting are Paul Ranker's puerile advances. He came back here last night to soft-talk me into supporting him. To replace George as trustee. He said George had agreed. I went along, except I thought the whole thing was a lost cause already. Thanks. You have beautiful hands.' She leaned over to him as he lit her cigarette. She kept her fingers touching his for a long moment when she took away the box.

'All this was before George Evan died, of course,' said Treasure.

'Poor George. You reckon he killed himself after doing in lover boy?'

'It's one explanation. There are others.'

'Hm. They say it takes all sorts. You found the two of them, though. You and Marian Roberts. You'll be careful of her, won't you? Makes trouble for men, as well as being disappointing in bed. Or so I've always gathered. Inhibited, poor love, despite her looks. Perhaps you've found that out already.'

'You're very forthright.'

'And dead common with it. Did they tell you? Also that I

168

drink too much, which isn't true. Only when I get depressed, like yesterday. And if I fancy a man, I tell him so. Marian's approach is more subtle. She got to my husband with a marketing plan. Load of horse manure.' Mrs Evan pulled on her cigarette, then slowly blew out the smoke.

'I gather your husband was against selling the company to Segam.'

'And he was wrong. For a bit I thought there might be some sense in getting rid of Paul, and giving Joshua the lead. But it wouldn't have worked.'

'Segam will sell you back the shares at four pounds.'

'Darling, you've got to be joking. Why should I want the shares back? So, it's less money than expected. Did you know I inherit George's entitlement? To the second payment? That's a laugh now.'

'I heard it suggested.'

'You mean Sybil told you? She was on the phone earlier telling me to give in gracefully. Sybil and I understand each other. We don't like each other, but then we're different types, wouldn't you say? Not much in common. Tough old lady.'

'I think you're pretty resilient yourself. Losing your husband that way must have been a great shock. Whatever your relationship.'

She shrugged. 'He'd lost me long before. Marian was welcome to him. It was the cunning way she got to him that burned me.' She looked up and straightened, drawing a hand down between the open top buttons of the blouse. 'So, Mister Rich Banker, you can report to the others I'm ready to go quietly. Michael Chard's also been pouring advice into my shell-like ear this morning. He rang to say there's no way in the world I can make anyone push to get that pension surplus. Not any more. And no way without it anyone's going to make the second payment. So what the hell?'

'I think you're being very sensible. But I'm not reporting to anyone, only helping to put together a plan for the company. It may be possible to keep it going. I need to know who'll be holding the shares.'

'Not me. I guess I'll be able to rub along on what I already got

169

for Joshua's holding. I don't care to remain a director, either. Not with Marian being made one. There wouldn't be room for both of us round that table. Anyway, I don't suppose anyone'll be pressing me to stay.'

'I couldn't say about that.' The directorship was hardly significant, but for the second time in less than an hour he found himself searching for the reason why anyone with such a huge financial expectancy should surrender it with such incredible grace.

'You're very tactful. I was only meant to be a stand-in director after Joshua died.' Her unblinking brown eyes carried a wistful look as she added, 'It's sad he's not around any more, poor sod. If there's a new deal. He'd have wanted to be part of that.'

Treasure allowed a pause before he asked, 'Satisfy my curiosity on something, will you?'

'I'll try.' The smile became mischievous. 'How disappointing it's only your curiosity you want satisfied.' She ran a finger down his arm.

'Tell me, where did Joshua sleep the night before he drowned?'

The smile promptly faded. 'At his mother's flat. Why d'you ask?'

'I told you, curiosity. It seems no one saw him there.'

'I know that. He told me that's where he was going. I believed it. So did the coroner.'

'He couldn't have slept here without your knowing?'

'Hardly. And I still don't understand why you're so deeply interested.'

'I'm interested in your husband's frame of mind before the accident. If it hadn't been for his death the train of events later might have been quite different. I probably wouldn't be here now.'

'So is that it?' Her tone had become very matter-of-fact.

'Not quite. If he really wasn't where he said he'd be that night, hypothetically, can you guess where he might have gone?'

170

She stubbed out the cigarette. 'Hypothetically or otherwise, that wouldn't be too bloody difficult.' She looked up at him coolly. 'I shouldn't give her the satisfaction of saying so, but I'd say it was obvious he was in bed with Marian Roberts.'

16

Detective Inspector Thomas beamed out through the office window. 'Smashing sea view you've got here, Mr Chard. It'd stop me working, I can tell you. Specially on a sunny day like this with the tide in.' He turned about to face the accountant who was seated behind an untidy desk, impatiently stroking his sparse beard with a stiff forefinger. 'Come in every Saturday, do you?'

'When I'm busy.' The phrase came over promptly.

The offices of Chard & Company occupied the upper floor of a fifty-year-old, two-storey, small commercial building at the unfashionable end of the sea-front at Pentre Beach. The ground floor accommodated two shops – a newsagent's on one side and a wine store on the other. The door and stairway to the accountancy firm was in the middle.

Michael Chard's private office was a functional affair, large, but furnished without care or much cost. The desk was made of deal, and there were three very worn upholstered chairs around it, two of them matching and all of them armless, plus the castered pedestal chair that Chard was using.

Against one wall was a bank of triple-tiered, grey metal filing cabinets, and opposite, a white painted table stacked with box files. The faded carpet had traces of an orange and green pattern, and might once have been arranged to fit wall to wall, but not to the walls of this particular office since it stopped at varying distances from all of them. Exposed surfaces were painted a sickly cream, except for the off-white ceiling, and the yellow-tiled surrounds of the fireplace that framed a fairly up-to-date gas appliance.

The three strip lights were all suspended from the ceiling on dusty lengths of chain at slightly different heights and angles. The two windows were uncurtained, but fitted with Venetian blinds for privacy and not against the sunlight since the office faced north.

It was a room suggesting that little of the firm's income was dissipated on creature comforts, or else that there was little income to dissipate – the inspector wondered which. 'I read about your partner Mr Wilks retiring last year. Left a lot of work for one man to do I should think,' he offered, seating himself on the least shabby chair – the unmatching one – and flipping open a small notebook, while still taking in his surroundings. It went through his mind that perhaps Wilks might have taken all the good furniture with him. 'Anyway, good of you to see me so quickly. After I'd put the phone down, I realised you might be making a special journey in for me. I could have called at your house later.'

The other drew his chair closer to the desk in an abrupt, hopping movement. 'I was just leaving home when you rang.'

'Fine. I won't keep you long. It's about the deaths of Mr George Evan and the young man Owen Watkins. You've heard some of the details I expect?'

Chard looked grave. 'Paul Ranker telephoned me first thing.'

'Yes, he would have done. You being auditor to the company, and close to Mr Evan. I saw Mr Ranker earlier this morning.' Thomas paused briefly while making the decision not to enlarge on the circumstances of that encounter. 'Just one or two questions, then. I understand you were at the G. L. Evan factory yesterday?'

'Yesterday, and at different times on the previous two days. I'm doing a special audit for the new owners.'

'That's Segam Holdings, which in turn is owned by Mr Lewis Bude. He just told me so. Small world, isn't it?' He had volunteered the knowledge to avoid any temptation for prevaricating by the accountant: Thomas preferred the straight-forward approach. Now, since there was no rejoinder, he continued. 'A special audit, you said?'

173

'To find out the current worth of the business.'

'I'd have thought Segam would have had one of those when they took over the company.'

'Things may have changed since then.'

'I see,' the inspector commented slowly, but in the way of someone who didn't see at all. 'That's not a job the company's own accounting department could do?'

'Possibly it is. But the Segam management asked me to do it.' The answer was decidedly dismissive, implying the question had been ill judged.

'Wanted an outside, objective opinion, I expect.' Again Thomas looked for a comment, but again failed to elicit one. He had nearly added something jocular about the extra audit fee probably making a nourishing bonus with the holidays coming, but decided against it. Chard wasn't the bantering sort, as well as being a bit stuck up. The two had met before – three years earlier, and shortly after Thomas had come to live in the town. He'd been a sergeant at the time. The accountant had been distant in his manner then, and he was no different now. 'So you were at the factory yesterday, sir?'

'In the office block, from ten in the morning till three fifty in the afternoon.' This had come with unexpected alacrity and exactness.

'You weren't in the main building?'

'No. Not yesterday.' Chard punctuated by looking pointedly at the time.

'Thank you. I understand you have keys to all the buildings.'

'The two main ones. The keys have been on temporary loan since last Wednesday. So I can get in at any time.'

'Like after hours?'

'Yes, if I want. With any members of my team.'

'You have assistants on this particular job?'

'On most. Only one on this one, at the moment. A pupil accountant. But she was away ill yesterday. It's why I was such a long time in the factory myself. I was trying to get the work finished.'

174

'You weren't there after hours yesterday, sir?'

'No, I wasn't.'

'Nor was any . . . any member of your team?'

'That's right.'

'And you finished the work?'

'No, but I brought away all the ledgers I needed to carry on here over the weekend. These are two of them.' He indicated the big loose-leaf ledgers before him on the desk.

'They look at bit pre-computer age.'

'G. L. Evan was that sort of company until recently. Until Mr Ranker arrived. They're gradually switching to electronic systems.'

'Better for you, I expect. About those factory keys, have they left your possession since you got them?'

'Not once.'

'Good. And can you tell me what time you got home last night, sir? To St Asaph? Approximate will do.' He looked up from his notebook with the sort of smile a policeman or doctor uses to indicate his question is only a matter of routine, and nothing to worry about.

'At eleven eighteen. My wife remarked on it. She'll remember it too, because of the attack on the baby-sitter.'

Thomas made a note – and a mental one about the built-in corroboration. 'Nasty, that was. About the girl.' They had touched on the event when he had first arrived.

'As I said, she came to no real harm in the end.' The accountant's tone was dismissive. 'If she'd only waited I'd have driven her home. My wife tried to make her stay, but she wouldn't listen. Impetuous. I explained that to the policeman who came to see us. At midnight.'

The inspector gave the reassuring smile once more. 'Must've had your fill of being interviewed by coppers.' Even so, he had looked for a good deal more concern about an attempted rape. Probably Chard's attitude stemmed from a sense of guilt for not being back in time to drive the girl home. 'I understand you and your wife had spent the evening at Mr Bude's house, sir?'

175

'That's right. My wife left before me. She had her own car.'

'And what time did you leave?'

'Around ten fifteen.' He swallowed, noting the other's still expectant expression. 'I didn't go straight home. I came back here. To check something in these ledgers. Then I locked them in the safe. That's in the next office. Mr Wilks's old office. I drove home afterwards. Must have left just before eleven. At night, it takes about twenty minutes from here.'

'Thank you. That's very clear.' Thomas put the rush of embellishment down to anxiety, rather than the earlier contrived impatience. For the first time Chard was showing signs of being rattled. 'Oh, you'll have been asked, probably, if you noticed anything unusual when you got to St Asaph. Around the cathedral?'

'I certainly have been asked. Several times. The town centre was completely deserted when I came through it.'

'I see. Sorry to bring it up again. Not my case, anyway. Just interested.'

'Well, I couldn't help your people. I was nowhere near when the girl was attacked.' Chard paused, blinking frequently, and pulling harshly on the wispy beard – unconsciously probably, because the action looked painful. 'My wife's very upset.'

'Naturally. Hope we catch the man. Well, now, did you happen to meet anyone you knew while you were here in Pentre Beach? That would be, let's see, between ten thirty and eleven?'

'No one that I remember. This area's quite deserted at that time of night, except in full season. Since you live here you'll know that, Mr . . . Thomas.'

'Quite so. Well, perhaps one of the neighbours saw the car. Parked outside, was it?'

'No, in the lane at the back. It might not have been seen from any of the buildings occupied at night.'

'Well, no harm in enquiring later, if necessary.'

'Why should it be necessary?'

'We may need to account for the movements of relevant people between those times.'

'Relevant people?'

'People with factory keys, sir. And I can tell you, there are an awful lot of them.' He made a friendly grimace intended to reassure but which did nothing to lighten the other's now undisguised apprehension. 'One last point, Mr Chard,' the policeman continued, 'I suppose you had to know about the two-part share sale by G. L. Evan shareholders?'

'That was something between Segam and them. I was never a shareholder.'

'But you did know about the arrangement?'

'Not officially. No.'

The inspector looked mildly pained. 'But you knew unofficially?'

'Only quite recently.'

'Thank you. But as a trustee of the pension fund, I understand there were G. L. Evan shares in your control? The ones owned by the fund.'

'They were in the joint control of all three trustees, yes. They were sold to Segam at the full price. Twelve pounds a share. They weren't subject to any two-part sale.'

'I see, sir. Very interesting. So you personally had nothing to lose if the second payment didn't go through? And nothing to gain if it did?'

'Nothing whatsoever, Mr Thomas. Not as a trustee nor as an individual.'

But intuitively and also from long experience in questioning people, the inspector was disinclined to accept the last statement. It was the eyes that usually gave people away when they were lying.

Thomas was also concerned to know where the accountant had really been between ten thirty and eleven the night before. Michael Chard was too pedantic to be true – and too worried.

Brenig Jones drew up his Ford Transit outside Albert Shotover's semi-detached bungalow, slid back the door to let in some air, and gave a short blast on the horn before stopping the engine.

The well-built young engineer wiped his brow, and ran a large hand through his flaxen hair. It was getting warm and he didn't intend walking up the little driveway and ringing Shotover's doorbell if he could avoid it. He wasn't lazy, only he sweated a lot – and anti-perspirants didn't always seem to help. He was here as arranged, on time, and ready to drive the older man to Hafod Bay. Then he had a more important appointment, which was why he was wearing the new striped sports shirt and blue linen trousers. His mother had said he looked like one of those beefy American golf professionals, which was exactly how he wanted to look.

After a further minute's wait, resignedly Jones slid out of the van and approached the low wall that separated Shotover's tiny front garden from the pavement. From there he peered closely across into the window of the living room. The curtains had been opened but there was no other sign of life. Shotover had to be up: it was gone ten thirty.

'Good morning, Brenig,' boomed Basso Morgan who had appeared from the other side of the road. He was wielding a walking stick. 'There's shocking news about Mr Evan and that boy. What are we coming to? Is Albert about?'

Jones nodded a greeting and an agreement in one. 'Can't seem to raise him. I'll try the bell. I'm supposed to be taking him down to the boat store at Hafod. I promised after we cancelled the staff meeting. He can't have forgotten.'

'Is that where he keeps that great rubber dinghy? In the old Hafod lifeboat house?'

'That's right. I've got his outboard motor in the van. Been mending it. God knows what he'd done to it. I promised to see him start it. In the water. In case it needs adjusting. He's not all that mechanical.'

'Good of you to fix it for him.'

Brenig Jones had mended the Morgans' electric lawn-mower a month before. He never charged his friends for such services.

'It was the challenge, really.' The younger man smiled as he opened the gate and led the way up the narrow cement path to

178

the partly-glazed doorway at the side of the building. 'To be honest, I'm not much good at petrol engines myself. I've had it going all right on the bench. It was full of sand. And he'd bent the drive shaft. Hello, what's this?'

There was a small brown envelope clamped under the brass door-knocker. It was addressed simply to 'Brenig'.

'He's left already. Must be walking. Wants me to meet him there.' Jones looked up from the note he'd taken from the envelope. Then he grinned. 'I'm to bring the note, and not tell anyone where we are. Think he's joined the Secret Service?'

Basso shook his head. 'Didn't want you leaving the note about. Not so a burglar could know the bungalow was empty. Lot of daytime break-ins round here. Dear me. What next?' he ended despondently.

'Well, Albert's secret is safe with me. And mind you don't tell any criminals we're down at Hafod.' Grinning, Jones stuffed the note into a pocket.

'So I could have saved myself the walk up,' said Basso, casting a critical gardener's eye at a badly pruned rosebush as they went back along the path.

'Jump in, then, I'll drop you at your place.'

'No, no. Don't mind going down. I was out for exercise in any case. Wouldn't have come uphill if I'd known he was out, that's all. Should have phoned before coming. I wanted a word with Albert about . . . about the deaths.'

'Dark horse, Mr George Evan, apparently.'

'And deeply evil with it, perhaps. That's if the report is right. Hard to credit, though.' Basso scowled and tutted twice. 'Will it make any difference to the pension arrangements, d'you think? To the surplus in the fund?'

'Don't see why it should.'

'Mr Evan was supposed to be coming over to our side, of course.'

'Frankly I don't think he mattered any more.'

'Good.' He hesitated. 'You know Albert and I were along there last night. Outside the factory.'

179

'What time was that?'

'Oh, well after we broke up at our house. Must have been quarter past eleven. Or a bit later.'

Jones's curiosity heightened. 'The two of you walked there, did you?' He closed the gate again after them as they emerged on to the pavement.

'Not together we didn't. Bumped into each other at the corner opposite. In Dewin Street.'

The younger man chuckled. 'Albert on the job again, was he? Been in the factory?'

'No. At least he said not.'

'Well, I suppose that's what he would have said, after the way Blodwyn Davies made fun of him, remember? For being a workaholic? He didn't like that, you could see.'

Basso pondered a moment after pulling his pipe from a jacket pocket. 'Awkward though, now. For anyone who did go into the factory. Later last night, I mean. Albert did say earlier he was having trouble with one of the vans. With the starter.'

'Which is actually not his responsibility.'

'I'm a bit out of date on what people do in the firm. You wouldn't be in charge of that, would you?'

'No, I wouldn't,' said Jones almost tartly. He was jealous of his graduate engineering qualifications, and not pleased to be taken for a mechanic or someone who looked after the innards of delivery vans. Pottering with engines as a hobby in his leisure time – or patching them up for friends – that was different. 'We have a transport manager for all that,' he added.

'Ah, he's away. On holiday. I remember Albert saying. And he was definitely bothered about that van.' Basso applied a match to his pipe while squinting at his companion over the top of the flame. 'So you could be right. He might have been in the van park in the yard before he met me. Despite what he said.'

'Behaving suspiciously, was he?' Jones grinned, but still waited expectantly for an answer.

'Looking devious, more like,' the other grinned back. 'But don't tell him I said so.'

180

'I won't.' The young man had already got into the Transit and started the engine.

Basso watched thoughtfully as the vehicle moved away. On the face of it, he thought, Albert Shotover had a far better reason for being in the yard then he'd had himself; Brenig had accepted that like a shot. So, Basso considered, would anyone else.

17

'If my becoming a director keeps the pension fund safe for the pensioners, then OK. Are you sure I'm ready for it otherwise?' asked Marian Roberts uncertainly.

She was looking cool and very becoming in a crisp white cotton shirt and flowered skirt. The sunlight from the window behind her was glinting on her auburn hair as she hurriedly arranged the spring flowers Treasure had brought with him.

'Protecting the pensions will be incidental. You can do a lot more than that. For the company in general. Your modesty does you credit, though,' he commented, glancing over to her approvingly from where he was browsing in front of a bookcase.

The two were in the living room of the upper-floor flat in Pembroke Square. It was arranged with mostly modern pinewood furniture and folkweave covers in pastel colours. There were several pictures – original watercolours by competent local artists. Alongside the overfilled bookcase was a complicated music centre, with a battery of switches and dials, housed in a black metal cabinet.

The banker moved on to examine the serious-looking record collection that went with the equally serious-looking equipment.

'Hm. Too much Wagner and Shostakovich here for my tastes,' he observed. 'Do you and Olive both go in for emotive relief at the tempestuous level?'

'Are we really that limited?' she questioned thoughtfully, while studying the set of the flowers already in the glass vase. 'I suppose we like to be stirred by our music – and other things. For the change it makes in our humdrum lives.'

'I don't believe that. Come to think of it, though, there can't be a world of difference between Olive's teaching biology and your running the chemistry in a sweet factory.'

'We're both governed by tight professional disciplines.'

'Swopped, it seems, after hours for rapture, noisy and unrestrained.' He grimaced at the cover of the Rimsky-Korsakov album in his hand. 'Only a theory.'

'I don't think it quite works that way. Except in special circumstances. Last night was special,' she added carefully.

'And in part quite horrifying, as I remember.'

'I hope you're thinking of the wrong part. I was meaning the bit at the end.' She moved across towards him as she spoke, placing the vase on a low table.

'The tea and biscuits?' he said, turning to face her. 'Better for you than Spanish brandy. No . . . no hangovers. No harm done.'

She came up to him, put her arms around his neck and kissed him lightly on the lips. 'And no hang-ups.' She waited, looking straight into his eyes.

'Why should there be?' He didn't try to stop her as she moved from his arms and out of his reach. 'Incidentally, last night you were quite sure about becoming a director and a trustee.'

'The tea had built up my confidence.'

'Well, since then Segam have ratified the idea. Informal but definite. I left that report of yours with the penitent Lewis Bude. It's very logical. He'll see that when he reads it.' Treasure had already explained about the now effectively abandoned two-part sale of the shares, and Bude's intention to be helpful.

'And you're not prejudiced? You're not being rapturously unrestrained because this whole weekend is sort of after hours for you?' She looked around from where she had gone to close and bolt a window.

'I'm very dispassionate when it comes to management decisions.'

'Paul Ranker and Barbara Evan . . .'

'Will be in a minority on the board from now on. And I have

183

the feeling they won't be here for long anyway.'

'Barbara must be furious about the whole thing.' She screwed up the paper from the flowers, taking it to the kitchen with her.

'Not as much as I expected,' he called after her. 'And I don't understand why, unless . . .'

'But pretty awful about me?' Now she had returned and stayed framed for a moment in the kitchen doorway.

He watched her expression carefully as he replied: 'In unexpected ways. She's not questioning your promotion. But she still has it in for you over your relations with Joshua. She's even convinced he slept here the night before he died.'

'But he was at his mother's flat!' The surprise seemed genuine.

'There's quite well founded, if hearsay, evidence that he possibly wasn't.'

'Well, he wasn't here. I'd have known.' She smirked, going to her bedroom to get something then reappearing. 'Come to think of it, Olive was here all that weekend, so I have a witness. Which rather puts paid to Barbara's little concoction.'

'I wonder where he did sleep?'

'How about at home?' she suggested pointedly, then looked at the time. 'I think we'd better go.' She picked up her handbag, white with a shoulder strap, then motioned him towards the little hallway. 'I'm sorry, we could have lunched together after all, after we've been to Blodwyn Davies.'

'I'm sorry too. But I can't stand up the inspector now. It was my idea. You can join us if you like?'

'Mm, better not, if it's semi-official as you said.'

He didn't press the point. 'So what happened to your date with Brenig Jones?'

'He's wanted at the factory.'

'By the police or the management?'

'He didn't say. Rang in a hurry just before you got here. From a call box. I'm not desolated. I only agreed in the first place because he gets so frighteningly upset if I refuse too often. You know he's proposed to me twice already this year? I think he was building up for a third try today. I've always figured whoever marries Brenig will probably have to spend her honeymoon in that red van. He seems to do everything in it. And that includes making frequent proposals of marriage.'

'Do we drive to the Davies' house? The car's outside?'

'Not worth it. It's just around the corner.' She let him out through the front door, then locked it behind them. 'It really is good of you to make the time for this.'

'I'm here on good works. Might as well wring out the last drop.'

'That's unfair to yourself. And your unsung motives. You could be swimming at the Budes' or . . . or playing golf if you chose, instead of indulging one of my committee members and her stage-struck daughter.'

He paused at the top of the outside staircase. 'I've been swimming already. First thing. And there wouldn't have been time for golf. You and I might manage tea later, of course.' He looked at her in a speculating kind of way. 'So you think my motives deserve wider advertisement?'

'Well, I'm not sure that one does,' she answered in an undertone, while acknowledging the wave of an interested neighbour, and aware she had started to blush, despite herself. She hurried on ahead of him down the steps.

'I offered to send for the doctor, Mr Treasure, but she wouldn't have it. Made me promise I wouldn't fetch him.' Mrs Blodwyn Davies sighed. 'But she's so upset. I didn't know she was that fond of Owen. They hadn't seen each other for ages. She's still only a child, really, after all's said and done.'

'I still think you should go up to her, Mark. If you could bear it,' said Marian. 'Otherwise she'll be bitterly sorry she didn't meet you, just as soon as she's over this shock.'

The three were in the kitchen of the small, rusticated-stone, terraced house in Sheep Street.

The banker had promised Mrs Davies he'd try to fit in a chat with Gwyneth; that had been on the day before. Both mother and daughter had been anxious to take up the chance of advice from the husband of one of Britain's most prominent actresses.

On their arrival Treasure and Marian had learned that Gwyneth was in her room, inconsolable over the death of Owen Watkins – and sure she wouldn't improve her career prospects by seeing anyone in the state she was in.

'She was recovering so well, too. After that experience in April,' added the strained Mrs Davies. She never referred to Gwyneth's near rape in terms more specific than the one she had just used. 'If you could see her, just for a minute, I'd be ever so grateful. The doctor said she could get nasty complexes. Emotional ones. This could be the same, I suppose? She needs taking out of herself, I expect.' She glanced from one visitor to the other. 'Basso Morgan was here just now. He did his best, but he didn't get through to her. Too old. Out of touch. It's a father she needs, not a grandad.'

Treasure shrugged. 'Of course I'll do what I can.' In truth, since his talk with the Reverend Handel Hughes he had reasons of his own for wanting to meet Gwyneth.

A minute later he was on the landing outside her door. He knocked before calling, 'It's Mark Treasure, Gwyneth. Can I come in? I shan't eat you.' There was no response so he knocked again. 'I think we should talk. The show must go on, and all that, you know. Almost the first thing a budding actress needs to learn,' he completed, feeling awkward about the banalities.

'Please go away. I'm not dressed,' the whimpered, unconvincing plea came from the other side of the door, and was followed by the sound of something falling over and some muffled, hurried footfalls.

'Are you all right?'

'Yes,' came slightly stronger.

'Well, make yourself decent, because I'm coming in,' but he waited a moment before doing so.

The girl was sitting up in bed, hair dishevelled, eyes puffed and cheeks tearstained. She was wrestling to do up the bow of a negligee which she had probably just grabbed from some other part of the room and pulled on over her nightdress. At the same time she was trying to straighten the quilt with her feet. The chair in front of the dressing table was overturned. Treasure picked it up and sat on it, facing the girl.

'What a pretty room. You're pretty too. More than they told me, and even under all that fret. Right now you look ready to play Ophelia in deep decline. Do you know your Shakespeare? You'll need to if you're serious about the stage.' He waited before continuing on another track, and after realising that doomed Ophelia had perhaps not been the most appropriate of characters to choose. 'I'm very sorry about Owen Watkins. We all are.'

There was an unpromising silence, then the girl uttered weakly and with obvious effort. 'I've read *Hamlet*. Twice. And seen it. At the theatre in Mold. It was marvellous. I'm very serious about my career. It's nice of you to come here. I'm sorry . . . I'm sorry I'm not . . . Oh . . .' then the words stopped. Sobbing, she buried her face in her hands.

'I'm sorry, it's a rotten day for you. I won't stay if you don't want,' but he made no move before adding: 'In any case, it's my wife you really need to meet. You should drop in on her in London. At the theatre, if you'd like. We can arrange it the next time you're down. She's very good about helping young people. I gather you're already entered for a drama school.'

Slowly the heaving and sobs had begun to ease, and the hands dropped away from the face. There was the hint of some sparkle in the still lowered eyes. 'Two drama schools. All depends . . . on my O levels . . . and . . .' there came a late sob before ' . . . and on the auditions.' She wiped both eyes, then applied the tissue to the end of her nose.

'Don't rub your nose. It'll stay red for ages.'

She flashed him a watery, grateful smile.

'Molly will give you tips on audition technique, and quite a lot else.' He stretched out in the chair with his hands behind his head. 'Look, Gwyneth, I know what you're going through. It's foul losing a friend. Especially unexpectedly. Especially someone one saw recently, all hale and hearty. Doesn't seem real.'

'That's right,' she answered but tentatively, while picking at the front of her negligee.

187

'Won't for some time, either. Owen was here yesterday evening?'

She looked up slowly. 'How did you know?'

'Guessing. By putting two and two together.'

'Mam doesn't know. She'll be mad with me when she does. You won't tell her?'

'Not if it'll upset her. But why should it?'

'There's a reason. I can't tell her that either.'

'Want to try me instead? It won't go any further. Not without your permission. It usually helps to share problems.' He took her silence to indicate a tacit consent. 'It was just the two of you? You and Owen?'

'Up here.' She hesitated, looked at him for a moment, then went on, still in a low voice. 'The police wanted to see him, he said. It was awful. He swore he hadn't done anything. Not anything serious. I said he could stay. Till it was dark. Mam was out. I was too, later. With her.' The tone was more resolute, as though she had made up her mind to something, although the gaze went downwards. She said nothing more for a moment, until she asked, 'D'you reckon God takes it out on people? For being bad?'

'What they call divine retribution? I've never thought so really. Sounds too mean and spiteful, don't you think?' He leaned forward. 'You a believer?'

'Sometimes.' She hesitated. 'I've . . . I've been trying to pray about what's happened.'

'Oh, Saturday's absolutely the right day for that.'

'Praying?' She looked up in surprise.

'Sure. Gets you ahead of the Sunday rush. You know, when all the lines are busy?' He watched for a smile and got one. 'How . . . er, how bad had Owen been?' He had tried to put the question in a casual way.

'Both of us.' There was a catch in her breath. 'We had sex when he was here. It was the first time for me. I think for him as well. It was nice. When we were doing it.'

'It usually is.'

188

'But I never meant to. Not ever. I mean not till I got married. Not till I was older. I'd promised my Mam.'

'I see. And Owen talked you into it?'

'Not really. It was me. I wanted to prove something. Like on the spur of the moment. And now he's dead. And I could have been having his baby. And I didn't even love him like you're supposed to. And my Mam'll go spare.'

Treasure frowned. 'So what's worrying you most? Not being a virgin any more? The chance you could be having a baby? Your mother's anger? Or Owen's death?'

'It's everything.' She was on the brink of tears again.

'Well, physically you can't return to being a virgin, but you can mentally. That's if you want. If you feel it was that important. Why not just go back to your first plan, which I'm sure was sound?'

'How d'you mean?'

'In future, save yourself again for someone special. Someone you really care for, and at least till you're older. Old enough to cope more easily.'

'But it's too late. I told you . . .'

'Because of one experiment? Not at all. Especially as it's made you see the good sense of what you'd intended. Try it. If you put your mind to it, I think you'll find it works.' He watched her reaction, which seemed to be positive. 'Now tell me, did neither of you take any precautions last night?'

'Owen did.' She frowned. 'I did too, except he didn't know.'

What she went on to tell him made it clear that the fear of conception had been a dramatic embellishment to fit her deep despond. It also made him feel even more like a family doctor.

'So I don't think you need worry about having a baby,' he concluded, in what he imagined was a sound bedside tone. 'As for your mother, if you'd like me to tell her about what's happened, and so she understands, which I'm sure she will . . .'

'Would you? I can't lie to her. I love her so much. She's made ever so many sacrifices for me. Since my father left us.'

'I'll do it before I go. And get it out of your head that Owen

189

was struck down by the vengeance of God or anything so unlikely. You'd have dropped that idea by tomorrow in any case. Someone took his life, and we all owe it to him to find out who. Agreed?'

She nodded.

'I think we'll have to tell the police about his being here, but you can leave that to me too, if you like.'

'Will I have to tell them about everything we did?'

'No. Just what time he got here, and what time you think he left. The rest is entirely your business.' He made a mental note to ask Inspector Thomas that she shouldn't be pressed. 'D'you know if Owen went from here to the sweet factory last night?'

'I expect so. He was meeting someone there. At eleven.'

'Did he say who?'

'No. It was the one he'd seen at the sailing club. The night I was attacked. He wouldn't say the name.' She paused. 'It was someone with a rubber dinghy with a motor. Who took Mr Evan's boat from the club that night. Towed it away, Owen said.'

'Mr Joshua Evan's boat?'

'I think so. Whoever it was, was going to help Owen for not getting him involved.'

'Him? It was definitely a man?'

She shook her head hurriedly. 'I'm not sure. I just thought . . . Well, he could have meant a woman, I suppose. He just said someone.'

'What sort of involvement was it? Did he say that?'

'Something to do with the inquest they had on Mr Evan. Except Owen couldn't really tell on . . .' she stopped speaking, biting her lip instead.

'Because Owen had broken into the club himself?'

'I think it was only for a dare.'

'I expect so,' he said, to spare her illusions.

'But I think it's why the police wanted him,' she added quietly.

'Probably. And this person was going to help Owen by giving him money?'

'Lending him enough to leave Llanegwen. To get a summer job. He'd been offered one. In Scotland. He didn't think the police would bother to go after him. He was going straight from the factory. To get a lift.'

'A lift with the same person?'

'He didn't say.'

'Well, did he say anything to suggest he was meeting Mr George Evan?'

She shook her head slowly. 'No, nothing. I've thought about that already.'

'And d'you happen to know anyone with a motorised rubber dinghy?'

'Only my Mam's friend, Mr Shotover. It couldn't have been him, could it? Owen would have said.'

18

Brenig Jones drove the Ford Transit under the narrow bridge and along the short, featureless area behind the beach at Hafod Bay.

Twenty yards on, where the broken-up road gave out altogether, he continued to nurse the van along the hard shingle below the railway embankment. Eventually, he stopped close to the wide stone breakwater – the original lifeboat slipway – at the western end of the beach. The tide was coming in, but wouldn't be high for three hours yet.

The beach was deserted, which was often the way here at the start of the season, at least in the daytime. Trippers liked amenities more than privacy. There was no promenade, no ice-cream kiosk, no café, and no public conveniences at Hafod. They had all those things a mile to the east at Llanegwen, plus carparks and a frequent bus service. They cleaned the beach on a regular basis at Llanegwen too.

Brenig was offended by the uncleared trash and debris above the water-line – disgusted by some of it. The tide and wind brought most of the rubbish, but not the stuff that lovers left to festoon the sheltered places, witness to the after-dark couplings that went on here. As he got out, he carefully avoided stepping on one shrivelled rubber discard, even though it looked to have been abandoned at least a season before.

Despite everything, Brening was still a puritan at heart, and fastidious with it.

There was no sign of Shotover. Grasping the outboard motor, the muscular young man scrambled up the side of the breakwater. He had changed out of his good clothes in the van after telephoning Marian. He was now dressed for work, in old blue jeans and a T-shirt.

He had been disappointed about having to cancel their lunch date, but what had diverted him could have a vitally important bearing on their future – his and Marian's: nothing could take precedence over that – everything he had worked for and waited for, would ultimately be justified by it. That was why he had needed to come.

The remains of the old lifeboat station at the landward end of the breakwater were fairly dilapidated. The soundest elevation was the one facing the sea, the one Brenig was approaching. The present doors were nothing like the size to admit for the launching of a lifeboat – even a mid-nineteenth century lifeboat, which was what the original opening had needed to accommodate.

After the station had been re-sited further along the coast – about a hundred years before this – the building had been used by fishermen until the back half fell down in 1910. It had then been occupied successively by tramps (moved off by the authorities), as a shallow beach shelter (with a new rear wall constructed only twelve feet from the then doorless front), and more recently as a lock-up store for municipal deck chairs (which was when the surviving double doors had been installed).

The deck chairs eventually proved as unfashionable as Hafod Bay itself had always been. The local council next sought a concessionaire ready to convert the structure into a beach shop of some kind – indeed, any kind. It was seeking still, but meantime had offered an annual lease at a nominal rent to any off-shore angler ready to keep the place secure and the doors painted a regulation olive-green. Albert Shotover had been the first to apply two seasons back, and had been the bargain lessee ever since.

Shotover would have preferred to keep his equipment in the sailing club at Llanegwen, except a still observed rule there banned powered craft of any description from the premises.

193

As Brenig Jones stepped nearer he noticed that even though the doors were pulled to, the padlock had been removed – a sign that Shotover was present. Brenig could have got in with the key he had been loaned, but he didn't fancy humping the boat and the motor down to the sea by himself. As he came up to the doors, the left-hand one was opened towards him a fraction, and a head was thrust out. He had to assume it was Shotover's head, since it was covered in a wide-brimmed soft felt hat, while the eyes below were disguised behind large and very dark glasses. There was something else different from what Brenig expected too, but he didn't place that straight away.

''Morning, Albert,' he greeted affably.

'Come in quickly,' Shotover ordered in reply, holding the door open a fraction more, and allowing the other man to squeeze through with what seemed an unnecessary degree of inconvenience considering he was humping an outboard motor. Shotover then pulled the door closed tight behind them, thereby considerably reducing inside visibility. The only light was coming from a narrow dusty window high up on the rear wall.

The inflated dinghy took up most of the available space. It was a substantial, sturdy craft, bought by Shotover in a sale of army-surplus equipment. He never deflated it because he had no adequate mechanical means here for blowing it up again. The only other objects the newcomer dimly took in were a canvas grip on the broken concrete floor and Shotover's jacket, folded on the dinghy's stern seat.

'Thanks for coming,' Shotover supplied, a bit late. 'Sorry I messed up the arrangements.' Nervously he stood on one foot, then the other, his face wrinkled with the effort of peering through the glasses.

'That's all right, Albert.'

'You saw the note? You didn't tell anyone we'd be here?' Shotover's shoulders were lifting, out of control.

'No,' Brenig lied, not wanting to seem unreliable. Basso Morgan hardly counted, and anyway the old man had promised not to tell anyone else. 'How did you get here? On your bike was it, or did you walk?' He set down the motor, his eyes now acclimatised to the poor light.

'Walked. I didn't meet anyone. I don't think,' It sounded as if the last doubt mattered. Shotover was still shifting on his feet, then, as if on a compelling impulse, clumsily he climbed into the boat and sat in the stern, where he looked oddly marooned. 'Want to sit down?' he asked, massaging his hands together.

'No, thanks. Why are you wearing those glasses? And the funny hat?'

Instead of answering directly, Shotover took off both objects. He blinked, fumbled in the jacket pocket for his steel-rimmed glasses, opened them carefully and just as carefully put them on. 'Outboard all right, is it?' he enquired, but sounding as if his thoughts were on something else.

'Right as rain on the bench the night before last. Want to get everything down to the water?'

'No!' the other stabbed back like a warning. 'I . . . I mean, not yet,' he stammered. 'Tide's too far out.'

'We can manage. Take the dinghy between us. I can cope with the outboard. Got much other gear have you? Rods and stuff?' On realising at last what else was different, he'd been about to put another question but decided against it. He would leave it to the anxious Shotover to explain in his own time why he had shaved off his moustache.

'I'm not fishing today, Brenig.'

'Just going for a cruise, like, are you? Nice day for it. Is Blodwyn coming down?'

Shotover shuddered. 'You can leave me to it now. I can manage.'

'No, no. I'd like to see that motor working in the water. Anyway, you don't want to be carting all the gear by yourself.'

'Tell you the truth, I don't know what I want. Except I don't want to be seen on the beach.' Now he made a noise that was somewhere between a sigh and a groan. 'I don't want to be caught.'

'What you mean, caught? Somebody after you?' He kept the tone light, but he'd known something was wrong from the beginning.

'The police, I expect. By now.' He made the same noise as

195

before. 'I'm in dead trouble, Brenig. You won't turn me in, will you? Not yet, anyway? I need help. Can I trust you? Oh dear.'

'*You* in trouble? Don't be daft. What you been up to? Parking your bike on a double yellow line?'

'It's serious.' The little Mancunian's head had now sunk tortoiselike between his shoulders. 'I did something terrible last night. Terrible.'

'At the factory?'

'In St Asaph.' He stopped, a thumb pressing a hinge of his spectacles into the side of his face. The upper fingers of the same hand spread across the forehead, the palm shielding his eyes from the other's view. 'I . . . I went after a girl. A young girl. By the cathedral.'

'Well, that's not so . . .' It was Brenig's turn to pause. 'You don't mean the girl somebody attacked? You didn't . . . ?'

Shotover nodded the reply. 'They'll say I tried to rape her.'

'I heard about the . . . the incident. In our paper shop this morning. Baby-sitter for Michael Chard, she was. They say she's all right. And that was you?'

'Don't know what came over me. Yes, I do.' Now both hands were on his bowed head, kneading the scalp. 'You see, it wasn't the first time,' he murmured. 'Last month . . .'

'Oh my God, Gwyneth Davies? That was you as well?' said Brenig in astonishment.

The other gave a breathy moan. 'Gwyneth's been my trouble all along. Driving me mad. I can't sleep for wanting her. Haven't for months.'

'But you and her mother ..?'

'I know,' the other agonised back. 'Blodwyn thinks we're getting married. Well, I couldn't go through with that. Not the way things are. Decided weeks ago. Not with wanting Gwyneth the way I do. Then I thought I was cured. After the scare.'

Brenig frowned. 'After the night you attacked her, you mean?' He could still scarcely credit what he was hearing.

'That's right. But ever since she's been back I have to fight to keep my hands off her. It started again in your van. On the way back from London. And because I can't have her, lately I've

196

needed to go after others. You can't understand. Nobody can. It's like a disease, Brenig.'

'So it was because of Gwyneth you went for this girl last night?' The tone was more enquiring than shocked.

'Not that one specially. Just a young girl. Oh, what am I saying? I didn't know where to put myself at Basso's last night, just looking at Gwyneth. I knew when the Chards would be likely to get home. From the dinner Marian said they'd be at. I knew where they lived. I knew they'd have to have a baby-sitter. I went there and waited. On the off-chance. She came out. I'm so ashamed.'

'So you planned that one?'

'Half-planned. I couldn't know if she'd be walking home by herself. And I tried to put off going. Because I was desperate, I asked Blodwyn earlier to come to my place. Better than nothing, I thought. That's when we were leaving Basso's. But she couldn't. She asked me back to Sheep Street instead. Imagine? In the state I was in?' Slowly he shook his head. Then he looked up. 'You'll tell me I should give myself up?'

'You say the police were onto you already?'

'They will be. I used the small van last night. Took it from the yard. It was mad. Anyone could have seen me. You could have seen me. Basso did. I ran into him after. But I had to get out of Llanegwen. To find what I wanted.'

'You were saying . . . about the van. It was parked at the back with the others?'

'Yes. When I took it back I was in a hurry. I forgot I left things in it. I went back for them after I'd walked home with Basso, but I couldn't get in the yard. The police were there already. I didn't know what to do then, but I went again this morning. I got in. I'd made up a story to see the police, but they wouldn't let me near the van. Then they took the ignition keys of all the vans. To search. I made them suspicious, I know that.' The confession seemed to have cleansed him in some way: the narrative had become more jointed.

'What are they going to find in the small van?'

Shotover looked pained. 'A woman's stocking, with holes in.

I used it as a mask. And . . . and a carpet knife. I left them under the seat. I wouldn't have hurt her, honestly. Not either of them. Not intentionally. Just threatened. Last night I let the poor girl go.'

'Let her go?'

'There was a reason. She's . . . oh, it doesn't matter. The police'll know what the knife was used for. And the stocking. They'll know they were mine. There'll be fingerprints I should think, but I tried to be careful.'

Brenig walked to the door, pulled it open a fraction and looked out. Then he came back and sat himself on the bow edge of the dinghy.

'They'll put you in prison if they catch you. You realise that?'

'It's what I can't face. I couldn't stand to be locked up. With criminals. And the disgrace. I think I'd rather die. Do myself in. I should have gone away. Months ago. After I attacked Gwyneth. Now it's too late.'

'Don't despair, boyo. Perhaps we can work something out,' offered Brenig with a forced cheerfulness, and wrestling with an inward dilemma. 'What's in the bag?'

'Clothes. After I saw the police, at the factory, I went home. Didn't know what to do. Then I thought I should run for it, so I put some things in there. And shaved off my moustache. Then I came down here. I wanted to see you, but I couldn't wait where they'd come for me first.' He hesitated, studying the other's expression. 'I suppose there's no point in running really, is there? They're bound to catch me. I've got my passport, and three hundred pounds in cash, though,' he ended, his face, like his words, advertising his indecision.

'I don't think you should give yourself up,' said Brenig suddenly and firmly. 'What if they don't suspect you after all? Better to see if they come after you.'

'But where shall I go?'

'Were you thinking of Ireland? The South?'

'Yes. About taking the ferry from Anglesey. From Holyhead to Dun Laoghaire. Could they extradite me from Eire?'

'Probably. But it'd give you a head start until we find out if they're looking for you. I could drive you to Holyhead in the van.'

'I don't want to get you involved.'

Brenig frowned. 'Come to think of it, if they're after you already they might stop my van. People knowing we're friends.'

'I could get to Holyhead in the dinghy.'

'That's forty miles by sea. The outboard only gives you six knots.'

'I don't mind. The sea's quite calm, and I'd be mostly moving with the current.'

'What about fuel?'

'There's plenty here. Two cans I can take.'

'You'd have to abandon the dinghy and the outboard when you got there. Risky. And costly. I could pick them up later, of course.' He thought fast for a moment. 'Tell you what. I'll come with you. You can lie in the bottom of the boat while we're in sight of land. If anyone wants to know later, I can say I was out testing the motor. I'll land you on this side of Anglesey, near Beaumaris or Amlych. You could get a bus then to Holyhead.'

'That'd be hours quicker,' agreed Shotover. Holyhead is at the far western extremity of the island.

'And safer.' Brenig stood up, countering the uncertainty in Shotover's voice. 'Come on, that's what we'll do. No one's going to see us put off from here.'

'You don't have to do this, Brenig,' said Shotover, but with the hope evident in his voice.

'Yes, I do. You're in trouble. I'm a friend. But if you stay free I want you to promise me you'll get treatment after. Proper therapy.'

'I will. I promise. I'll leave Llanegwen, too.' Earlier he'd half-decided to confess everything to Brenig – and to do as he advised. Now he was glad he had.

Fatalistically, Shotover had expected to be told to surrender to the police. He'd overestimated the rigidity of Brenig Jones moral attitudes. A lot of people did that.

19

'The village is called Pontnewydd. It means new bridge, but that one's been here since the early seventeenth century,' said Detective Inspector Thomas.

'Someone told me it may have been designed by Inigo Jones,' Treasure commented, admiring the graceful, stone structure that single-spanned the narrow river Elwy twenty yards downstream.

'Oh, yes,' the inspector replied, who, as a matter of patriotic principle, never dismissed local claims likely to promote tourism in his native Wales. As a responsible policeman he was also careful not to confirm fanciful conjectures either. 'It's a very well-proportioned bridge,' he offered guardedly. 'Used for sheep dipping in the old days,' which was an undeniable fact, witnessed by the dipping pit, part of the bridge structure and visible from where they were sitting.

The two had arrived almost simultaneously a few minutes earlier, in separate cars, turning off the main road, and over the bridge to the village. Now they were at a rustic table in the shady, riverside garden of the Black Swan Inn, about to wash down fresh bread, butter, cheese and pickles with pints of local ale, all collected at the bar.

Unspoilt Pontnewydd, five miles inland from Llanegwen, climbs up abruptly from the river course on to the mountain foothills. The village street comes off the bridge, passes the old thatched inn, and ascends through several twists, before starting an even steeper rise into the serious hill country beyond the little community.

The cottages, mostly slate-roofed, their walls rendered in

contrasting colours, are clustered in uneven, precipitous steps, and watched over by the long, low St Winifred's church on the highest levelled crest. You could say the setting is Italianate, but not to any of the inhabitants since Pontnewydd is quite as old as Monte Casino, if not so famous.

Altogether this is a tranquil place with the water rippling by, and sparkling, as it was now, in the midday sun.

'It's good to get away for half an hour,' Thomas said with feeling. 'Madhouse down there. *Iechyd da!*' He lifted the pewter tankard in salute, then took a long draught from it.

'Cheers! And thanks for suggesting Pontnewydd,' Treasure responded. 'Did you have a profitable morning?'

'Fished out a few worthwhile specimens, including Mr Ranker from that swimming pool. Oh, and there's been an interesting development on the rapist. Doesn't help me much. Not with the two deaths. Still.' He took another long swallow. 'So, what about you?'

As a result of a private conversation with the inspector, in the Budes' garden after the Ranker incident, Treasure had offered to report on further developments with his own interests that might have a bearing on the police investigation. It was then that he had invited the other man to a pub lunch.

'I got an instant assurance from Barbara Evan about the shares,' the banker offered. 'She's no intention of holding out for the second payment, even though she now controls a huge holding. That virtually clears things up from my point of view. There's only Ranker left gunning for the pension fund, and by himself he's too small to matter. With your permission I could now go back to London with an easy mind. At least over the business issues.'

'You don't need any permission, sir. Except I don't think you're ready to leave yet. Too interested in what's going on, I'd say.'

'You may be right.' Treasure smiled. 'Being super inquisitive can be a scourge, of course. Anyway, I'll stay around for a little while yet.'

'Good. That's quite a climb-down by Mrs Evan, isn't it?' the inspector commented reflectively. And, not being nearly finished with the previous subject, 'Leaving Mr Ranker to fend alone, despite his claim she was supporting him?'

Treasure spread a generous lump of butter on a quite small piece of bread. 'That was last night. She's changed her tune dramatically since then. Now *she* is using *him* for support. In a different cause.'

'Something to do with the death of Mr George Evan?'

'I'd guess all to do with a recent change in her priorities, Inspector. She was pretty anxious to establish with me that Ranker was with her at her place from ten thirty till after eleven last night. Of course, that's a fairly important time segment.'

'Critical, you might say, yes. Though I don't know exactly how Mrs Evan came to that conclusion.'

'Perhaps by simple deduction. Wouldn't be difficult.'

'I suppose not. Well, Mr Ranker corroborates what she's said to you.' The policeman looked about to ensure there was still no one placed within earshot. 'Very keen his wife shouldn't know, though. And it hasn't altered his attitude about the shares, not from what he told you and Mr Bude this morning. So why the change in the lady's priorities?'

'She's a potential beneficiary though George Evan's will. I'd say it was more important to her than anything else not to be seen as remotely involved in his death.'

'More important than eight pounds a share?'

'More important than getting caught up in your murder enquiry.'

The inspector looked sceptically at the bit of bread and cheese he was keeping poised in mid-air. 'I see,' he said. 'Or rather I'll take your word for it. For the time being.' He popped the edibles into his mouth like a conjuror completing a disappearing trick. 'Tell me, would you put your money on Albert Shotover as a rapist?'

'No, but I could believe a psychoanalyst might. Is that who you think it was? Of course I hardly know him. Doesn't a rapist need to be fairly strong?'

'Depends. But it could be why this one's failed twice. How about Mr Shotover as the killer of Owen Watkins and Mr George Evan?'

Treasure considered for a moment. 'Considerably less likely.'

'That's what I think. Anyway, he's got a few things to explain. Being brought in for questioning. Except we can't find him. He was at the factory last night. Around ten thirty. Took out a van, he said. We've since found a stocking mask and a carpet knife in it, possibly the ones used by the attempted rapist.'

'But surely if he was the rapist he wouldn't have left the evidence behind?'

'Sex maniacs do daft things. Some even have a subconscious wish to be caught. Anyway, we'll know when we pick him up. If he is the attempted rapist it doesn't exclude him from being involved in the other business. Less likely, though. Except he was there, at the right time. And he had keys to all the factory doors. You could say he had a motive, too.'

'To do in George Evan? Like every pensionable worker in the company.' Treasure thought for a second. 'The members of Marian Roberts's committee are keen, but I don't believe any of them would kill for the cause. In any case, George Evan had changed sides over who got the pension surplus.'

'But hardly anybody knew that.'

'Hm. I suppose Paul Ranker had keys too?'

'He also has Mrs Evan for an alibi, remember? Works both ways that one, of course. As things stand they cover each other. Mr Michael Chard probably wishes he'd been with them.'

The banker looked up from his plate. 'He had keys?'

'On loan, and he was by himself from ten thirty. In his office at Pentre Beach. Except no one saw him there. You've never come across him professionally, I suppose, Mr Treasure? Except in connection with G. L. Evan Limited?'

'No. Why d'you ask?'

'Offices look a bit down at heel. So does Mr Chard, for that matter,' the policeman observed while spearing another piece

203

of cheese. 'That is, for an accountant with important clients.'

'I don't believe he has many of those. G. L. Evan and Lewis Bude may well be the only ones of any size.'

'He's doing extra work for Mr Bude at the moment.'

'I know about that. It's a one-off job. He got it because he's handy, and speed is the essence.'

'He was involved in your pension business?'

'Very much so. As a trustee.' Treasure paused, frowning. 'And since this is a highly privileged conversation, I'll tell you I consider he's been a totally inadequate trustee.'

'And irresponsible, would you say?' The inspector asked with an insouciance he would only normally have applied to less slanderous propositions.

'Certainly that. He and Ranker could have rigged the G. L. Evan set-up between them. I mean the sale of the company to Segam, and the intended hijacking of the pension-fund surplus.'

'But Mr Chard wouldn't have gained anything himself if that had gone through. He's not a shareholder.' Thomas was watching the ale as he swirled it in the bottom of his tankard.

'Unless his complicity as a trustee was bought in advance, or was to be paid for on results.'

'And in the second case he'd have good reason for doing away with Mr George Evan?'

Treasure hesitated before answering. 'Also for doing away with Joshua Evan, if you think about it. But that applies to Ranker as well.'

The policeman looked up. 'That's an interesting observation. You could have included Mr Bude in it, too, of course. During the time that interests us last night, he was alone, walking his dogs,' he added slowly. 'His owning Segam makes quite a difference, of course.'

'I wouldn't have thought that much.'

'Perhaps not,' the other replied, but the comment was singularly lacking in conviction.

'If you suspect him of anything you'd better stop him flying to Liverpool after lunch today.' Smiling, Treasure pushed back his chair. 'Ready for a refill?'

204

'Just a half-pint for me, sir. Thank you.'

When the banker returned from the bar with the contents of both tankards half-replenished he asked: 'So you're working on the likelihood that Owen Watkins and George Evan were both murdered?'

'Because the evidence so far suggests it. Mr Evan was boiled alive. Either he jumped into that vat, fell in by accident, or he was pushed. I think he was pushed. He died at ten fifty-eight.'

'That's pretty exact timing.'

'His watch stopped then. It was the only thing he had on. Old but expensive lever-action watch. Must have clouted the side of the vessel as he went. The glass was spoiled, and boiling sugar did the rest. It stopped at ten fifty-eight and fourteen seconds. That wouldn't be enough on its own, but the time squares with the state of the undigested food in his stomach.' Beaming at the still substantial contents of his plate, the inspector piled mustard pickle on top of a cheese lump before enlarging. 'We got the time he finished his supper. Passed it on to forensic. So their fast report this morning included a time of death. They say, within two minutes either side of ten fifty seven. That method's pretty reliable. Even when the body's boiled like a lobster's. So I'll settle for the time shown on the watch.'

'Doesn't prove he was murdered, of course. Or that it wasn't him who killed the boy.'

The policeman beamed. 'Except there's more to come. The air-conditioning system in the factory was switched off at eleven three. It's operated from a complicated control panel in the production manager's office, and it has a print-out record attached to it. Someone switched it off, but no one's come forward to say so.'

'I understand the production manager . . .'

'Spent a blameless evening watching TV, uninterrupted, in the bosom of his very large family.'

'So your theory is that the boy switched off the system, and so must have survived George Evan?'

'We've another reason to think he survived Mr Evan, and to have switched off the system he'd have needed to know where

205

the panel was and how to work it.'

'Was the production manager's office locked?'

'No. But the boy didn't have any reason to switch off the system. It's much more likely somebody else did it. Somebody out to fool us. Seems Mr Evan was bonkers on saving energy. Never left a light switch on unnecessarily, let alone a whole air-conditioning system which he regarded as a massive waste of money, anyway. Everybody we've interviewed seems to know that.'

'So whoever did the switching off figured you'd accept Evan did it out of habit? Why? Was it just an embellishing touch?'

'We think so. That Mr Evan was supposed to have done it after he'd finished off the boy in the rock room, and as he passed the production manager's office on the way to the vat. Except we know he died before eleven three. It's not much to go on but it's fact.'

'And if the boy didn't do the switching off, there had to be someone else who did. So why hasn't he come forward?' The banker shook his head. 'And were you expected to believe Evan switched off the power to that vat before diving into it – also because he was a compulsive conservationist?'

'That's more likely than the other part, actually. It's not to do with saving energy. More because he might have been going for the . . . er . . . the dramatic ending you came upon. With the coagulation setting in.' The policeman winced slightly. 'I'm not buying it, even so.'

'But if all this is part of the murderer's scene-setting, it suggests we're looking for a failed improvisator.'

Thomas leaned forward. 'One who threw in any embellishment as he went along. Either because the whole crime was spontaneous . . .'

'Which in the circumstances seems unlikely.'

'I agree there. But it was either that or a new plan was being adapted to fit a previous one, with too little time to think it through.'

'The previous plan involving one murder not two.'

'Why d'you say that, sir?'

206

'Because it's the obvious starting hypothesis. Because murders usually come singly, and because of something I'll tell you about in just a second. Let's say one murder was intended. Two were committed because the second victim turned up as a convenient scapegoat. That was the big improvisation.'

'So who was the murderer's real victim?'

Treasure put down his tankard. 'My bet is the boy, who the double murderer wants us to believe was Evan's victim too, who Evan kills then commits suicide out of remorse. That's aimed to make us ignore any motive the double murderer had for killing the boy himself. But it's a scenario that only works if Watkins died first, of course.'

'Well, he didn't,' the policeman put in promptly. 'We know that from footprints. Bare footprints. Not as good as fingerprints, but good enough.'

'Weren't there fingerprints on the rails?'

'The rails had been wiped clean of prints. Except for a few of yours, Mr Treasure.'

'I see. But footprints weren't considered? More signs of careless improvisation. You've found prints of both men's feet?'

'Mr Evan's from the showers to the vat. No return journey. And we've got the boy's from the showers to a spot on the gantry, but short of the vat. In some places they're superimposed over Mr Evan's prints.'

'Showing Watkins was moving behind him, so could have pushed Evan to his death?'

'The footprints stop slightly too far away from the vat to make that certain.'

'Because the prints could have been obliterated on purpose, or just by chance? By me, for instance?'

'Or by policemen.' The inspector frowned. 'And then we've got Watkins's prints back from the gantry to the rock room. What can't follow is that after he'd been in the factory he then went back, hit himself over the head with a blunt instrument, and battened himself down in that press.'

'You don't have a time of death for the boy?'

'Not exact. Not yet. It'd help if we knew when he last ate. Where he was earlier in the evening. On the basis of just the body temperature when we found him, he could have died any time between ten forty-five and eleven fifteen.'

'But the important point the footprints establishes surely is that it's pretty unlikely Evan could have killed Watkins. And even if Watkins killed Evan, there has to have been someone else there who did for the boy.' Treasure pouted into his tankard. 'And two killers make too much of a coincidence. Oh, and what I meant to tell you just now is I know where Watkins was most of the evening. You know I called to see his parents this morning? It was a painful interview and mercifully a short one. I must say, nothing I've heard about that lad suggests a violent disposition, and certainly not homicidal tendencies. You knew him, of course.'

'And I agree. Crafty young monkey. Boaster about experiences with women which he'd never had. And not above a bit of petty larceny, but I don't believe he went further than that.'

'Except I'm afraid he may recently have been trying his hand at blackmail. You were right, he did break into the sailing club that night. Just after he left Gwyneth Davies. And he did see something there. Actually *someone* who came from offshore in a powered rubber dinghy and took off Joshua's boat and sails. Watkins had arranged to meet whoever that was last night at eleven. In the factory yard. The person was to give him money.' The banker sniffed. 'We don't seem to be able to get away from Joshua Evan's death, do we?'

'Watkins's parents told you this? But they were questioned . . .'

'No, Gwyneth Davies, who I saw later. I'd hoped not to bring her into it, but I don't think it can be avoided. He was at her house from six to about ten last night. She was only there till sevenish. We can ask her if she fed him before she left. Incidentally, the curate had already told me he'd seen Watkins going in that direction earlier.'

'The Reverend Hughes?'

'Mm. Who volunteered he doesn't believe Joshua slept at his

208

mother's flat the night before he died.' Treasure recounted what the cleric had said in detail, together with Barbara Evan's contention that her husband had been with Marian Roberts, and Marian's countercharge that he had probably slept at home.

'Difficult to understand why Mrs Evan has been so anxious to prove her husband wasn't home that night if he was,' the inspector ruminated.

'Unless it involved her as any kind of witness. Or even as an accomplice to something.'

'Like what?'

'I think the clue to that could lie with knowing why his boat was taken that night.'

'You any idea?'

'Yes. To save someone time next morning. I've checked. Sunrise that day was at six nine. I gather Joshua is supposed to have died between six five and six twenty?'

'It was approximate because, again, no one knew what time he'd last eaten. For the stomach test, you see? They had to assume he'd had breakfast between five thirty and five forty five.'

'You told me someone living in Sea Road actually saw his car pass on the way to the sailing club just before six o'clock?'

'Saw the car through a bedroom window.'

'The car, not the driver?'

'That's right. Too dark still.'

'But if he started to get his boat out and ready no earlier than, say, six, he must have got a lot done to be knocked overboard senseless and drowned at sea possibly five minutes later.'

'Especially if his boat wasn't there. That's assuming whoever took it never brought it back. Of course, they didn't know any of that at the inquest,' said Thomas. 'That he might not have gone there.'

'But they knew his car was there. Or was it taken down by someone else? If so, why didn't that someone come forward to say so?'

'But anyone who brought his car down surreptitiously had to

209

risk being seen leaving without it. Walking away just as it was getting light. But no other cars were reported. And there were no other boats missing from the club-house.'

'He or she could have been taken off by the same powered boat that came the night before.' As he spoke, Treasure had been watching a tufted duck emerge from the river and waddle away along the bank parallel with the water. 'Or else,' he continued, 'whoever it was might have walked along the beach below the shingle bank to Hafod Bay. That must be pretty deserted just before dawn in April.'

'Totally. Whoever it was might still have used transport in the end. But driving or being driven up from Hafod would be a pretty inconspicuous exercise by comparison with Llanegwen.'

'So the way we're talking now, Joshua's death was very likely murder not accident,' Treasure pressed. 'Murder possibly involving two other people. And what about murder starting with a knock-out blow to the head made shortly after he had breakfast? At the place where he really spent the night?'

'Except the blow was definitely made by the wooden boom of his own boat. They found hair and scalp tissue on it to prove that, and boom splinters in his scalp.'

'Faked later? Or else the boom was taken to the same place. You'd need the right kind of transport . . .'

'And to move it afterwards with the unconscious body to the coast,' the inspector was concentrating hard as he spoke. 'To a spot where the body could be taken to sea with the dinghy. By a powered boat . . .'

'And body and dinghy separately abandoned while it was still dark. It could all be made to fit.'

The silence that marked Treasure's last speculation was broken by a female voice calling from the bar. 'Telephone for Mr Alwyn Thomas.'

It was some time before the inspector returned to the table. 'We've interviewed Mr Basso Morgan,' he announced. 'He's told us Mr Shotover took himself off to Hafod Bay this morning on the quiet. There was a note to say so apparently, but Mr Morgan wasn't supposed to have let on. Might be Mr Shotover guessed we'd find those things in the van . . .'

'The van,' Treasure interrupted. 'I've just realised something. If . . .' But he abandoned whatever he was about to say when his voice was drowned by engine clatter. A helicopter had suddenly appeared flying low overhead.

'Noisy contraptions!' the policeman shouted eventually, still looking upwards at the receding plane. 'On the shortest route to Plas Gwyn, of course. Well, just to finish what I was saying, Brenig Jones went down to meet Shotover at the beach. His van's still there, but he and Shotover aren't. They may have gone out in Mr Shotover's dinghy. Mr Jones had an outboard motor with him. I'm asking the coast-watch to look for them.'

Treasure was coming to his feet on the last words. 'I don't believe that'll be enough, Inspector. Look, I think I can prove Joshua Evan was killed, as well as who murdered the boy – and why.' He grasped the surprised Thomas by the arm and began propelling him towards the carpark as he finished his revelation.

'But that would mean George Evan's death was just incidental?' the policeman questioned incredulously as they reached the cars.

'Yes, poor chap. And if I'm right, we've got to move fast to prevent another incidental murder. Bude has to be stopped from taking that helicopter.'

20

'If you stay as you are, no one's going to see you,' said Brenig Jones to Shotover's outline under the tarpaulin in the dinghy's bow. He dropped the paddle he had been wielding. Since there was now a good two feet of water under them, he lowered the outboard motor over the stern. The engine fired with the first tug he gave on the pulley.

Ten minutes later they were nearly a mile offshore. Brenig glanced back while holding the northerly course, directly away from the land. There was still no sign of any movement on the beach they had left, nor of any boats off Llanegwen to the east. To the west, in the distance, there were sails beyond the Great Ormes Head at Llandudno, but nothing closer. Ahead the sea was quite empty.

'Can I sit up yet, Brenig? I'm getting cramp.' The top half of Shotover's face was exposed above the edge of the hard sheet which he was grasping with both hands close together, his nose protruding between the two sets of white knuckles.

'Better not move. Pity to spoil things,' the younger man cautioned. 'At this rate we'll be off Beaumaris in two hours.'

If Shotover had been allowed to sit up he might have queried why the boat was still heading for the open Irish Sea and not towards Anglesey, visible to port. But Brenig had his reasons for what he was doing.

'Are you sure you didn't go into either of the factory buildings last night, Albert?' he questioned over the noise of the outboard.

'Certain. The police asked me that. I said I didn't have my keys. There was nothing I really wanted in the factory.' He wished there had been – anything to have deflected him from giving in to his obsession.

'Did they ask if you saw anyone in the yard?'

'Yes. I didn't, though I told you, only Basso outside, when I was leaving, at the end.'

'You didn't mention who else *might* have been there?'

'How d'you mean? Oh dear,' was added despairingly. 'Do we have to go so fast? And you know in the rush we forgot the life-jackets?' Out here there was a cross-wind disturbing the sea's surface. Every time the boat bucketed, the flat bottom slapped violently against Shotover's spine. He was definitely beginning to feel queasy.

Brenig chuckled. 'Cheer up, Albert. Don't you realise you now own a superb, hand-tuned engine? Reckon we're getting nearly seven knots. Don't worry, you're quite safe. It'll soon be over.' He nodded encouragement to his non-swimming companion. Yes, it would definitely soon be over. 'And what I meant was, did the police ask you to name the owners of the vehicles in the yard?'

'There weren't any besides the company vans. Oh, there was yours of course, like you said. But I always think of that as company.'

'And you're sure you didn't mention it was there?'

'Certain. I should have, I suppose. Anyway, they'd have seen it there this morning. Do you often park it there overnight and go home by bus?'

'Sometimes, if I'm getting a lift in next day,' he lied.

'I'm surprised they let you take it away today. They wouldn't let me near any of the company vans.' Shotover took a deep breath, then let it out again. 'Oh dear, I do feel rotten. I think I'm going to be sick.'

But Brenig didn't reduce speed or alter course. Later, when they were out of detail sight from land, he looked around to check there were no other craft close enough to see what was happening in this one. Then he called: 'Why not try to throw up, Albert? Might help. Over the starboard side.' The wind was to port.

The other man emerged painfully from under the tarpaulin and looking very grim. He shifted to the side of the dinghy as instructed and leaned out.

'Keep well down now. Head right over,' Brenig ordered, while steeling himself to his next move. He knew that if the police ever caught up with Shotover again, then under close questioning there was no doubt he'd let out that he'd seen the Transit in the yard last night. The van was the only weak link. Brenig dropped forward off the seat and onto one knee, still with his hand on the tiller. This put him right behind the now retching Shotover.

The police hadn't seen the red Ford Transit in the factory yard, even when they had first arrived, after the killings. They hadn't seen it because Brenig Jones had driven it away some time before that, at eleven nine p.m., precisely.

'Can we try a sweep to the north now?' Treasure called into his microphone, still leaning well forward to the front passenger seat, as he searched through the massive arc of the windscreen.

'At a higher altitude? We're not seeing much down here. Practically water-skiing,' Timothy Wells answered lightly. They were nearing the Llanegwen shore again.

'Just one more try at this height. Surprise could be essential.'

'You're the boss.' Timothy banked the Jet Ranger around in a tight circle and set off again seawards.

The banker and Detective Inspector Thomas had parted at the Black Swan. Thomas had gone to direct the official end of the search. Treasure had driven the two miles to Plas Gwyn where he had been in time to stop Lewis Bude leaving for Liverpool, and to borrow his helicopter and pilot. He knew he would be in the search that way faster than anything the inspector could arrange on sea or in the air – and he was working on the ominous conviction that minutes counted.

The machine was almost skimming the wavelets as it streaked

214

over the water at 120 miles an hour. The first sweep had been made on a north-westerly course and had produced nothing. Then they had spotted a mastless dinghy further west of them, but on close inspection it had revealed two elderly fishermen not in the least grateful for the fish-frightening attention they were getting from the Jet Ranger.

'That it?' called Timothy suddenly, pointing.

'Could be, but it's going the wrong way.'

The dinghy with the outboard spiral at the stern was a mile off, slightly to port, and closing fast because it was heading south, directly for Hafod Bay.

As the boat passed nearly under them, Treasure caught a clear sight of the single person aboard. It was unmistakably the burly Brenig Jones – and the thought went through the banker's mind that the man could have gone out alone after all.

'Want to go around?' Timothy asked, throttling back.

Treasure had nearly answered in the affirmative when what was little more than a speck bobbing in the water caught his eye. It was some way directly ahead of them and beyond the dying wake of the dinghy. 'What's that?' he called, pointing.

'Could be man overboard.' The pilot increased speed dramatically so that they were quickly over the subject.

'It is a man. If it's the one I think, he can't swim. Can you circle him?'

'I can hover over him,' answered Timothy doing just that. 'Keep your belt done up, and open your door. Is he still kicking?'

'Don't think so. And he's gone under the water now. Can you lower me down to him?'

'No winch, I'm afraid. We can drop him a lifebelt and inflatable dinghy.'

'No use in the state he's in. I'll go with them.'

Treasure was already kicking off his shoes. As he positioned himself to drop out of the craft, suddenly the head appeared again above the water. It was Shotover. There was a glassy appeal in the eyes, and a hand lifted feebly.

* * *

215

'As I hit the water, I suddenly wondered why I was risking all to rescue a fugitive rapist,' Treasure said, over his third cup of breakfast coffee.

'You don't mean that,' answered his wife who was paring French beans on the other side of the table. 'You could hardly have done anthing else. But I'm sure it was very brave.'

'No, it wasn't. Not much of a drop.' He reflected for a moment, then added: 'The water was cold, though.'

It was Sunday morning. Treasure had got back to Cheyne Walk from North Wales late the night before. The two had breakfasted on the patio in the sunshine, where they still were. Molly had invited friends to lunch and she preferred to get food preparations over early.

'I told you Mr Shotover was a weird little man after he was here. Harmless though.'

'Sex maniac,' Treasure insisted firmly, while scanning a section of the *Sunday Times*.

'He could hardly have been that. You said he'd tried rape at least twice and failed both times.'

'That's not the point. Anyway, he'll live.'

'No thanks to Brenig Jones. How quite dreadful that he's a murderer. Very attentive young man, and good-looking as I remember. Fine build. Fancy his pushing Mr Shotover in and leaving him to drown!' She shuddered.

'Because he was the star witness to Jones having been at the scene of the crime.'

'You mean the drowning of Joshua Evan?'

'No, to the two other murders. Joshua died more than a month before.'

'But that was the start of it all? And to do with someone trying to steal the pension-fund money?'

'Not really. That was incidental.' He put down the paper. 'It was to do with Barbara Evan wanting to get rid of her husband, and Brenig Jones being besotted with Marian Roberts, and certain he was about to lose her to Joshua.'

'But you said Barbara Evan had been bedding Brenig?'

'As a means to several ends. She got him to murder Joshua by

216

convincing him that was the only way he'd get Marian for himself. She also promised to cut him in for some of the money she'd come into after Joshua's death. I think seducing him was a necessary part of the strategy, and something she savoured as a snide way to getting her own back on Marian.'

'For stealing her husband?'

'Which Marian hadn't done, as it happens.'

'Marian told you that, of course?' said Molly, looking up from the beans with an indulgent smile.

'Yes,' he agreed, not rising to the implication. 'They were only involved together through the company.'

'I see. Why was Brenig Jones part of the delegation that came here about the pension? If he wasn't interested?'

'I should think primarily because it was an excuse to be with Marian Roberts.'

'Ah. And how exactly did he murder Joshua?'

'The night before it happened Joshua was supposed to have slept at his mother's flat. In fact he slept at home. When he was leaving there to go sailing before light next morning, Jones was waiting outside to brain him with the wooden beam from Joshua's own boat.'

'That's the pole that holds down the bottom of a sail? Bit cumbersome.'

'Not for Jones. He then drove the comatose Joshua to Hafod Bay where he had Shotover's dinghy with motor ready to take the body to sea and dump it. At the same time he took along Joshua's own boat which he'd towed over the night before. He set that adrift where he dropped Joshua and a loose lifebelt for effect.'

'And he'd put the beam back in place?'

'Yes. He'd fully rigged the sailing dinghy. He intended to get rid of Shotover in a similar way yesterday, except he didn't dare knock him out first. He wanted Shotover's death to look like suicide, brought on by guilt. When he was closer to shore, Jones intended to point the boat to sea again, before abandoning it and swimming back himself.'

'So it would have seemed as if Mr Shotover had gone out by

217

himself? And Joshua was definitely still alive when he was dropped in the water last month?'

'Alive but senseless. The official cause of death was drowning while unconscious, after being knocked overboard by the wooden beam and losing his lifebelt in the process. Splinters from the boom were found in his fractured skull. That seems to have fooled everybody.' Treasure paused to sip the coffee. 'Anyway, while Jones was taking body and boats to sea, Barbara Evan drove her husband's car to the sailing club where it was found later. She then went along the beach to join Jones. It was all carefully planned. And the plan would have worked but for a quite unpredictable intrusion.'

'The poor Watkins boy being at the sailing club?'

'Doing a burglary, yes. He spied on Jones and later tried to blackmail him. He thought he'd protected himself by telling Jones it was a friend who'd done the spying. Jones didn't believe there was any friend because he'd been told already the police were after Watkins over the break-in.'

'And the blackmail was over his murdering Joshua Evan? But . . .'

'No, nothing so serious. At least, that's what Watkins's girlfriend, Gwyneth Davies, says.'

'That's the budding actress? Blodwyn Davies's daughter?'

'That's her. Well, she insists that Watkins didn't believe the person he was getting money from had murdered anyone. Only that whoever it was hadn't wanted it known he'd taken Joshua's boat. You see, that hadn't come out in the inquest. Young Watkins had thought it fishy. Nothing more.'

'And that's why Jones murdered him?'

'There's no doubt. Arranged to meet him at the factory where a vat of cough-drop mixture had had to be kept on the boil because Jones had purposely gone slow mending a mechanical breakdown earlier.'

'Because he was planning an accidental death there?'

'Almost certainly intended to make it look as if Watkins had broken in, then fallen off the gantry into the vat. The police might well have assumed he'd gone senseless sniffing the heavy

218

vapour. It's strong stuff, apparently. Anyway, what seemed a better solution turned up when the boy appeared with George Evan, both naked, engaged in a kinky romp around the factory. It was almost too good to be true for Jones. He did in both of them, making it look as if Evan had killed the boy, then taken a suicidal leap into the boiling vat. Trouble was, unlike the plan to kill Joshua, this one had to be put together on the spur of the moment, and, significantly, without any input from Barbara Evan.'

'She really was the brains?'

'Unquestionably. Jones's extempore plan had faults in it – though like the first one, it came apart through another chance event. That was Shotover going into the yard and seeing Jones's van parked there.'

'And Brenig Jones has confessed to all this?'

'He and Barbara Evan couldn't unburden fast enough. Separately, of course. Each one's blaming the other, and pretending only to be an accessory. According to Detective Inspector Thomas, just before I left, it was an orgy of counter-accusation. He says it'll end with Jones taking the main rap, with Mrs Evan on a charge of conspiring with him to murder her husband.'

'Will that be fair?' Molly asked, eyeing the basin of sliced beans.

'Not in my view. She led Jones on. But I expect she'll get away with it. She moved much faster than he did to look after her own skin as soon as things started going wrong. When she last talked to me she was abandoning shareholder benefits like confetti. Ones in normal circumstances she'd have fought like mad to keep. That was because she knew which way the wind was blowing, and wanted to figure as an innocent bystander.'

'And did you buy the impersonation?'

'No. It was unnatural. But it took me far too long to fathom the relationship between the two of them. Even though it was virtually the first fact offered on arrival. When I flew over her house she was sunbathing naked on her pool. Jones was just about to join her.'

'Also starkers?'

'No. In a suit, which it seems he'd put on to be properly turned out for a meeting with me later. It was one of the reasons I didn't guess who it was. But the circumstances made it obvious he and Mrs Evan were more than casual acquaintances. He's now admitted to being her brief and unwilling lover.'

'So why did you have to guess at the identity?'

'Because I couldn't see his face. I did get a glimpse of his red van, without knowing then who it belonged to. Later, for a time, I was pretty sure it was Paul Ranker I'd seen.'

'The odious managing director? Because you suspected him?'

'Yes. But he really didn't have the substance for daring villainy. Total poseur. His sole concern was to make a pile by selling out the company. His buddy Chard, the other pension trustee I told you about, he got him his job in the first place. Ranker's now wangled another job in Australia, and good riddance, unless the Aussies find him out in time, as his wife has just done.' Treasure chuckled. 'Seems he forgot to tell her he was emigrating. He told the police, though, in the course of questioning, and they mentioned it to her, assuming she knew already and was going with him. It seems that caused quite a diversion.'

'Did Chard fix the G. L. Evan job for Ranker but really to help himself? I think that's enough beans.' Molly set aside the bowl. 'Perhaps I should do some carrots as well,' she added with a sigh.

'Why don't we go out to lunch?'

'Because it'll be much nicer here in the garden.'

'Chard is a fool,' said Treasure, returning to the subject. 'I suspect he's incompetent, and I know he's been an irresponsible trustee. Anyway, he's had a richly deserved lesson. Told the police he was at his office in Pentre Beach at the time of the factory murders. Actually he was with a young woman at her flat in the town. A pupil accountant who works for him. She was supposed to be ill. In fact, he'd given her the day off.'

'But not the night?' said Molly lightly.

'So it seems. The police interviewed her about some factory keys she might have used at a critical time. She panicked and insisted she and Chard had been together at her place. She rang him at home to tip him off afterwards. He was out, his wife answered, and the frightened girl unburdened on her. So another balloon went up.'

'Seems it's a highly sexed community up there,' Molly commented.

'Too little cultural diversion, I should think,' he answered firmly. 'Always bad, that. Only one proper theatre in the whole area, and the Liverpool Philharmonic's more than fifty miles away.'

This somewhat fanciful prognosis did nothing to convince Molly. 'That hardly justifies a wholesale reversion to primeval rollicking. I'm sure the Budes keep their urges under control. You didn't need to suspect Lewis of anything?'

'Not once I knew he has a nervous fixation with the knighthood he's about to be given. In the Birthday Honours List, next month.'

'He's to become Sir Lewis Bude?'

'Barring accidents,' Treasure nodded with a smile. 'Of course it's top secret, but Constance couldn't resist telling me all the same, last evening. Lewis is scared stiff about being involved in any bad publicity, anything antisocial before or after his elevation. But especially before. The knighthood explains a lot of things, like his huge gifts to charity.'

'And why he didn't really intend to pinch the surplus from the pension fund?'

'Oh, no, you're wrong there. He certainly intended to pinch it. What he felt he couldn't afford was to be *seen* to be pinching it. Literally stealing from widows and orphans.'

'There's a difference, I suppose?'

'Tremendous, and a clear one, as soon as we rumbled what was up, and he had to admit he owned Segam Holdings. After that he couldn't do enough for the G. L. Evan pensioners, or the company. He's even ready to help raise extra loan capital.

221

To get the business back on its feet.'

'Is that what will happen?'

'It's more likely we can arrange a merger with a bigger outfit.'

'So jobs will be saved, as well as the pensions? How very satisfactory. And what a good thing the committee enlisted your help.'

'Hm, that's one way of putting what they tried to do to me.'

'Worthy people, though. Except for Mr Jones, of course,' Molly reflected for a moment. 'Oh, and Mr Shotover. There was an elderly Mr Morgan . . .'

'Who also turned himself into a suspect for a bit,' Treasure interrupted. 'He confessed during a police interview yesterday that he'd been into the factory late the night before. Thought someone might have seen him.'

'Was he doing anything wrong?'

'No. He'd only been in the yard. Got a prostate problem. He'd gone for a leak in the outside gents behind the offices.'

'Poor man.' Molly picked up a tray and began collecting what was left of the breakfast things, the French beans and the parings. 'Well, so long as the pensioners get the extra money, you got what you wanted. Keeping the company going will be a bonus. Does Marian Roberts feel badly, I wonder? About being the cause of three deaths?'

'Hardly. It wasn't her fault Jones was potty about her.'

'Or Joshua Evan?'

'We're not certain he was. And even if he was, we know both his and Jones's passions must have gone unrequited.'

'And unsatiated as well? Bit of a tease with men, would you think?' Molly conjectured, picking up the tray.

'Here, let me take that.' Treasure got up and took it from her, following her down the short flight of garden steps and through the open door to the kitchen. 'She lives with another girl,' he said.

'You don't mean she's . . .?'

'Certainly not.'

'That's good. And you expect her to be part of the new management of the company?'

222

'She will if the ultimate owners get her to stay.'

'Will you be making recommendations about her?'

'Possibly. And on management generally.'

'I'm glad. I liked Marian. Saw quite a bit of her, did you? Besides the time when you found the bodies?'

'Yes, a little. Over business mostly.' He put the tray down carefully. 'I'm not sure you're quite right about her attitude to men. Basically she's a fairly dedicated career woman. Ambitious too,' he added, a touch solemnly.

'At home arguing with computers but no good at making tea. Not your type at all, darling.' Molly came over and kissed him warmly.

Treasure smiled, then went back to the garden and the paper. It was clearly one of those situations when to crave the last word would have been churlish.